ABOUT THE AUTHOR

David Cliffe is a retired journalist who spent nearly five decades working on newspapers, magazines and public relations.

Born in North Staffordshire, he has a strong bond with Leek and the Moorlands, having lived in the town for many years. He is a former editor of several newspapers and magazines, including the *Leek Post & Times*. A local history enthusiast, David has a particular interest in Victorian and Edwardian photography.

Images of Revenge is his second work of fiction.

Also by David Cliffe

Fiction
The Buried Secret: Old Leek Mystery Nº1
A tale of death, deceit and detection in Edwardian Leek

Non-fiction
A Moorland Album: Leek, Cheadle and neighbouring villages in Edwardian times from the photographs of W.H. Nithsdale

Victorian Views: Leek & District's first photographers

For more information or to purchase any of the above titles email moorlandalbum@gmail.com

IMAGES *of* REVENGE

DAVID CLIFFE

ISBN 978-1-80352-519-8

Typeset and designed by David Cliffe
moorlandalbum@gmail.com

Published by Independent Publishing Network

Printed in Staffordshire by Rowtype Printers Ltd.

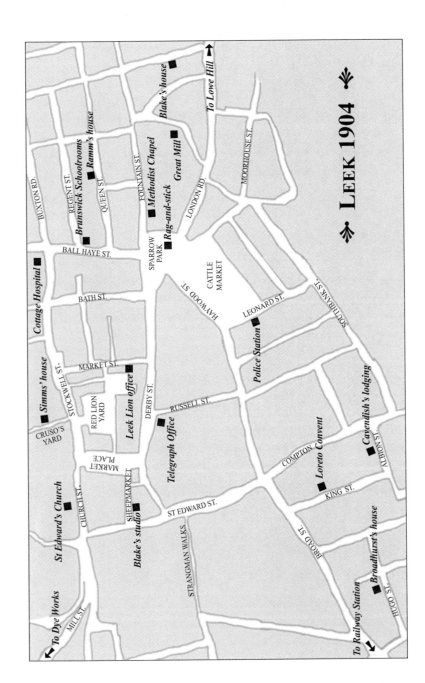

LEEK 1904

To Lowe Hill

Blake's house

Ramm's house
Brunswick Schoolrooms
REGENT ST.
BUXTON RD.
QUEEN ST.
FOUNTAIN ST.
Methodist Chapel
Great Mill
SPARROW PARK
Rag-and-stick
LONDON RD.
MOORHOUSE ST.
BALL HAYE ST.
Cottage Hospital
BATH ST.
CATTLE MARKET
HAYWOOD ST.
LEONARD ST.
SOUTHBANK ST.
Police Station
Simms' house
STOCKWELL ST.
MARKET ST.
Leek Lion office
RED LION YARD
DERBY ST.
RUSSELL ST.
CRUSO'S YARD
MARKET PLACE
Cavendish's lodging
ALBION ST.
Loreto Convent
COMPTON ST.
St Edward's Church
CHURCH ST.
SHEEPMARKET
Telegraph Office
ST EDWARD ST.
Blake's studio
KING ST.
BROAD ST.
STRANGMAN WALKS
To Dye Works
MILL ST.
Broadhurst's house
HUGO ST.
To Railway Station

A Word of Thanks

Images of Revenge would not have been possible without encouragement and advice from my wife Delia and my friend David Butler. I would also like to thank Leek artist Gavin Bowyer for his drawing which appears on the front cover.

I am indebted to the many readers who contacted me after the publication of my first novel. Their enthusiasm spurred me on to write a second murder mystery set in Leek and the Moorlands in times gone by.

David Cliffe, Leek, October 2023

CHAPTER ONE

July 1904

There was a buzz of anticipation as folk filed slowly through an opening in the canvas sides of the tent and looked for spaces on the wooden benches within. Oil lamps cast pools of light along the walls, but the interior was largely enveloped in gloomy shadows, adding to an atmosphere of mystery and suspense for the evening ahead. Outside, the sun had dipped behind the hills towards Cheshire and the faint sound of St Edward's Church bells chiming eight o'clock floated over the rooftops of Leek.

For the hundred or so people who had paid ninepence admission, the evening promised entertainment of a kind seen only occasionally in this market town on the edge of Staffordshire's moors. It was Friday night and the opening performance by Professor Kilner's Travelling Theatre Company was about to begin.

No one passing through the middle of town could have failed to notice the Travelling Theatre since its arrival the previous day. A procession of sturdy carts had come to a halt in Sparrow Park, the open space at the bottom end of the main thoroughfare Derby Street, and a substantial marquee had been erected. This was what local folk fondly called the rag-and-stick, the name referring to the canvas roof and sides supported by a sturdy wooden framework.

At one end of the tent, two carts were lashed together to create the stage, cloth being draped along the edge to hide the cart wheels. Rubber pipes were connected to the gas main in the street

1

and snaked inside the tent to feed lamps fastened to the front edge of the stage. A single row of sturdy wooden chairs were reserved for patrons prepared to pay an extra threepence for the privilege, but the majority of the audience were accommodated on benches or simply stood at the back.

The rough and ready construction took nothing away from the excitement generated by the theatre's twice-a-year visit to the town. Gaudily dressed members of the company, including Professor Kilner himself, had whipped up interest by strolling the streets and distributing handbills which advertised the performances over the next two weeks.

PROFESSOR KILNER'S TRAVELLING THEATRE

SPARROW PARK, LEEK
FRIDAY JULY 8TH FOR 14 NIGHTS ONLY

DRAMA!
THE CRIMES OF SWEENEY TODD.
MARIA MARTEN AND THE MURDER
IN THE RED BARN.

ROMANCE!
MY SWEETHEART.
A WONDERFUL WOMAN.

EXCITEMENT!
AS MIDNIGHT CHIMES.
THE HERO OF THE FLAG.

TRAGEDY!
OTTO THE OUTCAST.
TWO LITTLE VAGABONDS.

EACH EVENING AT 8 O'CLOCK PROMPT

As a taste of what was to come, some of the theatrical visitors performed impromptu songs and dramatic monologues from a wooden platform outside the tent, their strident tones echoing across the busy street and even above the hubbub in The Cattle Market and The Talbot, the inns overlooking Sparrow Park. Two more performers showed off their juggling skills as they wandered about Derby Street and the Market Place.

Friday was pay day in the town's silk mills so Professor Kilner had banked on a good crowd for the opening night and this evening looked to be living up to expectations. As late arrivals jostled to find standing room and children ran to join young friends sitting on the ground in front of the stage, the girl who had been taking money at the entrance gathered up a hefty bag of coins. Around her shoulders she tugged a shawl concealing the colourful costume she would wear on stage later in the evening.

Nathaniel Blake peered around inside the tent to see if he could spot anyone he knew in the audience, although it was becoming too shadowy to make out many of the faces.

Blake, who was in his late thirties, was Leek's leading professional photographer. He had already taken publicity photographs of the acting company shortly after they had arrived in town and was now wondering if it was practical to photograph an actual performance. Picture postcards of local scenes were an important part of his business and Blake had begun to photograph an increasing number of public events.

"I never thought it would be so crowded."

The comment came from Cora Blake, Nathaniel's step daughter, who was sitting next to him and fanning her face vigorously to stir the increasingly muggy atmosphere. The air inside the tent was an unpleasant mixture of the odour from the gas lamps, the pungency of a hundred bodies pressed close together and wafts of smoke from tobacco pipes.

A confident young woman of seventeen years, Cora assisted

her father in his studio in Sheepmarket in the middle of town. She helped to develop and print his pictures, and had also taken some photographs herself when Nathaniel allowed her to use the camera. But tonight, work was the last thing on her mind. Cora had a special reason to look forward to the performance and had made a note of the date as soon as she knew Professor Kilner's company was coming to town.

Years ago she had seen rag-and-stick shows aimed at children, chiefly clowning, juggling, songs and perhaps a performing dog. But tonight promised to be something rather different. For the opening performance Professor Kilner had chosen an old favourite with his audiences in Midland towns, *Maria Marten and the Murder in the Red Barn,* and Cora was keenly interested to see how the melodrama would unfold.

"Who would have thought an evening of culture would be so popular," mused Blake, with heavy irony.

Before either he or Cora could say any more the tent became even darker as one of the crew turned down the oil lamps on the tent walls. This prompted murmurs amongst the adults and whoops of excitement from the children, most of whom had sneaked into the tent and were too young to have any idea what awaited them. There were occasional shafts of dim light from the doorway as late comers hurried through the canvas flap.

Curtains were now slowly drawn back to reveal a shadowy scene on the stage lit by the lamps along its edge. Cora leaned forward to focus on what appeared to be an arrangement of straw bales and a couple of rickety chairs. Straw was scattered around the floorboards. "This must be inside the Red Barn," she thought. Her eyes darted from side to side, looking for the action to begin.

Then she noticed a dark shape that seemed to be suspended above the stage. At first she thought it was a bundle of rags, then she realised it was a figure in some sort of costume. Cora instinctively reached across and gripped her father's arm.

Blake, like most of the audience, was looking ahead intently, struck silent and trying to take in the scene. At first he scanned the props and then focused on the dark shape in the shadows above.

A woman screamed. Not on stage, but in the audience. "Dear Lord, it's a body!" she shouted.

Blake almost chuckled. This was going to be a quite a night of drama if the audience was screaming already, he thought.

Then the shape above the stage – it had become clear now that it was a person – slowly twisted round so that he or she faced the audience. And the next scream came from Cora.

"Oh Father, it looks like..." she began, her voice choking in shock.

Blake swivelled round to his daughter. "Why Cora, what in heaven's name is wrong?"

"That looks like Sarah! No it can't be… but it is, it's Sarah!" Cora cried.

One by one the audience realised this was no theatrical performance. A young woman was hanging far too realistically from a rope above the stage. The ghastly appearance of her face showed without doubt that she was dead.

Pandemonium broke out in the tent. Women screamed and some fainted, men leapt to their feet and shouted for help, children cried out in fear. Actors then appeared from both sides of the stage and rushed forward, reaching up to the stricken figure above them.

Cora buried her head in her hands as tears streamed down her face. "It's my fault. It's all my fault," she sobbed.

CHAPTER TWO

As chaos descended on the gathering in the tent, Nathaniel put an arm around his daughter and quickly led her through the jostling crowd. Once they were outside the fresher evening air seemed to revive her a little, but Cora was in a state of shock as they walked to the Blake family's terraced home in Portland Street. With not a word to her father, she stared straight ahead, almost in a trance.

She barely reacted when her mother Edith, startled to see Nathaniel and Cora home so soon, tried to comfort her.

Taking his wife's hands in his own, Nathaniel told Edith briefly what had gone on at the rag-and-stick. He knew the news would hit her hard as they had lost a daughter of their own only a year before. Although it had been just as harrowing for the family, three years old Emily's death was in far different circumstances. She was victim of an outbreak of scarlet fever that had claimed many young lives in the town.

Leaving Edith to comfort Cora, Blake hastened back to the tent. He expected that the local police, in particular his friend Inspector Albert Ramm, would be there by now and it occurred to him he might be of some assistance.

Refusing her mother's offer of a cup of tea, Cora trudged upstairs to seek refuge in her attic bedroom. She carried a candlestick because there was no gas mantle in her room. She flopped down on her bed and tried to come to terms with what she had seen on the stage.

"It's my fault," Cora murmured to herself again.

An evening which she had looked forward to so eagerly had

turned into a nightmare. To make matters worse, she felt she was to blame. For she had been responsible for her friend, Sarah Hulme, joining the travelling theatre in the first place.

Cora sat up and felt in the drawer of her bedside cabinet, pulling out a bundle of letters and birthday cards. Near the top was a cutting from the town's weekly newspaper, the *Leek Lion*. It was the scrap of paper that had started it all off.

By the light of the candle she read through the advertisement which she had neatly cut out from the *Lion* and saved. Her feelings were far different from three months' earlier when she had first shown it to Sarah.

Wanted Immediately!

Talented young ladies for summer tour of Midlands. Are you confident, musical, nimble on your feet? Can you recite, sing, charm an audience? Permanent situation. Money assured. Also required: heavies for scenery, cart work. Apply Kilner's Travelling Theatre c/o General Post Office, Stone, Staffs.

Cora pictured that Saturday morning which now seemed so long ago. Her father had spotted the advertisement as he browsed the *Lion* at breakfast. He read it out, teasing Cora that this could be her chance of fame and fortune. Months earlier she had begun music and dance classes with a few friends. Of course, her father knew that she had never wanted to go on the stage, but Cora couldn't help smiling at his joke that morning. Later she had snipped the notice from the *Lion's* front page crammed as usual with advertisements of all kinds, and had taken it to her Saturday afternoon class at Signor Manfredi's School of Music, Dance and Deportment. She knew that there was one person who simply had to see it. Her friend Sarah Hulme.

Sarah had been the reason Cora decided to go along to Signor Manfredi's in the first place. Sarah had attended music and dance lessons for three years and was now the star of the school. All the other pupils envied the way she could master even the most difficult dance steps. She and Cora had been friends since starting at St Luke's School when they were four. Now the two often talked about their dreams for the future: Cora working as a newspaper photographer and Sarah breaking free of her long hours in a braid mill to go on the stage.

As soon as Cora had arrived at Signor Manfredi's that Saturday, she had thrust the advertisement into Sarah's hand and urged her to apply. She had even helped her to write the letter to Professor Kilner secretly in case her mother tried to dissuade her. When Sarah had been accepted by theatre owner, everyone – well, almost everyone – at dance school had been so excited. Even her parents had realised it was her dream. But the dream had ended tonight.

Cora crumpled the newspaper cutting and looked away, her eyes filling with tears again.

The audience had demanded their money back and left by the time Blake reached Sparrow Park again. The rag-and-stick tent was darker than ever, but Sarah's body was no longer hanging above the stage. Members of the theatre company had climbed on the straw bales to release the rope from around her neck and lay the young woman gently onto the planks below. Someone had covered her body with a sheet.

Two men were standing beside the white shape on the stage. Blake recognised both. One was the burly, uniformed figure of Inspector Albert Ramm, senior officer of Leek Constabulary. The other was the pot-bellied proprietor of the theatre, Orlando Kilner, whom Blake had photographed with the rest of his company the previous day.

Ramm was looking intently into Kilner's face as the actor

spoke animatedly, making gestures to emphasise his words in a suitably dramatic fashion. To Ramm's mind there was something strange, almost sinister about Kilner's unnaturally flushed cheeks and his deep-set eyes, but then he realised the man's appearance was most likely the result of a liberal application of stage make-up.

"No Inspector, you must understand that none of us had any inkling of this. We are all *literally* in shock. I'm absolutely *horrified,* I had no idea the girl was going to do away with herself," the theatre owner was saying, or rather declaiming.

"Well, I shall need to take a proper statement from yourself and anyone else in your troupe who may have seen what went on. I want to get to the bottom of this tragic affair as soon as possible," Ramm replied.

He reached down and drew back the sheet to study Sarah's face. He shook his head sadly and then looked back at Kilner. "Please present yourself at the station at nine o'clock tomorrow morning and inform your colleagues that I will also want to speak to some of them. We will try not to disrupt your performances, but obviously police business must come first."

"*Certainly* Inspector. We will do *all* we can to assist. This is a tragedy for us all," said Kilner, mopping his forehead with a colourful square of cloth, removing both sweat and a layer of make-up. He turned away and strode to a group of performers at the side of the stage who were exchanging whispered comments and glancing towards the body. A woman with red ribbons in her long black hair was dabbing her eyes with a small handkerchief, tears making ugly streaks down her heavily made-up cheeks.

Blake approached the stage, his eyes drawn to Sarah's face which was still uncovered. The young woman had been so full of life when he and Edith had watched her perform at the dance school alongside Cora a few months ago. Now she lay lifeless and, even by the light of the gas lamps, Blake could see her discoloured features bore grim evidence of strangulation.

He was momentarily lost for words, then pulled himself together to speak to the policeman. "Inspector, I don't know if I can be of any help. I am sorry to say that Cora and myself were in the audience tonight."

Blake and the officer had formed something of a working relationship over the last two years, the two drawn together when the photographer became entangled in a previous shocking crime. Inspector Ramm was far-sighted enough to recognise that photographs could aid police work and had begun to make regular use of Nathaniel's services. Not only did Blake photograph men and women held in the police cells, he was also called upon to record the scenes of crime and accident. Such incidents frequently involved death or injury, and Blake had learned to put aside his natural squeamishness and get on with the job.

Inquisitive by nature, Blake had come to relish being involved in police business. For Ramm's part, he not only appreciated the photographer's professional skills, but found him a useful sounding board for his ideas, even if Blake was sometimes a little too enthusiastic about his own theories.

The Inspector looked down from the stage, relieved there was at least one reliable witness on this most unusual evening. "Ah Mr Blake, I would appreciate hearing what you saw. It's a sorry affair," he said.

"It is indeed. We have a personal connection, you see. The young lady..." Blake nodded hesitantly towards the girl's body, "was a friend of Cora's. Quite a close one, in fact."

Ramm sighed. One of the advantages – and challenges – of being a police officer in a small town like Leek was that everyone seemed to know everyone else. If not related they probably worked together, they were either lifelong friends or sworn enemies. Such a web of relationships sometimes made an investigation easier, sometimes much harder.

The Inspector rather awkwardly clambered down from the stage to join Blake. His cheeks puffed out as he almost lost his balance, but he quickly regained his composure. "Mr, or should I say, Professor Kilner tells me the young lady's name is Sarah Hulme. Is that correct?" he asked.

"Yes, Cora knew her from school and then dance classes. The family lives in Grosvenor Street."

"Tell me what went on, but be brief, because I want you to photograph the stage, the ropes and whatever, before these things are disturbed. And also the body, if you please, Mr Blake."

"Of course, Inspector, I shall collect my camera forthwith," Blake replied. Casting a hasty glance around the stage he realised he would need his latest gadget, a flash-lamp, to illuminate the scene. The lamp could be tricky to handle and Cora usually helped, but tonight that was out of the question. He would have to manage on his own.

Blake proceeded to give an account of what had gone on: the curtains opening, the shocking spectacle, the pandemonium.

"So it appeared the young lady was already dead by the time you saw her?" asked Ramm.

"Sadly, yes. It was shocking, especially for Cora."

Ramm knew from past experience that Blake's daughter was both sharp-witted and observant. She might make a useful witness, he thought.

"In due course I may need to speak to Miss Blake too. At present, however, this has all the signs of the young lady taking her own life, and the investigation should be relatively straightforward," the policeman continued. He called to a constable standing near the entrance and ordered that nothing be moved before Blake returned.

It took Blake only five minutes to walk to his studio in Sheepmarket, a small street that branched off the Market Place. He collected his hefty camera and tripod and into a leather holdall he put a dozen glass photographic plates, his new flash-lamp and a tightly sealed tin of combustible flash powder.

Making his way back towards the rag-and-stick Blake spotted the theatre owner strolling up the street. Professor Kilner was dressed in the colourful costume of an earlier era, presumably intended for that evening's abandoned performance, and was in animated conversation with another member of his company.

Kilner halted abruptly outside The Cock Inn, a public house that locals called Munro's – one of many town hostelries known by the name of their landlord. From within came the sounds of a raucous Friday night, drinkers with coins in their pockets after collecting their wage packets that afternoon. A similarly lively hubbub came from the half-timbered Roebuck Hotel, The Cock's arch rival on the opposite side of Derby Street. Kilner put his arm round the shoulders of his fellow thespian and guided him inside The Cock.

When Blake reached the makeshift theatre again he lifted his equipment onto the stage and mounted his camera on its tripod. He would start by taking a view of the stage, the ropes above and poor Sarah's body where it lay. Draping a black cloth hood over his head, he squinted at the inverted image on the screen at the back of the camera, but could make out little detail. The light was simply too poor and he knew he would have to prepare the flash-lamp.

Blake had known photographers who had scorched their hair when using a match to light the lamp's trough of explosive powder. He felt safer because he had invested in the latest version which ignited the chemicals with a spark from a dry cell battery. Although he could trigger the lamp from the camera, it was still awkward to hold the trough at arm's length while operating the camera with his other hand.

Cora had shown little fear in holding the flash-lamp handle, though she would usually squeeze her eyes shut. Blake now wondered if he should ask the constable to help. He unscrewed the tin of flash powder and was sprinkling it carefully into the zinc trough when someone spoke from the shadows.

"Would you like a hand with that, Sir?"

Blake turned to see a tall young man stride from amongst the sheets of scenery. Barefoot, he wore a torn shirt, ragged trousers and battered straw hat, but he appeared confident and well spoken. One of the actors, Blake guessed.

"Well, that would certainly be useful," said Blake, looking warily at the newcomer, "but this flash powder can be tricky. You will have to take care."

"Have no worry of that, Sir, I'm used to that stuff. We use pots of it on stage. Flash, bang – it can be quite dramatic," the young man replied.

The actor, who appeared to be in his early twenties, moved closer and Blake recognised him from the group he had photographed the previous day, although then he had looked rather different in a shirt and tie.

"Are you sure you're happy to help? This must be quite distressing for you. I'm afraid I don't know your name," said Blake.

"My name is Thomas, Thomas Kilner, Sir," the young actor replied solemnly. Blake saw that Thomas was now staring at the body, apparently unable to tear his gaze from Sarah's discoloured face.

"This should never have happened," said Thomas, his voice barely above a whisper. "Sarah deserved better than this."

Nathaniel was intrigued. Inquisitive as ever, he wondered if the young man could give a clue as to why Sarah had died. "Are you all right?" he asked.

Thomas regained his composure. "To be honest, I'm glad to do something to help," he said.

Blake loaded a glass plate into his camera, passed the flash-lamp to Thomas who was standing at his side, and connected its cable. With the click of a switch the powder ignited and the stage was illuminated in a blaze of harsh white light. Blake pressed the camera's shutter. Thomas stood impassively, showing little reaction to the explosive flash in front of his face. A puff of smoke rose towards the roof of the tent.

Blake removed the photographic plate and slid it into a protective case. After two more flashes and two more exposures, he moved the tripod nearer Sarah's body, focusing downwards towards her face. He knew Ramm would expect as clear as possible image of the young woman and her injuries.

Standing this close to the body he could detect, distinct from the fumes of the flash, a trace of the scent Sarah must have been wearing that evening. A hint of lavender, a poignant reminder of a vibrant life ended so tragically.

After refilling the lamp, Blake asked Thomas to reach closer so Sarah's face would be better illuminated. Another explosion of light and the task was done. Blake emerged from beneath his hood and glanced across to see Thomas, blinking from the flash but apparently unable to look away from Sarah. Finally, he handed the lamp back to Blake and walked away quickly before the photographer could thank him.

Blake watched him go. Sarah's death had been a shock to everyone that night, he thought, and this young man was struggling to contain his emotions.

Back at the Blake house, Cora lay on her bed knowing there was no chance of sleep. She stared at the low sloping ceiling, its plasterwork yellow in the flickering light from the candle. Her mind was filled with vivid images of what she had seen in the theatre tent. She tensed as she was struck by a sudden thought. Sarah could not have done this, she decided. No, Sarah was a victim. That was the only way to make sense of what had happened!

Cora sat bolt upright and picked up the bundle of letters again. She opened a small envelope and read the letter Sarah had sent a couple of weeks earlier.

Dearest C, I have the most exciting news. We are going to perform in Leek in July (Professor K had said we would be there in September but now he has changed his mind). I do hope you can come. Life with the theatre is everything I was hoping for. It is hard work learning parts and rehearsing, and we have to get used to new lodgings every week. But everyone seems so very friendly – although old Professor K is quite strict! But it is all worth it when the audience claps and cheers. Hoping to see you next month, S.

Cora read the letter twice. Those were not the words of someone desperately unhappy with life.

After the letter arrived Cora had told her parents how wonderful it would be see her friend when the theatre came to Leek.

Then Cora picked up a second envelope, also in Sarah's handwriting. This one had arrived three days ago, but this time she had not told Mother and Father what her friend had written.

Dearest C, I so hope you will come to see me when we are in Leek. I <u>must</u> to talk to you. Either after the show or find out where we are lodging and meet me there. But please tell no one – keep it a secret. Something has happened, I am very worried and I do not know who else to talk to. S.

When she received the second letter, Cora had felt disturbed and confused. Surely Sarah's secret couldn't be that bad, Cora told herself.

But after what had happened tonight Sarah's words seemed horribly ominous.

She fell back on her pillow, realising she had to tell someone. More than that, she had to do something. "I must find out what happened, for Sarah's sake," she said to herself.

She would tell her father, she would go to the theatre or the lodgings, she would speak to her friend Oliver Finch, she would ask questions. Cora's mind was in a whirl. She needed to find out who had done that to Sarah. Morning couldn't come soon enough, she thought.

Professor Kilner was the centre of attention in the snug at the front of The Cock Inn. The pub's small adjoining rooms were all crowded and were thick with the tobacco smoke that had, over the years, soaked into the paintwork and the upholstery.

Word had spread quickly about the shocking events at the rag-and-stick and now it was the chief topic of conversation amongst drinkers, many of them finding an excuse to poke their heads around the door of the snug where the theatre owner was holding court.

After his theatrical show of sorrow in front of Inspector Ramm, Kilner's natural ebullience now seemed undimmed by the tragedy. Leaning back on the bench, his richly embroidered Regency tailcoat was open to reveal a vivid scarlet waistcoat stretched tightly across his paunch. Around his neck was a voluminous white cravat tied with an extravagant bow.

Having been quick to secure credit with the landlord prior to getting his hands on the ticket money, Kilner had fortified himself with a succession of whiskies and was now sounding forth on a variety of subjects, ranging from cricket to politics. For him, attracting attention in a town was an important part of promoting his theatre and regardless of that evening's misfortunes, the show would go on.

"Sadly everyone is not suited to the life of the thespian. We make many sacrifices, many indeed, to provide entertainment for others, but we soldier on," Kilner announced solemnly to whoever might be within earshot. Turning towards the bar he held up his empty glass and shouted: "Landlord, another glass of your fine Scottish spirit, if you please. And one for my companion."

He dipped his hand into a bowl of raw peas on the table in front of him and tossed half a dozen skilfully into his mouth. A hawker with a bucket of peas, fresh out of the pod at this time of year, had just called in at The Cock selling his produce for tuppence a bowl.

"Shouldn't we turn in for the night, Professor?" asked the other actor. Like Kilner, this man was dressed in his stage costume. In his case he appeared to be a sea captain, sporting a navy blue jacket with polished brass buttons, resplendent with medals and a roll of sea charts poking out of his pocket.

"Perhaps, Hudson, perhaps. After one last tipple," replied Kilner, stroking the elegant waxed curls of his black moustache.

"That were a rum affair in yer rag-n-stick t'night," commented one of the locals, peering questioningly at Kilner.

"Yes ...indeed," Kilner sighed and fell silent. Onlookers were unsure whether he was overcome with grief or by 'Scottish spirit', however he managed to regain his thread. "Such are the challenges that face us all. Thankfully our art gives solace at times of trouble. We shall persevere, be sure of it."

Kilner was now back in full flow and continued without waiting for a reply. "Tell me, gentlemen, what did you think about Prime Minister Balfour's speech last week? Can we trust him? Can we trust any of them?"

The locals exchanged puzzled looks about this rapid change

of subject, not quite sure what to make of this odd character or what he was talking about. Lord Balfour rarely entered the conversation at The Cock.

The rambling conversations continued, but gradually the snug emptied and Kilner and his companion, their tumblers drained and the peas eaten, wandered off towards their lodging house. The theatre owner knew the following morning would bring another interview with that police fellow. He normally preferred a more leisurely start to the day, but he realised that tomorrow he would need to have his wits about him. He had already lost one evening's performance and he was determined to lose no more.

CHAPTER THREE

C ora Blake woke early to the sound of the occasional cart on the London Road near the end of their street and the heavy steps of mill workers trudging towards their Saturday morning shift. She had slept little and now lay staring into space, going over the horror of the night before. She felt the only way she could come to terms with her friend's death was to find out its true cause.

She heard the day beginning in the Blake household as her mother made her way downstairs to the kitchen to clean the ash from the cooking range and light it anew. Cora thought she could hear her young sister calling from her little bed in the room below and then realised she was imagining it, for she would never hear poor Emily's voice again. Providing Emily with a room of her own was one of the reasons they had moved to Portland Street last year, but she had died in the Fever Hospital just a few weeks later.

Cora rose, picked up a ewer and half filled the pottery bowl that stood on her chest of drawers. She put both hands into the bowl and dashed cold water onto her face, as much to revive her senses as wash the tear streaks from her cheeks. She didn't need to get dressed, she had fallen into bed in her dress the previous night and at the moment she couldn't bring herself to change.

She went down the narrow stairs and into the kitchen. Her mother turned from the range with an expression full of concern.

"Cora my dear, how on earth are you feeling? You must have had an awful night – didn't we all," said Edith, wrapping her arms around her daughter.

Cora buried her face into her mother's shoulder and willed herself not to start crying again. Then she pulled back from the embrace.

"It was horrible, Mother. I can't get it out of my mind."

"It will take time, my girl. I know you'll get over it in the long run, but at the moment if you want to cry, then let it all out." Edith's thoughts flashed back to losing little Emily – she knew only too well what Cora must be trying to cope with.

"It's heart breaking. But I'm angry too," Cora replied.

"You must not blame Sarah, or yourself…" Edith began, but Cora cut in, her voice rising.

"Blame? It wasn't Sarah's fault! I just know it wasn't, Mother!" She was almost shouting.

By now Nathaniel had come into the kitchen. He had also risen early, intending to go to the studio and print the photographs from last night as soon as possible.

He tried to soothe his distressed daughter. "Cora, I'm sure that whatever happened to Sarah will be sorted out. And then we can all remember her for the talented girl that she was," he said.

Cora spun round to face her father. "Sorted out, Father? Somebody did that to Sarah, I'm sure of it. I'll show you why!" she said, dashing past Blake and stamping upstairs.

Nathaniel and Edith barely had time to exchange a word before Cora was back in the kitchen, the letters from Sarah Hulme in her hand.

"The first time Sarah wrote to me she said how well things were going at the theatre," she said, waving the letter animatedly. "She wasn't unhappy or anything of that sort."

"Yes, dear, you told us," said Edith, hoping to calm her.

"But I didn't tell you what Sarah wrote this week," Cora went on, thrusting the second letter towards her father. "Here, you must read it! It was private, but you might as well know now. There was a secret she wanted to tell me. I'm sure she was frightened of something. And that's why all this happened!"

Blake took the letter from his daughter and read it through, then passed it to Edith.

"Well, I can see that Sarah did want to speak to you privately about something. But are you sure you're not reading too much into this, Cora? It might have nothing to do with last night," said Nathaniel.

"Going on stage was Sarah's dream. She would never have..." Cora began, then faltered, "...done *that* to herself." She sat down abruptly on a kitchen chair and looked away from her parents, wringing her hands in frustration.

Edith gave Nathaniel a worried look and shook her head slightly. They both knew how stubborn their daughter could be when she got an idea into her head. It might be a long time before Cora accepted her friend's death.

Blake read through Sarah's second letter once more. He had to admit there was something curious about it. Perhaps Cora was right and there was more to this sad affair than at first appeared.

Across town, Fellowes Jeremiah Finch, editor and proprietor of the *Leek Lion*, was in his cluttered office bright and early. The office, piled with back copies of the newspaper, books, directories and odd pieces of paper, was at the top of a three storey building in Market Street.

Finch, known to his friends as FJ, and his sole reporter, his son Oliver, were leafing through the latest edition of the weekly newspaper which had gone on sale that Saturday morning. The previous evening had been the usual rush of typing, proofreading and correcting before the press on the ground floor was cranked into motion. Now the two had chance to take stock of their work and consider what would create the greatest stir in the town.

However they both knew the *Lion* did not have the story everyone in Leek would be talking about that morning: last night's incident at the rag-and-stick.

Finch had learned of Sarah Hulme's death when he called at The Roebuck for a late glass of ale on Friday night. By that time, the latest edition of the *Lion* was already piling up next to the press and illicit copies being bought direct from the printer in charge. Finch knew he would have to wait a full week before he could report on the incident.

"And the whole affair will doubtless be cleared up by then," Finch thought.

As a father himself he was disturbed to hear of the young woman's death, but as a journalist he could not help being disappointed that he had missed the story.

Oliver, who shared his father's unruly red hair, restless manner and hunger for news, was also thinking of the tragedy as he read the *Lion's* item publicising Professor Kilner's Travelling Theatre.

"This piece about the theatre might look in rather poor taste after what happened last night," he said.

Kilner had taken a prominent advertisement on the front page and FJ Finch had obliged with a glowing report of the theatrical delights that awaited the town over the next fortnight. Above the report was the photograph which Nathaniel Blake had taken when the cast had arrived on Thursday. Amongst the performers was a beaming Sarah Hulme.

"How were we to know what was going to happen? It's a tragic affair, sure enough, but Professor Kilner will have no trouble filling his seats. Such macabre events attract the public's attention," Finch senior replied. He knew only too well how tales of death and mystery kept his readers interested, which was why he included several every week although they usually referred to events far outside the moorlands.

Twenty years old, Oliver had yet to become as thick skinned as his father and was shaken by the tragic death of someone just a couple of years younger than himself. He looked closely at the photograph. Despite the poor quality of the print, he had recognised Sarah easily. His friend Cora Blake had told him all about her and he could see in the girl's eyes her excitement at performing in her home town.

He wondered if Cora knew what had happened last night. He dreaded to think how distraught she would be and realised he should see her as soon as possible.

He and Cora had known each other for two years, brought together by mysterious events in the town. Back then he had been impressed by her determination and her confidence. Gradually he found there was no one else he would rather spend his time with. Not that a young reporter had much spare time.

Scanning the newspaper's broadsheet page filled with tiny type, something else caught his eye. "How long will you allow this 'John Bull' character to keep stirring things up, Father?" he asked.

British newspapers were printing an increasing number of articles and letters, often anonymous, about "The German Problem" and the *Leek Lion* was no exception. Reports were raising fears about the Kaiser's plans to expand the German navy. Even respected politicians were claiming that foreign spies were at work in England. Britain had signed a new alliance with France and many people were starting to take sides.

In the *Lion*, suspicions were being stoked by a regular

correspondent calling himself John Bull. His latest contribution was a new call to action.

"Don't you think these anti-German claims are going a little too far? Surely it doesn't have much to do with Leek? And besides, who is John Bull?" Oliver asked.

"Oliver, you know there is nothing like controversy to keep our readers happy. The more argument, the more argument, the more folk will want to buy the *Lion*," FJ replied. Seeing his son was unconvinced, he went on.

"Obviously John Bull gave me his real name when he first started writing the letters. If there's going to be a public meeting

24

next week, I presume that is when everyone else will find out who he is. As far as I'm concerned, the man has a point – there is sense in being vigilant about what's happening in Europe. I have real fears about what we might be dragged into on the Continent, young man," he continued.

"But surely warmongering won't help things, Father?"

"Let's hope it doesn't come to war now we've got the French on our side. But I can tell you that Bull is a respected citizen and he's entitled to his opinion as much as anyone else," Finch senior went on. "Provided his letters don't land us in any legal trouble, then I'm going to continue printing them."

Finch said no more, but his son's comments had given him pause for thought. Should he rein in John Bull? He would wait to see what happened at the public meeting. That was bound to make a good story.

At Leek Police Station, Inspector Albert Ramm checked his pocket watch against the clock on the wall of his office, growing more impatient by the minute. He stood up and pushed his chair back irritably, its legs scraping noisily on the polished parquet floor. He went to the door and shouted along the corridor.

"Knowles! If that fellow Kilner is not here in five minutes I want you to find his lodgings and haul him out of bed. I distinctly told him nine o'clock."

"Damned theatrical types," he muttered as he sat back at his desk.

The tragedy at the rag-and-stick had been witnessed by many and he knew the town would be talking about it. He was determined to handle the investigation correctly, but neither did he want the case to drag on. Shocking as the young woman's death had been, his gut feeling was that she had taken her own life, plain and simple. The town's Coroner had been informed, a post mortem was taking place later that day and an inquest should settle the matter within the week.

Although there were ten officers based at Leek's impressive, turreted police station in Leonard Street, there was no dedicated detective. Ramm had to squeeze in his investigative work alongside many other duties – managing his force, appearing at court hearings and public occasions and, of course, paperwork. He could ask for support from Police Headquarters in Stafford, but was loathe to do so. As far as he was concerned, this was his station, his town and he was perfectly capable of handling matters himself.

But if he was to deal with such investigations satisfactorily, witnesses had to be punctual and Professor Orlando Kilner was late. Unforgivably late, in fact. Ramm sighed deeply when he finally heard the theatre manager's commanding tones at the far end of the corridor.

As Kilner was ushered into his office, Ramm appraised his visitor with a steely expression. Holding a silver topped cane in one hand, Kilner was using his brightly coloured handkerchief to mop his brow vigorously. Although lacking the make-up and exotic garb of the previous evening, he still cut a striking figure. All his features seemed to be emphasised in some way. His hair was longer than currently fashionable and was unnaturally black for a man doubtless past sixty. His prominent moustache was finely clipped and twirled, his deep set eyes were surmounted by bushy black brows. His tweed suit was of a vivid check that would stand out in a crowd. A showman indeed, thought Ramm.

"Mr Kilner. Good of you to attend," said the Inspector curtly, deliberately avoiding the word "Professor" which he was sure was pure showmanship.

"Inspector, *many* apologies. So much to attend to this morning, so much. This tragedy has thrown us into complete disarray I'm afraid."

"Yes, yes, that's as it may be, but we too have important business," Ramm cut in before Kilner could waste any more time. He took up a pencil to make notes and ploughed on. "Let us begin with some background. I gather Miss Hulme was a recent recruit?"

"Yes, she joined us in May. A promising young performer, although, of course, it was going to take all my skill and experience to raise her to the standard the Kilner Travelling Theatre expects. But I always have time for the younger generation."

"And was she happy in her new position?"

Kilner was taken aback. "Why should she not be happy? What more could a budding performer hope for? It was the opportunity of a lifetime."

"There were no disagreements with other theatre members?"

"Not that I am aware of."

"And what about yesterday? Were things as normal? What was her demeanor? Was there any indication of what was to come?"

"It's a fearful scramble on the first night in a new town, you understand Inspector, but as far as I am concerned there was nothing untoward. Of course..." Kilner's reply tailed off as he his was searching for the correct words.

"Of course what?"

"Well, to be *truthful*, Inspector, entering our profession can be a challenge for anyone, even for someone of Miss Hulme's talents. She never said anything directly to me, but she may have been finding life, how shall we say... *difficult*."

Ramm stroked his moustache and frowned as he considered the statement. "What puzzles me is why no one saw what Miss Hulme was up to last night and tried to stop her. Presuming she did away with herself, that is."

Kilner, seeming to take exception to the "presuming", launched into an excitable response.

27

"Inspector, surely there's no doubt about it? The poor young woman is a great loss to us, but she *must* have done it herself last night.

"None of us saw what was happening on the stage, unfortunately. I was certainly not aware of anything. Obviously I have a lot on my mind before curtain-up... readying the cast, inspecting the costumes and so on. I barely have chance to catch breath, let alone to look what's happening out front!"

Ramm thought it seemed rather convenient that Kilner had not looked on stage before the performance had started.

"So *who is* responsible for checking the stage and scenery?"

"Why that's Conrad, our stage manager. He looks after all the equipment while I'm busy with the performers."

Seeing the theatre owner was going to offer little more assistance, Ramm said he could leave. "But tell this Conrad that I shall need to speak to him. The same goes for anyone else who might have information about Miss Hulme. Surely someone must have seen something," he added.

Alone again, the Inspector mused on how animated Kilner had become when denying any knowledge of the young woman's predicament.

With a sigh he rose from his chair. Next he intended to talk to Sarah Hulme's parents and the conversation was likely to be a delicate one. He was about to leave the station when Nathaniel Blake arrived with prints of the photographs he had taken the previous evening.

Taking the brown envelope from Blake, Ramm spread the photographs on the reception counter. The ten inch prints were barely dry after Blake's hasty work in the darkroom, but thanks to the flash-lamp, they showed a surprising level of detail. He examined them in silence, holding them up one by one to scrutinise particular features.

Ramm had learned from experience that a vital detail could be

28

missed at the scene of an incident and the chance to take a second look was most valuable. So it proved this morning as he considered the ropes above the stage, the way the props were arranged and the livid marks on the young woman's pale neck.

Ramm turned to the photographer. "Mr Blake, could I ask you something? Last night when the curtain was drawn back, were any of these straw bales below Miss Hulme's feet?"

Blake tried to recall the scene as he first saw it.

"Well, much of the stage was in shadow," he began cautiously.

"But the bales, Mr Blake. I presume she must have climbed on them to reach the rigging. Or perhaps she used one of those chairs?"

Blake shook his head. "I can't be sure. Like everyone else, I couldn't take my eyes off the body."

Ramm studied the photographs again, trying to picture how Sarah's death had unfolded. How had she managed to reach the rigging and do so without anyone else seeing her. He was silent in thought for some moments.

"No matter," he said finally. "I'm sure we will be able to sort it out to the Coroner's satisfaction. Now, I must press on." With that, he turned to the door, but Blake raised a hand.

"Inspector, a moment if you please. As I said last night, Miss Hulme was a good friend of Cora's," Blake began, thinking how best to introduce a delicate topic.

"And?" asked Ramm, his hand on the door, anxious to leave.

"Miss Hulme wrote to Cora twice in recent weeks. Once to say how happy she was and then earlier this week she wrote again. It's a rather strange letter as you will see," Blake went on, handing Sarah's second letter to Ramm.

The policeman took the small sheet of notepaper and read it, frowning as he studied the tiny handwriting.

"Cora is convinced that Miss Hulme would have not done this to herself," said Blake.

"May I keep this? It is certainly an unusual missive from the young lady, and I am sure that Miss Blake must be sorely distressed. However..." Ramm paused and looked directly at Blake, "...I would not want to complicate matters with too many wild theories, Mr Blake. My feeling is that this is a very sad case, but a straightforward one."

This time the Inspector did make it through the police station door, leaving Blake to ponder whether he had done enough to convey Cora's concerns. He doubted Ramm's reaction would pacify his daughter.

The Hulme family home in Grosvenor Street was relatively close by. The house was like many others in Leek's terraced streets with two rooms upstairs and two down, although Ramm noticed it was a good deal tidier than many he had seen. Spotless from the gleaming black-leaded range to the polished red tiles on the floor. Edgar and Gladys Hulme were wearing their Sunday best to receive the many callers they expected that morning. But they could not disguise the utter devastation on their faces.

"We still can't believe it, Inspector," said Edgar Hulme, staring blankly across the room. His wife sat red-eyed and speechless beside him.

"I don't mind telling you, we was worried when Sarah said she was going off to the theatre," Hulme went on. "Don't get me wrong, we were ever so proud of her. Sing, dance, you name it, she'd been like that since she was a little 'un. She loved it, that's why we scraped together the money so she could have lessons with that Signor Manfredi. But she wanted a way o' life that we knew nowt about. We wondered how she'd cope. And now..."

Edgar Hulme's voice trailed off as he rubbed a fist in his eye. He looked at his wife and shakily grasped her hand.

"We were supposed to go to see her last night, weren't we Gladys? We were looking forward to it. But then I was moved to the late shift at the bakery and so we said we'd go tonight instead.

We knew nowt about what had 'appened until your man came round and told Gladys – I was at work, you see. But by then... it was too late to do anythin' about it."

"I suppose Sarah had kept in touch since she joined Mr Kilner?" asked Ramm.

"Letter every week, regular as clockwork. And that's the thing, Inspector. As far as we knew, she was enjoying every minute of it."

"No indication that anything was wrong? It seems she wrote a letter to her friend, Miss Blake, saying she was worried about something."

The Hulmes exchanged a surprised look and then faced Ramm again.

"If there were summat wrong, Inspector, we knew nowt about it," Edgar Hulme replied.

Ramm could see that Sarah's death was as much a mystery to her parents as it was to everyone else.

CHAPTER FOUR

It was early Saturday afternoon when Edith Blake heard a knock on the front door and found Oliver Finch on the step.

"You must want to speak to Cora," she said. "She's terribly upset, the poor girl."

Cora, who had spent most of the morning on her bed, straightened her blouse and long skirt before going into the parlour to speak to Oliver. She didn't want to look a mess, but she could not hide the dark rings under her eyes following her sleepless night.

"I was so sorry to hear about Sarah. It must have been awful when you found out," Oliver began. He could see his young friend had none of her usual vigour.

"I was there, Oliver! I saw her!" Cora blurted out.

"Oh heavens! I didn't know you were at the theatre. How terrible," Oliver managed to reply.

Their conversation dried up. Oliver wanted to take Cora in his arms and comfort her, but knew it would be inappropriate in the Blakes' front parlour. Cora did her best to hold her emotions in check, determined not to make a show of herself in front of the young man. But there was something she just had to tell him.

"Sarah didn't do this," she began abruptly. "I'm sure of it."

Seeing Oliver's surprise she told him about Sarah's letters, then went on quickly: "We need to know what really happened. Sarah was worried. I told Father and he said he would tell the Inspector, but I need to find out for myself." After a pause, she looked pleadingly at the young reporter. "Oliver, will you help?"

He took a moment to digest what she had said. Saying someone else was responsible for Sarah's death was a serious business and he didn't know if he should encourage it. On the other hand, he knew how determined Cora could be. Two years ago it had nearly cost her her life and Oliver could not let her put herself at risk again. He may have to get involved simply to watch out for her.

"Cora, you know you should leave this to the police," he said. "But I will help, if I can."

Cora squeezed his hand, her thoughts already skipping to what Oliver might find out. She glanced at the clock on the mantelpiece and saw it was approaching two o'clock.

"It's dance class this afternoon, but I don't think I can face it," she said.

Seeing the time, Oliver realised he had to leave. He was supposed to be covering that afternoon's Poor Children's Outing to Endon for the *Lion* and would need to dash to the canal wharf to be in time.

"You might feel better to get away from the house, see some of the other young ladies," he suggested.

Cora hesitated. Before Oliver had called she had simply wanted to shut herself away from everyone, but seeing him had given her new confidence. She decided she would go to Signor Manfredi's. She was in no mood to dance, but at least she would see some of the others. One of them may even know more about Sarah.

33

Nathaniel Blake smiled as he watched hundreds of the town's poorest children milling around excitedly in a field beside Leek Canal Wharf. Some were as young as five and the oldest probably ten. Most were shouting, laughing and running in all directions, although some of the more timid ones were already standing on the towpath beside four brightly painted barges which were tied to iron mooring posts.

The occasion was the annual summer treat organised by the Leek Poor Children's Outing Fund and Blake was there with his camera to capture proceedings for posterity.

Leek's better-off residents arranged a number of initiatives to make life a little easier for the town's poorest families and the youngsters looked forward to the annual outing almost as much as the stew that lucky ones were served in the Poultry Market Hall twice a week. This year, four hundred children were to be taken by canal boat to Endon for an afternoon of games and a picnic tea, hence the gathering at the wharf. Most were from families that could not afford a day trip, let alone a holiday, so it was the first time they had been out of Leek and certainly the first time by boat.

Keeping that number of children under control was quite a task and Inspector Ramm was present, along with two of his constables, to ensure that none of the young ones either strayed onto the lines of the neighbouring Leek Railway Station or fall into the canal. Ramm also saw it as his public duty to be seen at worthy events such as this.

Seeing Blake set up his tripod on the towpath Ramm walked over to speak to him.

"What a commotion! I hope they settle down when they're on the barges," said Ramm.

"I doubt it. These young folk are determined to enjoy

themselves and, let's face it, they deserve a spot of fun," Blake replied. "It's good to see there is something so kind hearted happening in town," he added.

"Certainly, Mr Blake. None of us want to see tragic affairs like that one at the rag-and-stick too often. I talked to Mr and Mrs Hulme this morning and they are heartbroken."

"Well, let's hope you manage to find out what was behind it, Inspector," added Blake. Ramm simply nodded and then moved off to speak to one of the committee members, a white-bearded man in an immaculate suit.

Nearby, Oliver Finch had his notebook out and was interviewing Miss Wint, the chief organiser of the outing. She was resplendent in a full length outfit made of many layers of cream coloured cotton with lace at the edges, a matching wide-brimmed bonnet and long gloves.

"What a splendid afternoon," she said, looking up at the sun and then around at the boisterous throng.

"It should take ninety minutes to reach Endon, barring any mishap," she explained. "There will be games on the lawn in front of The Plough Hotel before tea is served in a tent. Each child will get pork pie, plum cake, tea and such. Then there will be sports on a field that has been kindly loaned by Mr Fogg. The children should be back by nine o'clock this evening."

Miss Wint, obviously a stickler for details, made sure Oliver had noted it all down before she continued. "Please be sure to mention Mr Tomlinson from Stockton Brook who has provided the barges, Mr Platt, our host at The Plough, and, of course, Mr Fogg who has loaned us his field."

Ramm took out his whistle and delivered three shrill blasts in the style of a Royal Navy officer. It brought a smile to the face of some of the adults and shocked most of the children into silence. Then, using his most commanding voice, he called the young voyagers to order and instructed them to line up ready to board the barges. His constables acted as marshals.

Children had learned at a tender age to obey orders from a 'Bobby' or risk a slap of his cape or even a cuff on the ear, and so the queues quickly formed on the towpath, although not without a certain amount of pushing and wriggling.

Blake took multiple photographs as the children climbed into the barges, accompanied by men and women in straw boaters. He took more when the boats moved off from the wharf, puffs of smoke rising as their steam engines chugged into action. A voyage of fun had begun.

Cora steeled herself as she climbed the stairs of the Brunswick Schoolrooms in Regent Street. The building had been erected to accommodate the Sunday School classes of one of the town's biggest Methodist churches. However, for two days a week the top floor was let out to Signor Manfredi for his music and dance sessions on the strict understanding there would be no activity which offended Methodist principles.

On the second floor, wooden benches had been pushed to the side creating an expanse of polished floorboards for the dancing. At this time on a Saturday afternoon, the room would normally be filled with excited chatter as young women gathered before the lessons began. But today there was barely a whisper. Sarah's death had stunned the class into silence.

The dance pupils came mostly from the town's better off families – Sarah Hulme, a working class girl, had been an exception. Even so, they were used to friends and relations dying young. That was usually the result of some kind of illness. Sarah's death, however, had been shockingly sudden and brutal.

Cora approached a small group of the young women. Looking from one sad face to another, she couldn't summon the strength to speak.

36

At the far end of the room, Giuseppe Manfredi stood with his back to an upright piano and cleared his throat with a sound like a long and rasping gargle. Strands of dark hair were plastered across his balding head.

He was tall and decidedly bony, his tight jacket and trousers emphasising the sharpness of his elbows and knees. But despite his wiry appearance, he was surprisingly strong – his students had often seen him move a stack of benches or the heavy piano with ease.

"Young ladies, young ladies. Attention if you please," he shouted. Manfredi's students were used to his thick accent and his singsong way of talking, although most of them had never heard anyone else from abroad speak, apart from the occasional hawker selling exotic goods on market days.

"I decide that we not dance today. We too upset about Miss Hulme, we not concentrate on our steps," the dance teacher announced.

Most of the girls exchanged looks of relief. One put her hand up and asked timidly: "Signor Manfredi, do you know what happened to Sarah?"

"Me? I only know what I am told. It best we not talk about it. I know nothing of rag-a-stick!" Manfredi's voice rose in agitation. All eyes were on him now, the dance master seeming as deeply affected as the rest of them, although he appeared more annoyed than upset.

"Soon we think happy things again. Then we dance," he continued. "I sorry, but please you all go home now."

Cora's mind went back to those happy times when Sarah twirled across the polished floor. And she also thought about how Signor Manfredi had reacted when Sarah announced she was joining the travelling theatre.

"Kilner Theatre? What is this?" he had said, making no attempt to conceal his dismay. "You waste your talent. Stay away from them, Miss Hulme, stay well away. They no good for you."

Perhaps Sarah should have taken his advice, Cora thought sadly.

With no dancing to take place, the young women began to disperse. Cora joined the others making their way back down the stairs. Outside she found that some were waiting for her, eyes wide with anticipation. These were her usual dance partners and Sarah had also been friendly with them. Cora could tell that word had spread that she had been at the theatre last night.

"Cora, whatever was it like? Do tell us," asked a girl called Martha. She had not been particularly close with Sarah, but was often first to gossip.

"I... I really can't talk about it," Cora stammered.

"I can't believe it. That Sarah would do something like that," Martha went on, shocked and yet anxious to hear the details.

Cora was unsure what to say. She wasn't going to start spreading Sarah's secrets around. Instead, she thought she would try to find out something for herself.

"Did any of you hear anything from Sarah?" she asked. "Did she write to you?"

The girls looked at one another blankly and shook their heads. Some were wishing they had been close enough to Sarah to have received a letter from her. How they would treasure such a memento after what had happened.

"None of us heard anything except what *you* told us about the theatre coming to Leek," Martha replied pointedly. They were all looking at Cora and waiting to hear more.

Cora realised she was the only one Sarah had trusted with a letter and now she must repay that trust. She said she was too upset to talk any further and headed for home.

Two floors above, Giuseppe Manfredi stared bleakly around the empty schoolroom. His students had gone and he was left alone with his thoughts. He slumped down on the piano stool and put his head in his shaking hands, elbows on the closed piano lid.

It had been difficult facing the young women who had danced with Sarah, but he knew he had to keep up appearances. He focused blankly on the swirls in the instrument's walnut veneer, trying to clear his mind of dark thoughts about the young woman who had once been his star pupil.

He looked up and saw his copy of the *Leek Lion* on top of the piano. It was open at the page with the photograph of Professor Kilner's Travelling Theatre. He picked it up and looked at the picture again, the smiling Sarah.

"Why did she have to go to the Kilner Theatre, of all places?" he whispered in his native tongue. "I tried to warn her, but she would not listen."

He looked again at the newspaper and read another item on the same page. Then he crumpled it and threw it on the floor.

Just like the previous evening, a queue was forming outside the rag-and-stick in anticipation of the Saturday night performance. Except that people had started to gather even earlier. As FJ Finch had predicted, the tragic events of Friday had done nothing to keep the audience away and tonight would be a sell-out.

A poster announced the performance was going to be *As Midnight Chimes – A sensational domestic drama in four acts*. The melodrama had proved a favourite in other towns and Professor Kilner was keen to take full advantage of his theatre's new notoriety.

Amongst the audience was John Gibb, a bewhiskered Scots-man well known in the town. In years gone by, Gibb had been an unkempt 'man of the road' that many Leek folk would avoid. But his life had been transformed when he met Nathaniel and Cora Blake after mysterious goings on. Nowadays he was respected as a brave war veteran and something of a hero. He no longer slept under hedges, but in an outbuilding at Dieulacres Cottage Farm on the edge of town where he now worked.

Gibb did not frequent any of the town's numerous hostelries and had been busy in the fields all day. He had heard no word of what had gone on at the rag-and-stick on the Friday night. Neither had Rosa Carter, the widow he worked for. She had seen Professor Kilner's advertisement in the *Leek Lion* that morning and urged her labourer to take the evening off and walk into town for a spot of entertainment.

As a boy Gibb had watched theatrical performances and years later his comrades in the Queen's Own Highlanders would occasionally put on a show to raise spirits in the camp. But after becoming a tramp he had never been to a travelling theatre again and was now intrigued by what the evening would hold.

Waiting for the performance to start, he was struck by how animated many of the audience were. Did folk always get this excited before a play, he wondered, not realising that most of them were talking about Sarah Hulme rather than what was going to happen on stage. He peered around the tent trying to see if he recognised anyone, just as Nathaniel Blake had done the previous night. Though he didn't have a wide circle of friends he was a keen observer of local life and there were one or two familiar faces.

Then Gibb froze, his eyes fixed on a man standing at the back amongst those who had been too late to get a place on the benches.

"Surely it cannae be," the Scot said under his breath.

It had been nearly twenty years since John Gibb had last seen this man, in far different circumstances and a long way from Leek. But he was sure it was the same fellow. The slicked back hair was greyer and thinner now, the moustache a little longer. But the piercing eyes and the ramrod straight bearing were the same as ever.

A drum roll signalled the start of the play, interrupting Gibb's thoughts and drawing his attention to the stage instead. However he took little notice of what the actors were doing because he was now preoccupied with a real life mystery. How did that fellow come to be in Leek?

As the evening wore on, Gibb stole glances across the audience towards where the man was standing, his face just visible amongst the shadows. Now the Scotsman was certain he was not mistaken. As soon as the performance came to an end he intended to push through the crowd and speak to him.

As the final applause and cheers petered out, Gibb rose and started to make his way towards the back of the tent. But he saw that the fellow was no longer there. The man from his past had slipped away into the dark town.

CHAPTER FIVE

The brilliant sunshine on Sunday did nothing to improve Cora's dark mood. She had been so disappointed when her father told her that Inspector Ramm had shown no enthusiasm for her theory about Sarah Hulme. She vowed to find some sort of evidence.

Sitting at home puzzling over the tragedy would solve nothing, she realised, and when her friend Ellen Simms called at the Blake house, Cora agreed to join her for a walk over the fields to Rudyard Lake. An afternoon in the countryside would help clear her head, she decided, and it would also be an opportunity to talk things over with Ellen in private.

Ellen was the same age as her, but while Cora was slightly built, Ellen was a good three inches taller and becoming quite stocky. Sunday was her day of rest from work in the packing room at Leek's largest silk mill, the Great Mill, and Ellen enjoyed being out in the fresh air. Like most of her school friends, Ellen had started half day shifts at the mill when she was only twelve and she had had to grow up quickly. There had been some difficult times for her at the Great Mill, especially with the former owner,

Enoch Heathcote. This meant she was mature beyond her seventeen years and it also made her an ideal companion for Cora, as they both found themselves increasingly frustrated with the things that they felt were unjust in life.

Today, as they walked beside the gently flowing waters of the canal feeder towards Rudyard, there were important matters to discuss. It was a chance for Cora to unburden herself of her fears about Sarah's death. Ellen had not been a particular friend of Sarah, she was not interested in dancing and such luxuries belonged to a way of life that Ellen knew she would never have. However she was as shocked as the rest of the town to hear what had happened at the rag-and-stick. She was even more disturbed when Cora told her that she thought someone else was involved.

"So how are you going to find out?" Ellen asked.

She knew how determined Cora could be, but Ellen wondered what her friend could do about this new mystery, if it was a mystery at all.

Sensing Ellen's doubts, Cora became defensive. "Well someone's got to do something! Oliver says he will help, and my father too. And I might find some of the other actors, ask them about Sarah."

It took Ellen and Cora more than an hour to reach the lake, walking through lush grass dotted with wildflowers and making the occasional detour to avoid cows grazing placidly in the afternoon heat. Arriving at the dam head they saw they were not the only ones who thought it an ideal afternoon to visit Rudyard.

The railway line made the lake easily accessible for large numbers and it had become a favourite resort for visitors from the smoky streets of Stoke, Stockport and Manchester. Today Cora could see crowds of day trippers were enjoying its delights and, judging by their accents, most were from miles away.

Well dressed men and women sauntered arm-in-arm along the dam head, the ladies shaded under fringed parasols. A crowd of young men packed onto a landing stage, elbowing each other, impatient to clamber into a chugging motor launch. Courting couples sought a little privacy in rowing boats, young men in straw boaters hauling on the oars to impress their companions. "I wonder if Oliver could row like that?" Cora thought.

A few yards from the lakeside, attractions were clustered under the trees. There were wooden huts selling sweets, hats, handkerchiefs and china trinkets painted with '*A Gift from Rudyard*'. In another hut, lads jostled around amusement machines, watching excitedly as pennies were slotted in and the handles flicked to send ball bearings spiralling round.

A small bungalow that had been converted to a tearoom was doing a brisk trade, its customers taking tea in china cups while they looked out across the water. Leek Town Band, their brass instruments gleaming in the sun, were playing on the lawn in front of the imposing Hotel Rudyard, but it was a Sunday and so there was no one dancing on the grass as they did on a Saturday or Whit Monday.

"My, how busy it is," said Cora.

"Let's find somewhere to sit down. How about across there?" said Ellen, pointing to a neatly clipped area in front of Spite Hall, a tall stone house. Its owners ran a refreshment room and also operated one of the latest attractions, a petrol driven motor launch called the 'Grace Darling'.

As the two approached the house, Cora could see a group of cyclists picnicking in a corner of the lawn. Their gleaming black bicycles were parked against the hedge and tied to the machines was a canvas banner announcing '*Clarion Cycling Club – Potteries Branch*'. She realised this was no coincidence, Ellen had probably been hoping the Clarion cyclists would be there today.

Some weeks previously Ellen had told Cora she had met the Clarion 'scouts'. They were members of the Labour Party who toured towns and villages handing out pamphlets on workers' issues and looking out for new recruits to the Socialist movement. Ellen was convinced that workers, especially women in Leek's mills like herself, needed to fight for a better deal for themselves.

The Clarion Club had given Ellen new ideas about fair pay and more support for working folk and she had told Cora about it enthusiastically. Although Cora was fortunate enough to enjoy working in her father's studio, she knew many other young people were employed in the silk mills and she thought they should be treated fairly. Both she and Ellen had been stirred by trades union rallies that had been held in Leek, aimed at boosting membership especially amongst women workers.

One of the Clarion group waved and shouted a greeting as Ellen and Cora approached.

"Ellen! How nice to see you," said a woman with short dark hair and sharp features who looked to be in her middle twenties. Two of the male cyclists also acknowledged Ellen with a nod before returning to their sandwiches.

"Beatrice, I wondered if you might be here today. Spreading the word as usual!" Ellen replied and then introduced Cora.

"Pleased to meet you, my name is Beatrice Elliott. Do you work at the same mill as Ellen?" said Beatrice. She was immediately gauging if Cora would be another recruit to the cause.

Before Cora could speak, Ellen answered for her, obviously proud of her friend's work. "Oh no, she's a photographer. Well, she works with her father who's a photographer and she sometimes takes pictures."

"Photographer? How very interesting," said Beatrice, appraising Cora anew. "We are always looking for people who can help our campaign. Photographs could be very useful."

Cora did not quite know what to answer. She had only just met this woman and yet she was being approached to work for the Labour movement. Still, she couldn't help being a little excited at the thought of joining a real campaign.

"Well, I've only just started to take photographs myself. Father takes most of them and I do some developing, printing and framing. But if I could help..." Cora replied, realising that framing pictures sounded rather lame compared to taking photographs of important social issues.

"But Cora wants to change things, just like I do," Ellen jumped in, still keen to impress the Clarion scout.

"Change things? You know, Ellen, there's really only one way we can do that," Beatrice continued.

"By giving women the vote, you mean?"

"Exactly! There will be no fairness for women until we can vote for ourselves." Beatrice glanced across at the rest of the Clarion group. She knew that not all men supported Votes for Women, even in the Labour Party. Many believed it would be the upper class, not working women, who would be the first to benefit.

Cora did not need any persuading. She could see straight away that it would be a cause worth fighting for.

"So... how do you change things? Surely it's for the people in Parliament to decide, isn't it? What can we do about it?" Cora asked.

"Being allowed to vote is just the start, Cora," Beatrice replied, gripping her leaflets ever tighter. "Our chances in life are limited in all sorts of ways. Yes, there are many folk against us, including most of the politicians, so we are going to have to fight. Make protests, organise demonstrations, make sacrifices if we have to. Whatever it takes, we must do it."

Cora could see Miss Elliott was deadly serious and found herself in awe of this fervent woman she had met only a few minutes ago.

Realising that the two young women were keen listeners, Beatrice told them what some of the Votes for Women campaigners were doing already, although she admitted that progress was painfully slow.

"Manchester is where a lot of the protests are taking place at the moment. That's where Mrs Pankhurst lives, she's the one who's organising everything. She's amazing and so is her daughter, Christabel. Their speeches are so inspiring, although some people are trying to keep them quiet." Beatrice paused as she was struck by an idea.

"If you two want to know about the fight you should see what's really going on." Beatrice looked round and lowered her voice. "We've had word there's going to be a protest at Stockport market next Saturday. It isn't advertised in case the authorities try to stop it, but I shall be going. Why don't you two come? You could catch the train from Leek and I would make sure you were all right."

Ellen and Cora looked at one another uncertainly. The conversation had moved on so fast that they both wondered what they were getting into. Would they dare to go to Stockport on their own?

Seeing the doubt in their faces, Beatrice tried to reassure them.

"Look young ladies, I could meet you at Stockport station. You could listen to the speech and then I'd make sure you caught the train back. It's going to start about three o'clock, so you would need to be there by half past two. Think about it and if you decide to come, send me a note." Beatrice took a pencil out of her pocket, wrote her address on one of the pamphlets and pressed it into Ellen's hand. "Try to make it, you won't regret it!"

Beatrice went back to her companions to start handing out more pamphlets, and Ellen and Cora went to buy ginger beer from one of the refreshment stalls. At first neither of them spoke about what Beatrice had suggested. It was exciting and yet frightening at the same time. Beatrice had talked to them like adults and now she seemed to expect them to behave like adults, too.

Cora was the first to speak. They were on the dusty path beside the lake when she suddenly halted and turned to face Ellen.

"We've got to go to Stockport," she announced.

"Oh, I'm glad you've said that, Cora," said Ellen. "I so want to

47

hear Mrs Pankhurst or whoever it is. I'd be scared to go on my own, but if we went together…"

"Together," Cora said, "we can go there and we can join the fight for the vote."

On the walk back to Leek, Ellen and Cora planned how they would make the trip. It was going to be an adventure as neither of them had caught a train that far on their own before. Cora had been on day trips with her parents and Ellen had only been on a train to visit her grandmother in Stoke.

They decided that Cora would look for the railway timetable that was printed in the *Leek Lion* every week. On Monday she would call at Ellen's house with a note of the train times. It would be Ellen's job to send a postcard to Beatrice Elliott and tell her what time they would arrive at Stockport station.

The two also talked about what story they should tell to keep their trip secret. If their parents found out they would flatly refuse to let them travel on their own to a town miles away, to meet a group of strangers in some protest that might be illegal. Cora hated keeping things from her mother and father, but this time she would simply have to do so.

As soon as she reached home she found that week's *Lion* and told her mother that she was going to look at it in her room while she rested before supper. The railway timetable filled about a third of a page and, after deciphering all the symbols and footnotes, she copied out the times of trains between Leek and Stockport on Saturdays.

Cora would have to miss the next dance lesson with Signor Manfredi, but dancing was the least of her concerns at the moment. Then it struck her that she had not thought about Sarah Hulme since she had been to Rudyard. Her mind had been full of the women's campaign and the adventure to Stockport. She felt a little guilty. She knew she must not let this new scheme with Ellen get in the way of what she had sworn to do for Sarah, so the next thing she needed to do was to contact Oliver Finch.

Cora found another piece of paper and quickly wrote a note to Oliver asking him if he knew where the theatre people were staying because she wanted to talk to them about Sarah. She put it an envelope and dashed downstairs.

"I'm popping to the post," she shouted towards the kitchen door and left the house before her mother could reply. Minutes later she slipped the envelope through the letterbox at the *Leek Lion* office.

Voices were raised more than usual that Sunday night at The Hare and Greyhound in Warslow, a village on the moors half a dozen miles from Leek. The bowling alley at the back of the inn was always popular and tonight a match versus The Black Lion from neighbouring Butterton was in raucous progress.

The narrow room was filled with the smell of sweat, beer and tobacco. Young men were bowling the chipped wooden ball with ever greater force, flexing biceps built by hauling stone and or wrestling rams. All were red in the face from the exertion and from the ale. Each time the skittles went flying there was a roar of approval from one side or the other and a dog barked excitedly. Village pride was at stake.

In the bar at the front of the low ceilinged inn, old timers sat around a small circular table, in turn sucking their clay pipes and taking a sip of ale. All were long past being able to graft in the quarry or on the farm and needed to make a pint of Sixpenny Best last the whole evening. They met most Sundays to put the world to rights and tonight's conversation turned to the gypsies who had set up camp on land on the edge of the village.

"I don't like the look of 'em. Be glad when they're gone," said one curmudgeonly chap, gazing unhappily into his glass.

"Come on Walter, what 'arm does they do?" commented a fellow called Samuel, a fuzz of white hair around his chin but none on his head.

"Gypsies been comin' since I were a lad," Samuel went on. "Granted, some look a bit rough and you 'ave to keep an eye on anything that might go missing. But them gypsy women are fair enough. I 'ad me some beautiful mushrooms when they come knockin' the other day."

Walter was not persuaded. "Never liked strangers round Warslow. And they're talking foreign. I've 'eard 'em."

"Well, they're German, that's why. 'Orse dealers, lookin' for bargains," explained a third man in an authoritative tone. He always wore tiny wire-framed spectacles, the presence of which his fellows took as a sign of his learning. He reckoned the visitors had arrived not only for the village's own livestock sale, but for the big horse fair being held in Leek the next week.

"German? There ye go... we've got to watch our backs and no mistake. Kaiser Bill's sent 'em!" Walter continued.

"Well, I know nowt about Kaiser Bill, nor do I want to. 'E should stay over in Germany, if you ask me," Samuel declared. "But some of them gypsies know more about 'orses than the rest of us put 'gether. Aye, and folk say they drive an 'ard bargain."

"What about what that John Bull writes in the *Lion*? 'Ave you seen his stuff? Spies for the damn Kaiser, all o'er the place. War on the way. It's the same in that there *Daily Mail*," Walter continued.

Although he could not afford to buy a newspaper himself, nowadays Walter spent much of his time studying what was going on in the world thanks to the periodicals in the village's tiny Reading Room, especially when it was too wet for him to sit outside the front door of his cottage.

"That's why we're making friends with the Frenchies," he added with a wag of the finger.

"I don't know nothing about politics, but ye might be right, Wally. We might all need to keep a look out fer trouble – at least until these foreign folk have moved on."

Those words from Samuel were greeted with grunts of approval. Then discussion moved on to another pressing matter – whether The Grouse, a village inn that had become a 'temperance hotel', would ever serve ale again.

Albert Ramm leaned back in his armchair and closed his eyes, nodding appreciatively as Edna picked out tunes on the piano in the parlour of their Queen Street home. Last Christmas, Albert had bought his wife a copy of *Favourites from Gilbert and Sullivan* and she had been studiously working her way through the album.

Sunday was a time when many folk stayed at home, catching up on housework and quietly occupying themselves, often with the Bible, particularly if they were churchgoers. Although Albert and Edna were regular members of the St Edward's congregation, they had decided that a little music on a Sunday was in order and these evening recitals were now a regular occurrence in the Ramm household.

"Edna dear, that was charming," said Ramm encouragingly as his wife lifted her hands from the keys. She turned and smiled her appreciation.

The scene of domestic harmony was disturbed by a heavy rapping at the front door. Ramm looked at the clock above the fireplace and frowned. It showed half past nine.

"Who on earth can this be?" he said, his heart sinking. Callers so late usually meant some kind of trouble in the town. Friday night at the rag-and-stick had been bad enough.

"Not again," he muttered as he pulled himself up and strode to the door, watched nervously by Edna.

The visitor was Constable Knowles. "You must come to the

station, Sir. There's been a call from Headquarters, Chief Superintendent Johnson, I think he said it was. He wants to speak to you straightaway," he said.

Although two officers patrolled the town through the night, it was Knowles, unmarried and lodging in an upstairs room at the police station, who had the job of dealing with enquiries when the main door was closed. However to receive a telephone call at such an hour was highly unusual, as Knowles' excited expression showed.

"Headquarters? At this time of night?" Ramm was bemused, but hoped it was something important enough to disturb his Sunday evening. Grabbing his uniform tunic and cap from a peg in the hallway he called a farewell to Edna and hurried after his constable.

Once Knowles unlocked the station's front door Inspector Ramm made straight for the gleaming black and brass telephone on the reception counter. He snatched up the heavy handset, wound the handle to reach an operator at the exchange and asked to be put through to the County Police Headquarters in Stafford.

Knowles watched intently, anxious to find out what was going on. However the Inspector's curt questions revealed nothing.

"What?" a startled Ramm barked into the mouthpiece.

"When?"

"How many?"

"For how long?"

"Where to?"

Knowles looked expectantly when Ramm finally dropped the handset into its cradle. The Inspector stared blankly across the room and spoke almost in disbelief.

"The King is coming to Leek!"

CHAPTER SIX

"His Royal Highness will be passing through Leek on Friday of next week. There are no plans for him to actually stop anywhere in the town. At least, that is what I have been told."

Inspector Ramm announced the Royal visit to his team at their Monday morning meeting. The news was greeted with surprise and not a little concern from some of the officers.

"Next week, Sir?" asked Sergeant Reynolds, second in command at the station.

"That is right, Friday the twenty second. The King's motor car is due to leave Swythamley Hall at around quarter past eleven, no doubt His Royal Highness will be taking a sizeable breakfast."

The last remark lightened the mood and Ramm paused before continuing. "He should arrive in Leek sometime after twelve noon, depending on the speed of his vehicle. The King and his party will be on their way to Alton Towers and that means he will be on our patch for quite a period of time. We will have to make sure all our rural constables know exactly what they need to do."

"Rather short notice isn't it, Sir?" Reynolds persisted.

"Well Sergeant, I didn't find out myself until ten o'clock last night and I haven't had much sleep since. I am sure this visit was arranged weeks ago, perhaps months, but now that we *have* been informed, we must do our best. There will be plenty of eyes on us, including from Headquarters."

"Will there be reinforcements, Sir?" asked a young constable, clearly uneasy at the work they now faced.

"That I do not know, Phillips. I intend to make an immediate start on a plan of who needs to do what and where. In the meantime, what else do we have to deal with?"

Ramm looked across to Sergeant Reynolds who gave a brief summary of incidents over the weekend, which were thankfully few: a couple of drunks, a missing cow and a gold watch stolen at Rudyard. Then the Inspector spoke again.

"You will all be aware of what went on at the rag-and-stick. I should receive a post mortem report on the poor young woman today and we should try to find more witnesses. However, I expect the inquest to be held before the week is out and the whole matter settled."

In the light of the King's visit, it was obvious that Ramm hoped Sarah Hulme's death would not occupy too much of anyone's time at the station.

"And there's the Horse Fair coming up on Thursday, Sir," Reynolds interjected. "That always brings a fair old crowd into town. We will have to keep an eye out for pickpocketing, drunkenness and the like."

"Very good point, Sergeant. We may need extra men on the beat that day. The Horse Fair has drawn a few ruffians to town in the past."

Returning to his office, Ramm took up a pen, dipped it with precision into the bottle on his inkstand, and began a list of what was needed for when King Edward VII travelled through the moorlands in barely ten days' time. The King's motor car would be accompanied by two others, he understood, one of them containing the young Philip Lee Brocklehurst, who had inherited the Swythamley baronetcy only months earlier. Ramm surmised that his force's main task would be to ensure the vehicles' progress went unimpeded.

The crowds along the route would be their biggest headache. He expected patriotic locals to be respectful; there were huge celebrations in the town when King Edward was crowned two years ago, following the grief at losing their beloved Queen.

However he knew the throng would be excitable, and excitement could bring unfortunate consequences.

He had written more than a dozen lines and was pressing the sheet on his blotting pad when Constable Knowles came in.

"This has just arrived for you, Sir," the officer said, passing him an envelope.

"Excellent," said Ramm, recognising the fine script on the envelope as the hand of Dr Handbridge, the town's Medical Officer of Health who had carried out the post mortem examination on Sarah Hulme.

Ramm unfolded a foolscap sheet and studied its contents, stroking his moustache, deep in thought. Finally he put the paper down and heaved a sigh of frustration. Dr Handbridge had confirmed that the young woman died from asphyxiation and marks around her neck were consistent with a rope noose.

But the Medical Officer also reported other marks on her neck, as well as bruises on her upper arms. Dr Handbridge suggested Sarah could have made the marks on her neck herself, perhaps in a last desperate attempt to free herself. However, and this is what troubled Ramm, the doctor could not rule out them being made by a third party.

Ramm reached into a drawer and pulled out the photographs Nathaniel Blake had taken on the fateful evening. He tried to picture the sequence of events and how they might fit with the post mortem findings. But he came up with more questions than answers.

How had Miss Hulme managed to reach the ropes? Had she been struggling frantically before the curtain opened? Crucially, if someone else had been involved, who was it?

He thought back to what Blake had said about his daughter's suspicions and the curious letter Miss Hulme had sent to Miss Blake. Perhaps the affair was not as clear cut as he had hoped.

"Knowles!" Ramm shouted through his open door, bringing the

constable hurrying back down the corridor.

"Go over to the rag-and-stick and find Mr Kilner. Tell him to gather his people together. I shall be there to speak to them in an hour."

Nathaniel Blake took care what he said to his daughter that Monday morning. He hoped her outing to Rudyard had done her some good, but he realised that Sarah's death would be on her mind for a long time to come.

Nathaniel knew Cora too well to believe she would simply drop her suspicions about what had actually gone on at the rag-and-stick. He was proved right when, soon after they arrived at the studio, she asked where he had put the photographs he had taken of the Kilner Theatre Company the previous week.

"Are you sure you want to look at those, my dear?" Blake asked.

"Please, Father, it's important."

As well as the publicity photograph which had appeared in Saturday's *Leek Lion*, Blake had printed out half a dozen other images of the actors and stage crew lined up in front of the tent.

Cora sifted through them, looking closely not only at Sarah but also examining the other faces, as if she was trying to read something in their expressions. Cora saw that her friend looked slightly different in each picture, serious in some, smiling in others. One in particular caught her attention. Sarah's face was turned towards a tall young man standing beside her. Her were eyes wide and she appeared to be laughing. The other person was looking at Sarah, his mouth slightly open, apparently sharing some whispered exchange.

Cora stared at the picture. The way Sarah was smiling at the young man, the way he looked back, she could see that there was something between those two that neither could disguise. Perhaps this was the secret Sarah had so wanted to tell Cora about. She was confused. Surely this couldn't have led to Sarah's death.

"Is everything all right, my dear?" Nathaniel asked, seeing his daughter frowning in concentration.

Cora hesitated. Best not to share her idea with her father, she thought. At least not until she had found out more about what had been going on between Sarah and this rather handsome young man. Instead, she handed Nathaniel one of the other photographs.

"I was wondering who this person is," she said, pointing to the young man.

Blake looked at the photograph and recognised him as the actor he had met on Friday night.

"The young man? Why, that's the fellow who helped me with the flash-lamp... er... on Friday night. He said his name was Thomas Kilner. I presume he's related to the Professor."

"Oh, I see," Cora replied, trying to keep her voice steady, but secretly excited. This clue might help her to find the truth. She must speak to the young man, as soon as possible.

When Cora went out to post some packages of photographs, Blake scrutinised the pictures of the theatre company for himself. Something had sparked his daughter's curiosity, though she had done her best to conceal it.

Studying and comparing the photographs, Blake now spotted the look shared between Sarah and Thomas Kilner. He thought how the young man had behaved on Friday night, when he was helping with the flash-lamp. The way he had been transfixed by the sight of Sarah's body. Surely young Kilner must know more how Sarah had been in the last few weeks.

While Cora was still out, he gathered prints of all the pictures relating to Miss Hulme. There were the theatre group photographs, the images he had taken on stage and of the young woman's body, as well as a copy he had made of her last letter to Cora before he handed it to Inspector Ramm. He also began to jot down his thoughts on the affair. He often did this when he was puzzling over

57

a police case, trying his hand at being a detective.

He tried to remember exactly what had happened on Friday night. He closed his eyes and reimagined the scene when the curtains opened: the shadowy body suspended above the stage, twisting slowly towards the audience, and what was below it. Blake's eyes shot open as he realised there had been no straw bale or chair near Sarah's feet. He was sure of it.

"That can't be right," he said to himself.

He knew this was a police affair, but now he shared Cora's suspicions and they both wanted to find the truth.

An hour later, Inspector Ramm had climbed onto the stage in the rag-and-stick and was looking down at the performers gathered in the tent, some standing, some seated on the benches.

Orlando Kilner stood to one side, looking back and forth between the officer and his company members. He had appeared flustered when Constable Knowles had told him that the Inspector wanted to speak to them all and now he could not hide his concern at what might be said.

Ramm cleared his throat, aware that his audience was much more accustomed to speaking from a stage than himself.

"Ladies and gentlemen, the tragedy of Friday night has upset you all, I am sure," he began. "You may prefer to move on from it, but we have to establish the circumstances surrounding Miss Hulme's death. I wish to hear from anyone who saw Miss Hulme immediately before her death or who may know something which would have a bearing on the matter."

The performers looked around, it seemed no one seeming wanted to speak first. Ramm saw several cast anxious glances towards Professor Kilner. Were they afraid of speaking freely, he wondered.

"I'm sorry, Sir, but I just can't understand it. None of us can," one young woman piped up. "Sarah seemed fine, as far as I'm concerned."

"I am particularly puzzled how Miss Hulme managed to reach into the ropes above the stage without any of you noticing what was going on and trying to stop her," Ramm continued. He looked from face to face for some reaction, but there was nothing to be discerned. He gave a sigh of disappointment.

"I think I will need to speak to you individually. Mr Kilner, is there somewhere I can conduct interviews in privacy?"

A small table and three chairs were set up in an adjoining dressing area where Inspector Ramm and Constable Knowles could be seated with one member of the company at a time. Kilner fussed over the arrangements, making a show of accommodating Ramm's needs while commenting: "I hope this is not a waste of your time, Inspector. I am sure there was nothing suspicious about the sad episode."

Ramm's interviews began with Conrad Mulder, the stage manager. Well over six feet tall and broad shouldered, he appeared ideally suited to the task of building the theatre each week. A stained grey vest was stretched tightly over his ample girth and a wide leather belt supported his black breeches. His long hair was greying and unkempt, his jutting chin had not seen a razor in days.

Mulder was of little help. He spoke haltingly in broken English and explained he was from Belgium. He claimed he had not looked on stage once the props were set out and so knew nothing of Miss Hulme's fate until the audience cried out.

Subsequent interviews followed in rapid succession. Most said the same thing: there had been no inkling of what would happen on the fateful evening. Some had been her friend, some barely knew her.

Ramm was particularly keen to question those who removed Sarah's body from the rigging. What emerged was a scene of general mayhem on the night. No one agreed on what had been moved to reach the young woman or precisely how she was freed from the noose.

When Ramm and Knowles finally walked back to the police station it was approaching lunchtime and the Inspector's thoughts were increasingly drawn to the hearty sandwich that awaited him in his desk drawer. The interviews at the rag-and-stick had revealed little. However, the very absence of information, similar to Professor Kilner's ready denials on Saturday, made him suspect that he was still not hearing the whole story.

John Gibb had pushed a handcart into the middle of Leek from Mrs Carter's farm on the edge of town. He collected two sacks of bone meal from Carding's Agricultural Stores in Derby Street and then went over to the knife grinder who parked his sharpening stone in the street twice a week. He waited as the man attended to a scythe that was needed on the farm and glanced across the street to where there was considerable activity outside the Town Baths. Several groups of women were standing talking, young children running about at their feet. The baths were always popular on Mondays with ladies wishing to swim, or to teach their youngsters, because they knew the water would be clean as it was changed at the start of each week.

Gibb then went into Skinner & Co. ironmonger's, the front of the shop festooned with galvanised watering cans, dustbins, buckets, coal scuttles, sieves, saucepans, mops, brushes, rope and a sign for Pratt's Motor Spirit. Its interior was equally crowded with everything the grower, handyman or cook might require. John bought two bags of nails and spool of twine and started to trundle his handcart back up Derby Street.

It was the middle of the day and the town's main street was busy with pedestrians and the occasional cart, but his attention was drawn to a group of men emerging from The Cock Inn. They were talking animatedly and at the centre of the group was a portly, dark-haired fellow he had seen on stage on Saturday evening. He realised they were all probably members of the theatre company, though some of them looked rather different without their stage costumes.

As the actors made their way noisily past Gibb he saw someone else come out of the inn. It was the man he had recognised in the audience at the rag-and-stick.

Gibb halted and watched the man look down the street, then turn in the opposite direction and walk off quickly. John was sure the fellow had seen him.

He decided to follow and try to speak to the man. Looking around, he saw a group of boys sitting on the edge of the pavement outside the Congregational Church.

"Here, you lads," he called, "watch this cart for a minute or two, and I'll give you a copper when I come back."

One of the boys tipped his cap and stood next to the handcart, determined to be the one to claim the reward. Gibb strode purposefully up the street, hoping to catch up with his quarry.

As he got nearer he saw the man turn towards the Market Place. Dodging an old lady bent over a walking stick, the Scotsman reached the corner in time to see the other man quicken his pace and then dart to the right again, disappearing into the alley that led to the stables behind The Red Lion Inn.

Gibb walked still faster, despite his heavy working boots, and went into the narrow entry between the Buttermarket building and the inn. He could no longer see the man he was following. He continued along the alley, but when he reached the Red Lion yard he could see no one.

He stopped and looked around. On the far side of the cobbled yard he caught sight of a hefty door swinging open. He advanced towards the low building and as he got closer his nostrils filled with the smell of raw meat. His steps faltered as he saw blood on the ground, until he remembered that this building was used by a local butcher as a slaughterhouse.

In contrast to the bright sunshine, the interior of the building was dark and, as he stepped through the doorway, he could see nothing in front of him at first. Then he perceived a bloodstained cutting block in the centre of the room and a row of cleavers hanging from hooks along the wall. He paused as he had the sudden thought that there might be danger in here.

As Gibb took a step further into the abattoir he heard a movement behind him and a hand grabbed his shoulder, spinning him around roughly.

"What's your game?" came a harsh voice from the shadows.

Gibb knew the voice, just as he had recognised the man's features at the rag-and-stick on Saturday evening.

"Major Cavendish?" he asked. He put his hand up to shade his eyes from the glare of sunlight in the doorway and tried to get a better look at the man.

Still grasping Gibb's coat, the other man said nothing.

"It's me, Sir. John Gibb, Sergeant Major Gibb, Queen's Own Highlanders. Do you not recollect me, Sir?"

The man dropped his hand from Gibb's shoulder, but his stony expression gave no sign of recognition.

"I think you must be mistaken, my man. Cavendish is not my name," he said quietly.

"But we both served Her Majesty in the Sudan. Khartoum… General Gordon…the siege. Surely it is you, Sir?"

The man raised his voice, now speaking forcefully. "I know nothing of what you are talking about. And I would be glad if you stopped following me. Otherwise, I shall have to do something about it." His eyes narrowed and he added: "Do you understand?"

Gibb peered into the man's face, baffled by the reaction. He was sure it was Major Francis Cavendish whom he had last seen at the hellhole that became of Khartoum. They had been from different regiments but had been thrown together in the infamous siege. And this was the man who had been awarded the Victoria Cross for his bravery. Yes, it was nearly twenty years ago, but soldiers did not forget such things, especially a man like Cavendish.

The other man showed no sign of recognition. If anything he became even more aggressive, seizing Gibb by the lapels of his jacket.

"Listen, you fellow. We have never met before, do you hear me? I do not wish to see you again. If you get in my way you will suffer for it. Now, be gone." He pushed Gibb back forcefully to make his point.

Gibb steadied himself. Momentarily he considered standing his ground, then decided against it. He believed he could handle himself against the man, but if Cavendish was truly deranged there was no telling how it might turn out, particularly when there was a meat cleaver within reach.

"If that's your wish, aye, I shall steer clear of ye. I bid ye good day," Gibb replied curtly, pushing past the man and walking out into the sunshine again. He didn't look back.

His was still frowning in confusion as he reached the main street and found the lad obediently guarding his handcart of farm supplies. Gibb fished a penny out of his pocket before seizing the cart and setting off again up the street, saddened by the bizarre behaviour of a man who had once been a hero.

The working day had ended when Cora called at the Simms' house in Cruso's Yard. The courtyard off Stockwell Street was crowded with some of the poorest houses in town. In one corner a pair of privies were shared by all the folk who lived there. It had been another hot day and, from the smell coming from that direction, Cora could tell the privies were long overdue being emptied by the 'bucket man'. She tried not to look in the other corner where a midden was piled with anything the families couldn't burn on their stoves. Several young children, most of them barefoot, ran back and forth chasing a hoop across the cobbles. Water dripped from a cast iron pump in front of one of the humble homes.

Ellen came to the door and ushered Cora back towards the street. "We must be quick because I'm helping Ma with supper," said Ellen.

There was no room in the Simms' cottage for them to talk and little privacy in the yard. The two young women stopped outside a set of stables which adjoined the houses and talked over their plans for the following weekend. Cora was pleased to hear that Ellen had not changed her mind and handed her the note of the train times. Ellen said she would write to Beatrice. They agreed to meet at the railway station at one o'clock on Saturday, telling their parents they were going on another country walk.

The plan decided, Cora was impatient to make another call. She hurried to Market Street and was glad to find the door of the *Leek Lion* offices unlocked. She had been here before to see Oliver Finch and she quickly made her way past where the great iron printing press stood silent on the ground floor and went up the staircase. On the next floor was where the *Lion's* pages were put together from thousands of letters made of metal and wood. This room was usually a hive of activity, but Alfred the compositor had gone home. She could hear the clatter of typewriters as she neared the second floor, the sound of father and son still at work.

When they first became friends, Cora had been embarrassed to speak to Oliver in front of his father. But she had learnt a few lessons in life since then. "Mr Finch, I hope you are well?" she said confidently as the editor looked up from his trusty Imperial typewriter.

"Miss Blake! A pleasant surprise," FJ replied. "I hope you are somewhat recovered from that sorry affair on Friday?"

"I am still very upset about what happened to my friend, Mr

Finch. She was wronged, I believe," Cora replied, her voice full of emotion.

Finch's eyebrows rose, sensing there must be something he did not know about Miss Hulme's death, something he would need to find out for the next edition. Before he could press Cora on what she meant, Oliver sprang up from his swivelling office chair and stepped between them.

"Cora, how can I help?" he asked.

She did not respond immediately and instead looked towards FJ. Realising the two young people might have something private to discuss, Finch senior decided to leave them to it.

"I must dash to the Telegraph Office, I have messages to send," he said, making for the stairs. When his father had gone, Oliver's gaze searched Cora's face, anxious to see whether she was faring any better.

"Have you found out anything for me, Oliver? You see, there is someone I especially want to speak to," she said.

"Well, I do know where most of Professor Kilner's performers are staying. They are at Warburton's Lodging House in Stockwell Street, although a few others sleep in the theatre's carts. But..."

"I must go there," Cora interrupted, "I need to see the one called Kilner, Thomas Kilner."

Oliver was a little taken aback. "Oh? Why him in particular?"

"I think he was Sarah's...friend. He might know more about what happened to her."

"Well, please be careful. Perhaps I should come with you." Oliver was unable to hide his concern. "Besides, you have no idea what sort of person this Thomas Kilner is. How old is he?"

"I think he's about the same age as you. And from his photograph, he looks friendly enough."

"Friendly? I know that Sarah meant a lot to you, but..."

Cora did not let him finish. "Oliver, I shall not rest until I know what was behind Sarah's death."

She turned to go, ending their conversation. As Oliver listened to her footsteps clatter down the wooden stairs he wished he had persuaded Cora to let him accompany her. He didn't like the sound of her meeting this person on her own, someone they knew nothing about.

On her way home Cora made a detour back into Stockwell Street and past Warburton's Lodging House. She had heard of other lodgings in Church Street where really poor people paid a penny to sleep standing up, leaning against a rope, but this house looked a little more respectable and she was sure the performers would need a bed. Standing outside the front door, she couldn't stop herself lifting the brass knocker. An elderly woman, whom she took to be Mrs Warburton, opened the door. In answer to Cora's question she replied that none of "those theatre folk" were in.

Cora could not face going round to the rag-and-stick to find young Kilner, in fact she didn't know if she would ever bring herself to go inside a theatre tent again, and so she turned towards home.

She had gone only a few steps further when she was nearly bundled over by a figure hurrying in the opposite direction. It was Signor Manfredi, head down, preoccupied, striding out with those long skinny legs.

"Signor Manfredi!" Cora cried, startled.

"Oh Miss Blake! Scusi! I hurry and not notice you."

The dance teacher was breathless, his eyes darting around the street, beads of sweat between his strands of hair. Cora felt a pang of sympathy – he was plainly still upset about Sarah's death. She must have meant so much to him.

"Monday night I give lessons on piano. Home, I must be home. My pupils, they wait," Manfredi explained, waving a thin hand vaguely down the street before making off again at a smart pace.

Cora watched him go and thought how she used to enjoy those lessons from this excitable fellow with the strange accent. She wondered whether the dance school would ever be the same again.

FJ Finch was in the Telegraph Office, part of the town's main Post Office in Derby Street. It stayed open until eight each evening and was still busy, hence Finch had to join a queue at the counter to send his telegrams. He planned to contact the Manchester offices of the *Daily Mail* and the *Daily Telegraph* to offer a report about John Bull's planned meeting on the 'The German Question'.

In front of him, a stranger was engaged in animated discussion with the telegraph clerk. Finch liked to think he knew most people in Leek, but had never seen this man before. He had the air of someone visiting the town on business, someone used to giving orders. The curious journalist could not help listening in on the increasingly heated exchange.

"But Sir, I can't understand what I'm supposed to be typing," the young clerk was saying, holding up a piece of paper on which the customer had written the text of his telegram. "It doesn't look like English to me."

"It matters not a jot whether you understand it, young fellow. That is the message I wish to send, it is urgent and it must be sent this evening," the man replied forcefully, stabbing his finger at the note. "Perhaps we should summon the Postmaster?"

At the mention of his superior, the clerk relented and went back to his seat at the telegraphy machine. Finch watched the young man alternately peer at the customer's note and press the telegraph keys. It was a laborious process, made slower as the clerk apparently did not understand the message he was supposed to be sending. The customer sighed impatiently.

Finally the telegram was on its way, perhaps to some far-flung destination where it would be delivered by a GPO messenger boy that evening. After the clerk had added up the number of words and worked out the cost, the customer scattered a handful of coins on the counter and stalked away.

It had been a curious exchange and Finch took a good look at the man as he left. Late forties, straight-backed and with a greying moustache, he walked with the confidence of a military man. His expression was uncompromising, menacing even.

"I wonder who he is?" Finch thought.

Later that week he would find out, thanks to John Gibb.

CHAPTER SEVEN

Soon after Nathaniel Blake arrived at work the following morning he asked Cora to look after the studio while he went to see Inspector Ramm. Unfortunately, when Blake arrived at the police station the harassed Inspector made it clear he could afford the photographer little time.

Ramm had much to do in preparation for the King's visit although, as details were still sparse, he was not yet prepared to share news of the occasion, even with Blake.

Nathaniel proceeded to explain why he thought Thomas Kilner should be interviewed and why he had doubts about Sarah Hulme's death.

"I've been going over it all again and I just cannot imagine how the young lady managed to reach those ropes above the stage," Blake went on.

"I must admit, Mr Blake, the same thought had occurred to me," replied the Inspector. "As for Thomas Kilner, I interviewed him yesterday and he had nothing for us. Perhaps I need to speak to him again and put a little more pressure on him."

After Nathaniel had left, Ramm leaned forward on his desk, head in hands. Blake's comments had added to his own misgivings about Sarah Hulme's death. There would be no swift inquest, he feared, and his inquiries would have to go on.

Cora Blake had spent the previous evening and most of the morning thinking about Thomas Kilner. By lunchtime she had decided to pay another visit to the boarding house. She was in the street outside her father's studio when she heard the sound of an accordion coming from the Market Place nearby.

Once she was in the square, she could see that members of the theatre company had made a temporary stage out of wooden crates and were giving an impromptu performance of songs and readings. As Cora got closer, three young women, including one with dark brown skin, started a tap dance routine.

Cora edged towards the front of the crowd that had gathered around the stage and immediately recognised Thomas Kilner. She found she could not to take her eyes off him. Tall with blond hair that fell across his forehead, he had a confident air as he recited his lines.

She took in little of the performance, however. Instead, her mind was on how she could attract his attention and whether he would even speak to her. Suddenly she felt less sure of herself, but she knew she had to do something if only for Sarah's sake.

There was a ripple of applause when the show came to an end and as the spectators began to drift away Cora stepped closer. Thomas Kilner jumped down from the platform and started to move the crates.

"Excuse me!" Cora called out. She was embarrassed at how small her voice seemed compared to how loud the performers had sounded. Thomas ignored her.

She cleared her throat and shouted a little louder: "Excuse me. Thomas? Could I speak to you?"

Kilner swivelled round to see who had called his name. He saw a young woman looking up at him with an earnest expression. She was at least a foot shorter than himself, her brown hair pulled back.

"Can I help you, Miss?" Thomas replied cautiously. He had no idea who she was. He suspected she was probably someone who wanted to ask about the coming night's show.

"I want to talk to you about Sarah Hulme," said Cora, regaining her confidence.

Now she had his full attention. As his deep-set eyes appraised her, Cora felt a frisson of nerves mixed with excitement. She understood how Sarah may have fallen for this handsome young man.

"About Sarah? I'm not sure what I can tell you, but perhaps we should find somewhere more private?" said Thomas, looking around the cobbled square.

"What about over there?" Cora suggested, pointing to the entrance to the Buttermarket. Although the indoor market hall was closed for business, the cast iron gates across its entrance hall were open. Thomas exchanged a word with his fellows and then followed Cora across to the market building.

"So. What did you want to ask?" asked Thomas, turning to face Cora, his eyes searching her features.

Cora clenched her fists by her sides, determined not to be disconcerted by the tall young actor, perhaps five years older than herself.

"My name is Cora Blake and Sarah was a good friend of mine. I encouraged her to join your theatre," Cora began. She paused and took a deep breath. "I was there on Friday night when it all happened. It was my father who took the photographs... of the stage."

"Oh yes, I think Sarah mentioned you. She... she wanted you to see her on stage," Thomas replied, looking away as he remembered Sarah's bubbling enthusiasm about coming back to her home town.

"So you were friends with Sarah, too?"

The question snapped Thomas back to the present. "You could say we are all friends in my father's theatre," he said smoothly.

"No, I think there was something special between you two," Cora challenged him.

"We all... liked Sarah," Thomas replied, a little less assured.

"But wasn't she worried about something? And why did she die?" Cora went on, her voice rising as she struggled to contain her feelings, sorrow mixed with anger and with her own guilt.

Thomas gulped as if he too was trying to swallow his emotions and looked away again.

"Yes, Sarah was a special person. And I know what it's like to lose someone who is close to you. Perhaps our theatre was not the right place for her." Thomas focused on Cora once more, his mood now different, determination seeming to burn in his eyes. "And you, Miss Blake, must stop with these questions. It would be best for all of us if you asked no more."

Before Cora could say anything else, Thomas turned and walked away.

Cora stared blankly at the brown glazed bricks of the Buttermarket entrance, her mind filled with what had just gone on with Thomas. She thought there was pain as well as anger behind his blue eyes. He had made it plain he didn't want to talk about Sarah, but she was determined to speak to him again. She was convinced there must be more to know.

Thomas was troubled by the conversation with Cora Blake when he met his father and Conrad Mulder later that afternoon.

The rest of the company were on stage, going over last-minute items for *A Wonderful Woman* that evening, including deciding who was to step into Sarah Hulme's part. They all knew not to disturb the theatre manager when he was engaged in one of his meetings. Occasionally one of them would try to listen in, but they could never make out what was being said.

Thomas, Orlando and Conrad had drawn their stools close together in a dressing area behind the stage. A fourth stool stood vacant. They were speaking in low voices.

"We not wait for our friend?" asked Conrad, nodding at the empty stool. He seemed much more confident than when he had spoken with Inspector Ramm.

"There is little time and much to discuss. Besides, he should be here soon," Kilner senior replied.

Conrad growled his consent.

"I have heard no more from the inquisitive policeman, so we can only hope that particular problem is going to go away," said the theatre manager. "By now he must believe there was nothing suspicious about this affair with Miss Hulme. Hopefully we can now get on with what we are actually here for."

"But we all know it should not have happened," commented Thomas. He looked less than happy with his father's breezy assurance. He knew it would not be easy to move on from Sarah's death, even if his father and the rest of the company were prepared to do so.

"Some young friend of Sarah's is asking questions," Thomas went on seriously. "She confronted me in the Market Place."

"Young friend? Who was this?" asked his father.

"The daughter of Mr Blake, the photographer. They were both here on Friday night and he took the photographs for the police," Thomas answered. "She wanted to know what had gone on with Sarah."

"And what did you say to her?"

"What do you think? I said that I knew nothing, of course."

"So what are you worried about, Thomas? Surely this young woman is of no consequence? What do you think, Conrad?" Kilner senior looked across at Mulder.

The stage manager, elbows on knees, leaned his bulk forward to ensure he had their attention.

"Weiter! Onward... we go on," said Conrad mixing his own tongue with English. "Ten more days and nothing stops. Then we pack and move. Forget police, forget fraulein." He spoke with an authority that seemed to leave little room for argument.

"I fear this young woman could be persistent," Thomas warned. The way Cora had looked so earnestly at him was fresh in his mind.

"Then you must make sure she does nothing to get in our way," Orlando told him. "Your brother always knew what he had to do."

Thomas clenched his jaws and nodded. Sometimes it seemed his father never missed an opportunity to refer to his brother, the one who had always done the right thing. Thomas knew they had probably not seen the last of Cora Blake and it was something he was going to have to deal with himself.

It was early on Tuesday evening and Francis Cavendish sat on the edge of his narrow iron bed, scanning his pages of notes. The three storey terraced house in Albion Street belonged to an aged clockmaker who let out his back bedroom to earn a few extra shillings. The old man spent most of his time in his attic workshop, the sort of space that was used for spinning, weaving or sewing in many similar Leek houses. Cavendish could hear the occasional tap and scrape of his tools through the ceiling.

Although the room was only big enough for a single bed, a small cabinet and a bentwood chair, it suited him. Ideally he would have liked to have found somewhere a little closer to the middle of town where the travelling theatre was set up, but at least this house was on a quiet street. There were no houses opposite, only the walled garden of some mansion, and the clockmaker kept himself to himself. Cavendish could come and go as he pleased without worrying too much about other people seeing him.

"Except for that fellow Gibb," he thought bitterly.

What were the chances of coming across someone who recognised him in a godforsaken place like this? Hopefully the Scotsman realised his mistake and would stay out of his way until he had left town, Cavendish thought.

"Curse the man!" he said under his breath, although he knew he should not blame Gibb. He shook his head, thinking back to those horrific days in the Sudan. The Sergeant Major had always been a stickler for proper conduct whatever conditions they found themselves in. The world had moved on since then, but the dangers remained. Nowadays Cavendish rarely met anyone he felt he could trust, even an old comrade.

"What must he think of me?" he wondered. Still, Gibb's opinions were of little importance at the moment. Cavendish had far more pressing matters to contend with.

He looked again at his papers. He had collected a telegram from the Post Office. It was addressed to the false name he was using so Cavendish believed he was safe from discovery there. But in a small town like this there was always tittle-tattle about strangers and he expected folk other than Gibb had seen him around.

He knew he could not relax. The death of that young woman had been unfortunate, but sometimes such things could not be avoided. Would there be consequences? Were the police even taking it seriously? He expected not, and it suited him to have no complications from the local constabulary.

His mind went back to a couple of hours earlier when he had been discreetly observing the younger Kilner in the Market Place. Cavendish had watched a young woman approach him and then they had gone through a gateway beneath the clock tower. Some sort of assignation, he thought.

"What was that all about? Is Thomas making a conquest?" Cavendish wondered. He decided he would need to watch out for that young woman, keep an eye on what she was up to.

He turned to his plans for the following day. First he would hire a horse and trap so that he could visit one or two local villages. He checked his list – Longnor, Warslow, Waterhouses, Ipstones – the names meant little to him. He fished out a map to see how far he would have to travel and to estimate how long it would take. There would be no time to waste. He needed to be back in Leek before the evening as he had important business to attend to.

What should he do tonight? He did not want to draw

unnecessary attention to himself, but thought it would be useful to visit one or two local inns and listen out for the gossip. Incidents like the one at the travelling theatre always set tongues wagging and he might hear something to his advantage.

"Over the next few days," Cavendish said to himself, "these folk might have a lot more to talk about."

CHAPTER EIGHT

Wednesday was always a busy market day and today the centre of Leek was heaving with activity as Inspector Ramm made his way to the courtroom where the inquest into Sarah Hulme's death was due to be held at ten o'clock.

Across the street from the police station, spirited bidding was under way in the livestock market, where pens were filled with cattle, sheep and pigs. Farmers in muddy boots and squashed trilbies prodded beasts with their sticks, or watched intently as the auctioneer called out the bidding.

Derby Street was lined with the carts of local carriers who had brought in customers from the surrounding rural area. Other carts had arrived laden with butter, cheese, eggs, fowl and produce to be sold in the Buttermarket and Poultry Market halls. In the Market Place the canvas-topped stalls were crammed together offering a huge variety of items, from kitchen tools to doormats, from pottery ornaments to pet rabbits.

Ramm threaded his way through a crush of people on the pavement, many of them farmers' wives carrying hefty wicker baskets for the day's shopping. Some of the women were selling rather than buying, and had laid out baskets of dairy produce and vegetables on the edge of the paving stones to tempt passers-by.

Adding to the busy scene were street hawkers pushing handcarts piled with summer crops and shouting "Strawberries, penny a scoop. Celery, ha'penny a stick." After touring the middle of town, they would start to walk the side streets and householders would often hear their calls until nightfall.

When Ramm reached the elegant Georgian building that was home to the town's leading solicitors he strode past a severe-looking clerk on the reception desk and took a corridor to the rear of the building.

Here was the wood-panelled room which served as the town's courtroom. On a summer's day such as this, there was no need for a fire in the grate because the air in the crowded room was stifling. Leather bound legal tomes lined all four walls and seemed to make the atmosphere even more oppressive. The windows were closed and could be opened only at the discretion of the presiding magistrate.

The inquest was scheduled to take place before a list of police cases were heard and so the room was crammed with a motley array of folk with many different reasons to be there: worried relatives, belligerent injured parties, hesitant witnesses, harassed lawyers. Sitting amongst them were Sarah's parents, looking around with bewildered expressions.

Inspector Ramm nodded to Edgar and Gladys Hulme as he entered, then turned to catch the attention of the Coroner, Herbert Evershed, who was about to start proceedings. The Coroner was seated on a raised dais at one end of the room, the position usually occupied by magistrates. He had to lean forward and tilt his head to one side to hear what the policeman was saying.

"Are you sure, Inspector?" Evershed responded, a frown adding to the creases on his wrinkled forehead.

"Certainly, Sir," said Ramm.

After checking that it was precisely ten o'clock the Coroner lifted a gavel and rapped twice with some force. The hubbub of conversation ceased and all eyes turned to Evershed.

"I am here today to conduct an inquest into the death of Miss Sarah Hulme of Grosvenor Street, Leek, who died in this town on Friday last, July 8th 1904. Let me remind you that these are serious legal proceedings and I expect silence and good behaviour from all present until their conclusion."

Many of those present for the later court hearings were unaware an inquest was to take place first. They now watched with interest, surprised to find themselves amongst the first to learn the truth about the tragedy at the rag-and-stick.

"I shall open proceedings by calling upon Inspector Ramm, senior officer of Leek Constabulary. Inspector, please take the witness stand," the Coroner continued.

Ramm took his place and addressed the courtroom.

"I wish to request an adjournment of proceedings so that inquiries into Miss Hulme's death can continue. Due to the nature of the case and the number of potential witnesses, we are not yet in a position to give a satisfactory account of the events of last Friday evening."

Edgar Hulme, perhaps realising the implication of what the Inspector was saying, looked startled. His wife leaned towards him and whispered "What's this all about?"

"Do you know how long it will take to complete your invest-igations, Inspector?" asked the Coroner.

"Unfortunately not, Sir. Our priority is to establish the truth no matter how long it takes."

"In that case I summarily adjourn these proceedings to a date to be fixed," Evershed announced. Looking directly at Sarah's parents he added: "Mr and Mrs Hulme please accept my condolences. This should not prevent your daughter's funeral from being held."

Chatter immediately broke out in the courtroom. Ramm went across to the Hulmes and promised to keep them informed of developments and then started to leave. Before he made it through the door he heard his name being called. The policeman turned to see Oliver Finch hurrying towards him. Oliver had been seated in court ready for a busy day of note taking.

"The adjournment, Inspector. Do you have doubts about Miss Hulme's death?" Oliver asked.

"I am afraid I cannot expand on what I have already said. Our investigations are continuing," Ramm replied.

"Does this mean you suspect foul play?" Oliver persisted, determined to get a story for the *Lion* as well as more information for his friend Cora.

Ramm grimaced. "Young man, I cannot answer that. At this time I am anxious to ascertain the full details. And when I have them the Coroner will be first to know." With that he strode off along the corridor while Oliver scribbled in his notebook.

As he walked back to the station, Ramm was aware that the Coroner would now expect to see results from the police inquiries, increasing the pressure on his limited resources. But plans for the King's visit would have to come first. He just hoped the remainder of the week was uneventful.

Francis Cavendish came upon what he was looking for as he approached Warslow.

Early that morning he had set out from Leek in a horse and trap, relieved to avoid the market day crowds and the risk of coming across John Gibb again. His route had taken him up the steep hill three or four miles out of the town towards Buxton, past rocky crags and over the moors tinted purple with heather blooms.

His first stop was the grey stone settlement of Longnor. He halted in the sloping square in the centre of the village and looked around to see three or four public houses and a surprising number of businesses: grocer, butcher, newsagent, shoemaker, undertaker, post office. The village even had its own market hall topped by an impressive stone crest and a table of tolls 'By Order of the Lord of the Manor': four pence for a stall, a penny tax on every pig sold.

He scouted around the narrow lanes which led off the square and saw no one except a couple of women in conversation on a doorstep. In the fields around the village he saw only cows and sheep, not what he was looking for.

Cavendish continued in the trap in the direction signposted for Warslow, the next place on his list. As he neared the village, he spotted smoke rising from an encampment and he surmised he may have found the German gypsies.

He halted the trap and secured the horse's reins to a tree near the entrance to an imposing stone house with 'Warslow Hall' carved on its gate posts. He walked on slowly staying close to bushes by the side of the lane, his eyes fixed on the camp ahead. He wanted to get closer without being seen himself.

The wagons of traveller folk from far across Europe had become a common sight in rural England over the last couple of years, particularly when large livestock fairs were being held. Farmers were often glad of the extra labour the visitors provided although others, like some Warslow folk, were suspicious of the foreigners. There had even been questions asked in Parliament about the influx of German gypsies.

Cavendish drew a small brass telescope from his pocket and focused on the camp. He had done this sort of thing many times in the past when he was in the army, watching the enemy from a safe distance.

There were four or five wagons, mostly lightweight affairs with roofs of canvas stretched over hooped supports. One was more substantial, a roof of corrugated iron and the bodywork pared down from an ancient wooden railway carriage, its windows covered with slatted shutters. Large sheets of canvas, perhaps eight or nine feet high, had been secured to wooden poles to screen the camp from the village. In the centre of the clearing a fire was burning and nearby a sow was rooting in the earth.

Cavendish could see mostly women and children. The women wore long frilled skirts, shawls around their shoulders and many had colourful headscarves. One was chopping vegetables with a hefty blade, another appeared to be stirring a wooden washing tub made out of half a barrel. The children, whose faces were even dirtier than young people he had seen in towns, were mostly barefoot and many wore baggy clothes that had presumably been passed down from older siblings.

Cavendish guessed that the menfolk were out visiting local farms, either labouring or bargaining for livestock that they could sell on at a profit. Then he tensed as he spotted someone he recognised. The man had bushy eyebrows and a black beard so dense that it seemed to cover most of his face in hair. On his head was an unusual black beret and, even from this distance, Cavendish could see the glint of a heavy gold watch chain that hung across his brown tweed waistcoat. Cavendish knew that the man was the leader of this group of travellers, the biggest caravan was his and perhaps, so were many of the children.

Cavendish settled into the shelter of the hedgerow. He had no need to visit the other villages now. He would stay here a while longer and watch what the man in the black beret was up to.

When the magistrates adjourned court proceedings for luncheon, Oliver Finch decided to call round at the photography studio to give Cora the news about Sarah Hulme's inquest. He found her on her own in the ground floor shop which sold prints of Nathaniel Blake's landscape photographs and as well as his many picture postcards. She looked up expectantly as he came in.

"Cora, I'm glad you are here. Are you on your own?" Oliver said. When Cora nodded he continued quickly. "I was in court this morning and the inquest into Sarah's death was adjourned. Inspector Ramm asked for it to be delayed."

Cora frowned.

"The Inspector said he wants to continue his inquiries. I tried to get more from him, but he wouldn't say," Oliver went on breathlessly. "Don't you see what this may mean, Cora? They might think that Sarah's death is suspicious after all."

"That's just what I said in the first place!"

"But now the police are investigating you can leave them to get to the bottom of it."

Cora could see Oliver wanted her to stop digging into the affair, but she was having none of it.

"I saw Thomas Kilner yesterday and I've decided I need to speak to him again," she announced.

"Why?" Oliver struggled to hide his exasperation.

"There was something about him..." Cora trailed off as she recalled the way Thomas's eyes had locked with her own. "It was how he looked at me, what he said. I'm sure there is more to it than he's admitting."

"The way he looked at you?" A twinge of jealousy spiced Oliver's concern for Cora. "But he could involved!" he went on, grasping Cora's hand. "You should steer clear of him. Let the police sort it out. I think it would be safest."

"Safest? Isn't it more important to find out what happened to Sarah?"

"Well, if you really must persist, I should come with you next time." As well as protecting Cora, Oliver wanted to take a closer look at this Thomas Kilner.

"Oliver, please don't alarm yourself. I shall not do anything unwise."

Cora wanted to see Thomas again and not just to find out more about Sarah. There was something about the intense young man, the way he looked both sad and angry at the same time. She would track him down and talk to him again, but it would have to be on her own.

It was later that afternoon and Cora was out on an errand when the dye house owner James Broadhurst arrived to have his portrait taken.

"I have been wanting to come to see you for some while, Mr Blake, and now seemed to be the right opportunity to have a new set of portraits taken. For business use, of course, and... publicity purposes, shall we say." The businessman was obviously in a talkative mood as Nathaniel led him upstairs to the where his studio and darkroom were located.

In his late fifties and balding, Broadhurst was well fed and well dressed, a sign of the success of his business on Mill Street. The dye works drew water from the River Churnet and Blake had passed the collection of buildings many times, but had never met the owner.

Broadhurst was certainly more expansive than many of the businessmen who were Blake's clients. The sort of men who owned the town's textile firms tended to be brusque in their dealings with tradesmen and suppliers. They were used to having their wishes attended to without need for idle chat.

This man, on the other hand, seemed keen to engage Blake in conversation and, as the photographer soon discovered, there was one particular topic on his mind.

"So, Mr Blake, what do you think of the German problem?" Broadhurst asked as he settled into the velvet upholstered armchair which Blake often used for his portrait sittings.

Blake poked his head out from the cloth hood at the back of his camera. "German question, Mr Broadhurst?" He was somewhat thrown by the rapid change of subject.

"Yes, surely you must agree that if the Kaiser keeps building his warships it's a threat to our nation, our livelihoods? Thank God we have the French on our side now."

"Well, I've seen the stories in the newspapers..." Blake thought he should be guarded in his response. Many shopkeepers and tradespeople tended to avoid the subject of politics in case they said the wrong thing and lost business.

"John Bull in the *Leek Lion*, you mean?" Broadhurst interjected enthusiastically. "He seems like a sound fellow, don't you think? Stands by his principles, talks some sense. Somebody has to, let's face it. We have the English way of life to protect!"

Blake, uncertain where he stood on the contentious issue, tried to change the subject. "Mr Broadhurst, could you look to the left and try to hold your head still. That's it!" he said, now behind the hood again.

As the portrait session progressed Broadhurst adopted a variety of expressions, from serious to contemplative. When it was finished he asked how long it would take Blake to produce prints.

"I shall require publicity photographs quite soon, by the end of the week even. I have some public engagements in the diary, you see."

"In that case I will send proofs tomorrow and you can select which you prefer," Blake replied.

Broadhurst checked the time on his pocket watch. "I need to return to the works," he said. "I'm meeting someone, a new customer, at six-thirty. The time is a little awkward really, because I have a public meeting to attend tonight, but I think it might be important."

When his client had left Blake pondered those last remarks. He surmised the public meeting Broadhurst planned to attend was the one Blake had read about in the *Lion*, called by the infamous correspondent John Bull.

The photographer himself had no intention of attending, he had other things planned for that evening. As it turned out, he could not have predicted how events would unfold.

CHAPTER NINE

From the number of people making their way towards Union Street, FJ Finch could see that the public meeting called by John Bull was going to be packed. Once inside the Temperance Hall he struggled to find a seat, even though there was still fifteen minutes before the meeting was due to start.

Finch gave a satisfied smile. An attendance like this not only proved the power of publicity in the *Lion*, it guaranteed him a good story for the next edition.

Perhaps local people were more concerned about 'The German Question' than he had realised, however he suspected that many of these folk were just curious to find out who John Bull was.

Rather than squeeze into the rows of wooden chairs, Finch decided to stand near the doorway, that way he would have a good view of both the stage and anyone who spoke from the audience. His position also meant that the *Lion* editor was easily buttonholed by people who wanted to make their feelings known.

"Appalling isn't it, Mr Finch?" began a red faced councillor looming up to FJ. "Who knows where this aggressive behaviour will lead?"

"Quite," Finch replied, not knowing whether it was German or British aggression that so distressed the man.

"We have to be on our guard, these German agitators could be anywhere," the councillor went on. "Had a gentleman in the shop last week, interested in a new bowler hat, he said. Accent was decidedly odd. Kept a close eye on him, have no worry."

As the councillor went to look for a seat, someone else approached Finch.

"Thank goodness John Bull is speaking up for us Englishmen," said a rotund character who Finch recognised as a leading Freemason. Leaning close enough for Finch to smell brandy on his breath, he went on: "Of course, I know who he is, this Bull character."

"Indeed?"

"Wouldn't do for me to say before he arrives, but mark my words, he's a silk man. I know for a fact that trade with the Continent has suffered thanks to the Germans. No wonder he's hot under the collar!"

Another man, whom Finch recognised as the owner of an ironmongers' shop, overheard what was being said and butted in. "Oh yes, I think we know exactly who Bull is. As good as told me so himself."

Finch realised that John Bull was perhaps not as anonymous as he had presumed, probably because the man could not resist self publicity.

The Freemason wasn't finished. "He's going to name names, you know, Mr Finch. Putting a finger on these dashed infiltrators in the town. And I sincerely hope that you will be printing it all in your newspaper."

Finch took out his watch and saw it was half past seven, the time the meeting was to start. "Surely Bull should be here by now," he thought, "unless he's planning some sort of grand entrance."

Just then someone stepped onto the stage which had been laid out with a small table and two chairs. It was Harold Harrop, a thin, white haired man with wire-rimmed spectacles perched on the end of his nose. Finch knew Harrop was on the local council and all sorts of other town bodies, and he also knew that he was not John Bull. The room fell silent as the audience looked at Harrop expectantly.

"Ladies and gentlemen," he announced in the commanding tone he used in the council chamber. "I am here to act as your chairman for tonight's proceedings, an impartial chairman, of course. I want to maintain good order so that important matters can be aired in a proper fashion."

Harrop glanced towards the door, consulted his pocket watch, then continued with a little less assurance. "Our host has yet to arrive. Until he does, I ask... er... I ask you to be patient. The meeting will begin forthwith."

Harrop sat down and started to fiddle with a piece of paper he had unfolded from his pocket. The audience started to talk amongst themselves again and Finch looked around the gathering to see who else he could put a name to.

People were still arriving and Finch glanced across just as someone else he recognised was slipping through the doorway. It was the fellow he had seen being impatient in the Telegraph Office the previous evening. Finch watched as the man, head down and avoiding eye contact, made for the back row of seats and managed to find a space.

Minutes passed and there was still no sign of the elusive John Bull. The volume rose as the audience discussed not only Britain's alliance with France and Germany's growing number of battleships, but also began to wonder whether the whole evening was some sort of ruse. Someone suggested it might even be a German plot to make fools of people of Leek.

Quarter to eight came and went. Harold Harrop called for order, conversation subsided briefly, then the noise grew again until finally someone stood up.

"Where's Bull?" the man shouted irately. "Is he coming or not? Who are these German spies he's going to tell us about?"

Soon there were more people on their feet, calling for Bull, calling for the truth, calling for a bigger army.

Finch could see tempers were rising, people were starting to feel hoodwinked and things could become ugly if John Bull, the man behind it all, did not show up soon. Several were muttering and nodding in Finch's direction and he realised that there was a risk the *Lion* might get the blame instead.

Looking around the hall, he saw that the stranger with the grey moustache sat impassively, saying nothing to his neighbours, but keeping a careful watch on what was going on.

On the stage, Harrop had a harassed expression as he repeatedly looked towards the door in the hope their host would arrive. Finch decided it was time to intervene and stepped across to the chairman.

"Councillor Harrop, I suggest you wait until eight o'clock and then call the meeting off. It looks to me like our friend John Bull is not going to appear."

Harrop appeared relieved that someone else had suggested what he himself wanted to do, and at precisely eight o'clock he rose to his feet and, shouting above the growing din, announced that the meeting was being abandoned.

"It appears our host has been unavoidably delayed. I am sure there will be an opportunity to discuss these matters properly in the near future," he said.

Finch made it to the door before the crush of disgruntled patriots and walked quickly to the *Lion* office to write up his notes on this strange turn of events. He had quite a story to tell, not only about the meeting that never got started, but just how suspicious of foreigners some Leek people were becoming.

"Let's see what the great man is up to now," Albert Ramm said to Edna as he settled into his armchair that evening, opening his copy of *The Memoirs of Sherlock Holmes*. Conan Doyle's stories were becoming hugely popular and the Inspector found himself fascinated with the fictional detective's methods, if a little jealous of his powers of deduction.

He had read barely a page when someone rapped on the front

door. Edna went to answer it and came back into the parlour with one of Ramm's colleagues. When the Inspector saw Constable Lowe, one of the two officers on night patrol around the town, he knew there must be trouble, yet again.

"Now what?" asked Ramm grumpily, rising from his chair. Seeing the constable's disconcerted expression, he added: "Apologies, Lowe. Do you need me?"

"Mill Street dye works, Sir, I think you need to go down there. Someone's found a body."

"What! Another?" the Inspector replied. He noticed Lowe was wearing his bicycle clips and so quickly fetched his own bicycle from the back yard and wheeled it down the dark entry at the side of the house and onto Queen Street.

"All right, Constable, no time to waste," Ramm said as he swung his leg over the high crossbar and pedalled off beside Lowe. Once through the middle of town the two officers were able to freewheel down Mill Street to reach the dye works. The Inspector was familiar with the collection of single storey buildings with saw-tooth roofs, although he could not recollect meeting the owner.

After the leaning their bicycles against the front wall, the two went through the main door. Ramm was immediately struck by the atmosphere inside the building, thick with the smell of chemicals and damp cloth. He pulled out a handkerchief and held it across his nose and mouth.

Constable Lowe led him through a series of connected buildings. A darkened warehouse was piled high with reels of silk cloth and twisted yarn. There were washing rooms where the reels would be plunged into large vats of boiling water and drying rooms with coal fired stoves that were still warm from the day's work.

Finally they reached the dye house itself. The dyeing was usually done in natural light but now the building was lit by a couple of gas lamps. Ramm peered into the gloom to try to understand what had happened in there.

He could see a row of copper tanks, shaped like larger versions of the individual slipper baths found in the cubicles at the Town Baths. The tanks were filled with black liquid and the room was littered with all manner of smaller containers and dye stained rags.

In front of one of the tanks, a body lay in a pool of what Ramm at first thought was an horrific quantity of blood, but quickly realised it was black dye. In fact the body itself was almost covered from head to toe.

Lowe unhooked his bull's-eye lamp from his belt, lit it with a match and handed it to Ramm. The Inspector leaned forward to look more closely at the figure on the floor. From its black surface, it could have been mistaken for some kind of bizarre mannequin but, by the beam of the lamp, he could see that it was indeed the body of a man.

Two men who appeared to be dye house workers stood silently watching what was going on. Both wore cloth caps and long brown aprons liberally splashed with black dye, as were their hands and faces.

"So what has happened here?" asked Ramm.

"This man found the victim, Inspector," said the constable, easing one of the men forward.

"And you are?"

"Higgs, Inspector. Elijah Higgs," said the worker uncertainly, apparently still in a state of shock.

"Tell me what has gone on."

"It was 'bout seven o'clock and I was locking up for the night. That's me job, you see, Sir. Came in 'ere and saw a sort of shape in the bark."

Ramm knew that a 'bark' was what the dyers called the copper tank. He let the man continue.

"I thought it were a bundle o' silk that should've been taken to the whizzes."

"Whizzes?"

"Aye, what whizzes the silk round, dries it out a bit."

"I see. Go on," said Ramm, anxious to move the story on.

"Anyway, I 'ad a closer look and saw it were a body. I ran for Charlie," Higgs indicated the other worker, who nodded, "and the two of us set about pulling 'im out. Thought we could save 'im, but there were no chance. Stone dead when we got 'im out. It were a struggle and a right mess as well."

"And one of you fetched help?"

"That were me," said Charlie, taking up the story. "Went across to The Spread Eagle. Bill Fisher, he's the landlord, sent his lad up to the police station but 'e met the bobby on 'is way there."

"Can't believe it," Higgs resumed, shaking his head as he stared down at the body. "We've 'ad accidents afore, but it's usually scaldings and the like. Never ever seen anybody drown in a bark. Can't think 'ow it happened, especially to Mr Broadhurst."

"Mr Broadhurst?" Ramm was newly alert.

"Aye, that's Mr Broadhurst, he's the gaffer!"

The clock on the mantelpiece had chimed nine and Nathaniel Blake was flipping through his copy of *The Photographer*, when Constable Lowe came to the house. The officer told him that Inspector Ramm required photographs of an incident at the dye works.

It was getting dark and the lamp lighter was working his way along Mill Street reaching up to ignite the gas lamps as Blake walked down the street a quarter of an hour later, equipment in both hands. He was filled with foreboding. It had been only days since he had to focus his lens on death at the rag-and-stick and now he wondered what distressing scene awaited him tonight.

A workman was waiting at the main door of the dye works to show him through the shadowy interior. Just as Inspector Ramm had done, Blake began to cough in the fume filled air. When they reached where the incident had occurred, he found the Inspector talking to a man in a waistcoat and white shirt. On the floor next to a copper tank, the body of a man lay face up, barely recognisable because of the blackness that coated his clothes and his skin.

It was a bizarre sight and, as he waited for Ramm to finish his conversation, Blake looked more closely at the body. A well built man in a three-piece suit, traces of hair plastered across the blackened dome of his head.

"Good Lord!" Blake gasped.

Ramm broke off from what he was saying and turned to Blake.

"A gruesome sight, is it not, Mr Blake?" the Inspector said. "It appears he drowned in a bath of dye stuffs."

"It's not only the dye that has shocked me, Inspector. It's the man. I met Mr Broadhurst only this afternoon," came the photographer's startled reply.

Blake sometimes had nightmares about the things he had to photograph for the town police. Occasions like this when he knew the victim were even more shocking. James Broadhurst had been full of vigour when he had seen him only hours ago. Now the man was reduced to a corpse lying in a pool of black dye.

"This afternoon, Mr Blake?"

"Yes, he came in to have his portrait taken. He wanted to see the prints as soon as possible, poor fellow." What cruel irony that he should be photographing the man again, so soon afterwards and in such circumstances, Blake thought.

"Aye, I remember the gaffer went out this afternoon," the man in the waistcoat interjected. "And he said he was seeing somebody after finishing up time, then he'd got another big meeting."

Ramm told Blake that this was Mr Clarke, the works manager whom he had summoned to the scene.

"Did he say where his meeting was?" the Inspector asked.

"No, but it was something he couldn't miss," Clarke replied.

"He told me he was due to see a new customer here," Blake

94

interjected. "He said it was rather awkward because the person wanted to come in at half past six."

"Do you know anything about who this new customer could be, Mr Clarke?"

"No idea, Inspector. The gaffer..." Clarke glanced at the body with a pained expression, "...used to keep stuff about new orders to himself. I only get involved when it's time to do the work."

"Would anyone else know?"

"You'd have to speak to Miss Grindey, the gaffer's secretary, she would know about his appointments. We all knock off at six, so there'd be hardly anybody else around by half past."

"Mr Clarke, do you have any idea how Mr Broadhurst could have finished up in this tank?"

Clarke shook his head, mystified. "The gaffer's been in and out of dye works since his was a lad. He knew what was dangerous. And you couldn't just fall into a bark – see for yourself, the sides are too high, surely? Unless you intended getting into it."

Ramm gazed at the copper tank and tried to imagine how and why James Broadhurst had pitched into the menacing black liquid. A bizarre accident, if indeed it was an accident. He would need to speak to the secretary, find this mystery visitor and interview anyone who was in the works that evening.

"Our inquiries will have to continue in the morning," said Ramm. "In the meantime, Mr Blake, I would be grateful if you could photograph what we have here: the body, the tank, the room as a whole, anything else that may catch your eye." Ramm knew he could trust the photographer to be meticulous.

And so, for the second time in a few days, Blake surveyed a shadowy scene of tragedy and started to unpack his camera and tripod. He had brought his flash-lamp and soon the blackened corpse would be starkly illuminated in an explosion of light. Images of death would be burned onto Blake's glass negatives and into his memory.

Having returned to the *Lion* office, FJ Finch made short work of his report about the aborted Temperance Hall meeting, writing as much from memory as from his notes. He used carbon paper to make extra copies of each sheet as he hammered away at his Imperial typewriter. When he had finished, he went to the pillar box in Derby Street to post copies to the newspaper offices in Manchester.

Although it was now well after ten o'clock, there were more people about than usual, many returning home from the performance at the rag-and-stick. On the spur of the moment, Finch decided to continue along the street and call in at The Black Swan for a quick glass of ale. He might pick up gossip about tonight's meeting, he thought.

Finch was about to enter the inn when he spotted a figure at the door of Blake's studio on the opposite side of Sheepmarket. The nearest street lamp was flickering badly, but Finch recognised it was the photographer himself. With his camera case and tripod at his feet, he was jangling keys as he unlocked his door.

"Nathaniel! You must have had a long day," Finch called out, crossing the cobbled street. From the slope of his friend's shoulders he could tell the day had been a tiring one.

"Yes, FJ, and I am not finished yet," said Blake. Even in the semi-darkness Finch was struck by the look on his friend's face, drained of his usual energy. He followed the photographer inside where Blake lit the gas mantles in the downstairs shop before sitting heavily on a bentwood chair. He gestured for Finch to pull up the other chair.

"I still have plates to develop tonight, but I think I need to take a moment before starting work in the darkroom," Blake began. Seeing Finch's questioning expression, he continued: "Another death, there's been another horrible death to photograph."

"Good grief, who has died? Not a murder, surely?"

"I don't know about murder, but it is certainly a strange affair. And I was only talking to the chap this afternoon, in this very studio," replied Blake, shaking his head. "James Broadhurst, from the dye works. You will know him, of course. Drowned, by the look of it, in a vat of his own dye. Tragic... and ghastly to see."

Finch's mouth fell open. He felt the breath had been knocked from him.

"Broadhurst?" he said incredulously.

"I have got to say, FJ, what with the affair at the rag-and-stick and now this... it has put me in low spirits."

"Are you sure it was Broadhurst?" Although sympathetic to his friend, Finch was focused on the facts.

"Yes, of course. It was at the dye house in Mill Street. Some of his men were there. They identified him and so did I."

"But, Broadhurst should have been at the meeting about Germany tonight," said Finch.

"How do you know that?"

"Because I was there Nathaniel, and Broadhurst was the one who called the meeting. He was the fellow calling himself 'John Bull' who has been writing letters to the *Lion*. He was going to be the centre of attention, but he never turned up. I can barely believe he's dead, tonight of all nights."

Shocked as he was, Finch realised that the *Leek Lion's* story about 'The German Question' would have to change. The affair had suddenly become even more complicated.

"That's a tragic coincidence," said Blake. He saw from Finch's frown that the editor thought differently.

"It could be more than a coincidence, Nathaniel," Finch replied sombrely, "much more."

He left Blake to develop his negatives. Finch no longer felt like that drink of ale. His mind was on James Broadhurst, found dead at the very moment he should have been addressing his supporters.

CHAPTER TEN

Leek's cattle market usually stood empty on Thursday with only the odd wisp of straw a reminder of the hustle and bustle of the previous day's sales. Today was different. Since dawn the market had been a hive of activity as labourers and stockmen prepared for the annual Horse Fair. Soon, buyers and sellers would be arriving from across the moorlands and beyond for a hectic day of haggling and hand slapping.

Inspector Ramm, glancing across the livestock pens as he approached the police station that morning, knew it could also be a day of argument, pickpocketing and drunkenness. And today was the very last day he and his men needed any extra work. There were more serious matters to attend to. Two unusual deaths in a matter of days with the second coming before he had chance to draw a line under the first.

"Any developments overnight, Sergeant?" asked Ramm, dispensing with any greeting as he entered the station. "Anything useful from Mrs Broadhurst?" he continued before Sergeant Reynolds had chance to reply.

Last night, Ramm had dispatched Constable Lowe to inform the dead man's wife.

"According to Lowe, Mrs Broadhurst was too shocked to say anything. Fainted apparently. There were three daughters in the house, so it was quite a scene," Reynolds replied.

"Anything else I should know about?"

"The rural lads have reported one or two things, nothing serious. Fight at Rushton, cow stolen at Foxt and someone broke in a store shed at Cauldon quarry."

"Very well. Let me gather my thoughts about Mr Broadhurst. There is plenty to sort out," said Ramm.

He was about to leave the front office when FJ Finch came in. It was much earlier than he was usually seen at the police station.

Ramm gave a sigh. "Mr Finch, I have no time for you this morning. Sergeant Reynolds will help, I am sure."

"But Inspector, I have something important to tell you. About James Broadhurst," Finch said before Ramm could escape to his office.

Ramm paused. "Broadhurst? I suppose you should come in then," he said, although wary that Finch wanted to pump him for information.

"You've heard about Mr Broadhurst then? Your sources are very efficient, Mr Finch," Ramm began when they were seated.

"Well... I happened to see Nathaniel last evening and..."

"Ah, that explains it," Ramm interrupted. "So what do you have to tell me?"

"I was at the meeting in the Temperance Hall last night, the one to discuss this fuss about Germany. James Broadhurst should have been there," Finch explained.

"That's as it may be, Mr Finch, but what does it have to do with the man's demise? He was in his dye house, not out and about in the town."

"Well, Mr Broadhurst had called the meeting," said Finch,

before adding rather sheepishly: "He was the person calling himself 'John Bull' who wrote the letters to the *Lion*. He was whipping up fears about the Germany navy, spies and so on."

"Interesting material for your newspaper, I'm sure Mr Finch, but surely this has no bearing on a works accident?"

"So you believe it was an accident?" said Finch, seizing on the Inspector's comment.

Ramm paused. He was unwilling to commit himself, especially to a journalist. James Broadhurst's death could probably be explained as an accident, a bizarre one admittedly. However until he had all the information, nothing could be taken for granted. Instead of giving a direct answer he fired a question back at Finch.

"Are you suggesting this nonsense is connected with Mr Broadhurst's death? German infiltrators in Leek? I think you're getting a little carried away." Ramm could not hide his scepticism.

Finch was hardly surprised. He knew many people would find it difficult to believe. However, he had convinced himself there must be a connection between Broadhurst's rabble-rousing and his shocking death. He was also beginning to feel uneasy that he had printed so many of John Bull's letters in the first place. Had he encouraged the man to pursue something that ultimately cost him his life?

"If it turns out to be an accident, then obviously it was a coincidence," Finch responded. "But please bear in mind what I have said, Inspector. Broadhurst had his supporters, but not everyone may have agreed with his opinions."

"I shall consider your point, however at first sight it seems unlikely that letters in the newspaper could lead to something like this." Ramm rose from his chair to show the conversation was over. "Come to see me tomorrow morning and I will give you a statement on the matter. I will also have some other important news for you."

Alone again, Ramm stared at the pattern of ink speckles on his blotting pad. He could not believe the cause of Broadhurst's death was as far-fetched as Finch had suggested, but the affair still needed to be untangled as soon as possible.

Nathaniel Blake was in his darkroom unpegging the prints of the scene at the dye house which he had hung up to dry the previous night. He had worked past midnight on the photographs and now intended to deliver them to the police station. He had not mentioned the tragedy when the family sat down for toast and jam that morning, however once he and Cora arrived at the studio, she was naturally curious about what her father was working on. When he told her that James Broadhurst had died, without including the gruesome details, she uttered a cry of shock.

"Mr Broadhurst from the dye works? That's Lucy's father!" she said.

"You know his daughter?"

"She used to come to dance class and so did her sisters. They stopped coming a few weeks ago. I think they all had piano lessons from Signor Manfredi, too."

"Well, I'm sorry for upsetting you, my dear." After what had gone on with Sarah Hulme, Blake regretted having to tell Cora about the new death.

"Mr Broadhurst was the one who's been writing to the newspapers, wasn't he?" Cora went on. "Lucy mentioned it after dance class a while ago She said he was always making notes about politics and writing letters to the *Lion*," she added.

Blake thought how, in a small town like Leek, so many people knew each other's business. Even pupils at the dance school were caught up with not one, but two tragedies in a week.

"Perhaps Signor Manfredi will cancel classes again this week," Nathaniel suggested, "with all this bother." He had seen the dance teacher hurrying along the street when he had finished at the studio the previous afternoon. The fellow had appeared preoccupied, his head down, and had not acknowledged Blake.

"He certainly seems upset about Sarah. He wasn't his usual self on Saturday, nor when I saw him on Monday. And he must have known Lucy's father," said Cora.

Mention of the dance school gave Cora her opportunity to introduce her plans for the weekend, or rather her alibi for her adventure to Stockport.

"Actually, I was thinking of not going to dance this week, Father. Ellen and I are planning another country walk – we thought it would do us both good," she said.

"That sounds an excellent idea." Nathaniel was relieved his daughter had something to look forward to, away from the dark events of the town.

Cora smiled at her father, determined that her real plan would remain a secret.

After delivering his photographs to the police station, Blake went to capture the busy scenes at the Horse Fair. He thought it would make an excellent set of picture postcards.

Horse sales had been held in the town for years, drawing keen interest from traders as well as farmers and carriers seeking new blood to haul their ploughs and carts. Colts and foals were tethered in long rows, each inspected from tooth to hindquarter by prospective buyers. Offers and counter-offers would fly back and forth until a deal was sealed with a slap of hands.

The spectacle attracted crowds of onlookers. Farmers' sons and bewhiskered old men argued over the relative merits of the animals. Every man was in a cap, a trilby or and bowler hat. Most were smoking cigarettes or pipes. The tobacco smoke coupled with the aroma of sweating horses and the stench of large quantities of manure, filled the air with a distinctive fug.

Women tended to keep a safe distance from the hurly burly of the horse trading. Mothers and grandmothers in bonnets and straw boaters lined the raised pavement in front of Cromwell Terrace. Some balanced infants on the stone wall which bordered the market so that even the youngest could watch the horses being led back and forth.

This year a different gang of horse traders brought new fascination for townsfolk. They were the German gypsies, marked out by their large trilbies, long coats and dark beards. Their argumentative haggling was less easy to understand because of their strong accents and limited English.

Blake was busy for an hour, moving from one side of the market to the other, capturing the animated scenes from different angles.

Inside the police station, Inspector Ramm was trying to ignore the noise through his office window while he concentrated on Blake's photographs of James Broadhurst's body. He tried to imagine what had gone on. Could the businessman have fallen or thrown himself into the vat of dye or was he pushed?

He decided he needed to speak to Broadhurst's secretary and was about to set off for Mill Street when Sarah Hulme's father arrived. Edgar Hulme was nervously twisting his cap in both hands as he was shown into Ramm's office.

"I can tell you, Inspector, me and Gladys were a bit put out when you stopped the inquest yesterday. So you still don't know what 'appened with our Sarah?"

"I am not satisfied I have heard the whole story, Mr Hulme. It appears that none of the theatre folk saw what she was up to, so I would still like to do some digging. Do you have any more to tell me?" Ramm replied.

"Well, Professor Kilner said we should collect Sarah's things out of her room at Warburton's. As well as her clothes and such, there was a box where she used to keep her precious bits an' pieces. This was inside it." Edgar Hulme reached into his jacket and produced a small book which he handed to Ramm. "It's her diary."

"Have you looked at it?" asked Ramm.

"Yes, Inspector, it were right upsettin'. Brought it all back, reading how happy she was. We thought you should see it in case it 'elps."

Ramm started to leaf through the diary which he could see Sarah had been keeping for some time. He was aware that Mr Hulme was watching him closely, and so, not wishing to appear to intrude on the young woman's private life, he skipped towards the end and the weeks since she had joined the theatre.

Turning from one page of closely packed handwriting to the next, he saw the brief entries seemed to reflect a largely happy life. Sarah often used initials rather than people's names and Ramm spotted repeated mentions of one person in particular – "T". Thomas Kilner, no doubt. He realised he would have to study the diary more carefully when he had the time.

"Did you find anything else amongst her things that might assist us, Mr Hulme. A letter perhaps?"

Edgar Hulme realised the officer was asking about something which might have indicated her intentions. "There were nothing, Inspector," he replied tonelessly.

Ramm asked if he could keep the diary to study and reassured Sarah's father that inquiries would proceed without delay.

When Edgar Hulme had left, Ramm ran his fingers over the diary's dark blue cover. He wondered if he would find any sign of the reason why Sarah had planned to end it all. That would certainly help him to tie up the case so that he could concentrate on James Broadhurst… and the King. However the young woman and her parents deserved his best efforts, so he would do what he should have done two days ago. He would speak to Thomas Kilner again.

FJ Finch arrived to observe what was going on at the Horse Fair and make arrangements to collect the sales results from the organisers later in the day. He went over to Blake who was standing behind his camera.

"If you get anything decent, I may be able to use a picture in the *Lion*. Although it looks like we will have no shortage of news this week," Finch said.

Only mildly amused, Blake responded: "Oh, they will all be 'decent', FJ! I plan to develop the plates straightaway so I will let you have something later."

Finch nodded his thanks.

"Any more thoughts on this Broadhurst affair?" Blake added.

"I spoke to Inspector Ramm and he didn't seem to think that Broadhurst's rants about Germany could have anything to do with it," Finch replied with a shrug.

"Apparently Cora and some of her dance school friends knew he was John Bull. So much for him being anonymous."

"I have been asking myself whether I should have reined him in," Finch went on thoughtfully. "But judging by last night's meeting, there are plenty of other folk who are hot under the collar about these threats to our fair nation."

Finch edged his way around the onlookers and came across John Gibb. Like many others, he respected the Scotsman for his bravery. Gone were the days when he was seen only as a tramp. Gibb told him that Rosa Carter was considering buying a new horse to work at Dieulacres Cottage Farm.

"She's sent me to see what there is here, though I have to admit I know precious little about horses, Mr Finch."

Before Finch could reply he saw that Gibb's attention was drawn to something across the market and he was now staring intently.

"Is there one that interests you, John?"

"Not a horse, no. It's someone I thought I knew once," Gibb said with a hint of bitterness.

Finch could tell that Gibb was not looking at the activity around the horses, but at the onlookers on the raised pavement at the side. There was a man, tall enough to look over the heads of the women in front. Finch recognised him as the stranger he had first seen at the Telegraph Office. And just as he had done at last night's meeting in the Temperance Hall, the man was watching keenly what was going on, eyes darting around as if making a mental note of everyone there.

"It wouldn't be that tall fellow at the back, the one with the grey moustache, would it?" suggested Finch.

The surprised look on John Gibb's face told Finch he was correct.

"It would indeed," said Gibb, but showed no inclination to say more.

"I wondered who he may be. I've already seen him myself twice this week and I'm sure he's a stranger in town."

"A stranger to Leek perhaps, but not to me, Mr Finch."

Gibb had been thinking about Francis Cavendish ever since his altercation on Monday. He had behaved so strangely toward him that Gibb was worried his old comrade was in some sort of trouble. He decided to unburden himself and, with a sigh, told Finch of his history with Cavendish. How the young major had distinguished himself at Khartoum and how Gibb had seen him for the first time in nearly twenty years at the rag-and-stick on Saturday. He ended his account with the way the man had warned him off.

"It was as if he was a different person. But the army can scar a man's mind as well as his body," added Gibb sadly. Although he didn't talk about it, he had been pursued by his own bloody memories since his days serving his Queen and country.

"I wonder what he is up to in Leek?" Finch replied as they both returned their gaze to Cavendish.

Meanwhile, Cavendish had seen Gibb in the crowd. He avoided making eye contact with the Scotsman, but was aware that he was now in conversation with a fellow with reddish hair who he had seen at the Temperance Hall.

He didn't want to be distracted by Gibb. He was there to watch the gypsies who were busy amongst the horses, and in particular, the one who wore a black beret.

When Inspector Ramm arrived at the dye works he found the white haired Miss Grindey, James Broadhurst's secretary, at her desk. In answer to his question, she produced the ledger where she noted the owner's instructions and appointments. An entry for the previous day stated simply "6.30 pm. Meeting."

"Mr James didn't say who it was, just that he had received a letter from someone and he needed to meet them. I thought it was about new business," she explained. She was obviously still in a state of shock and sniffed into a lace handkerchief between each sentence. The works had been run by generations of Broadhursts and Ramm guessed that Miss Grindey, who was probably in her seventies, had served "Mr James's" father, if not his grandfather.

"Trade has been a little thin of late, Inspector," she went on in a confidential whisper. "I think that's why Mr James was rather anxious to meet this person, even though it was outside usual business hours. He said he had never heard of the company."

"So was Mr Broadhurst worried about the business?"

"Well, if you must know, we used to dye a lot of silk for an important customer in Germany. But then the orders dried up and Mr James blamed it on politics, or something of the like. Just how bad things were I don't really know because he didn't tell me everything." Ramm got the impression Miss Grindey was disappointed Broadhurst no longer confided in her.

Last night she had left at six o'clock she had not seen the visitor herself. She suggested the letter might be somewhere on Broadhurst's desk but she had not had the heart to go in there yet.

In Broadhurst's office, Ramm found papers spread untidily across the large desk. As well as numerous pages of handwritten notes there were newspaper cuttings which appeared to be mainly about foreign politics. On the top of one pile was a list of names, some crossed out, some underlined. Ramm saw they were all traders and professional people in the town. There was no sign of the letter from the mystery client.

On the way out of the dye house, Ramm spotted Clarke, the works manager.

"I gather business was rather poor, Mr Clarke."

"Not too good, Inspector. The gaffer was worried but I'm sure he was trying to do something about it."

As he returned to the police station, Ramm ruminated on James Broadhurst's final hours. How had someone so familiar with the dye works made such a fatal error? If trade was poor, perhaps Broadhurst had had money worries. Could it have been another suicide? However, if that was his intention, the man appeared to have left no note, just like Sarah Hulme.

Back at the police station he found that Thomas Kilner had been brought in and was now waiting in the interview room. Ramm decided it was time to put some pressure on the young man.

"So Mr Kilner," he said as he strode into the room, "you will have guessed why I want to speak to you. I gather you knew Miss Hulme rather better than you admitted on Monday."

Thomas moved uneasily in his chair, however his pale eyes addressed the Inspector with a steady stare and he said nothing.

"You were close friends, were you not?"

"Yes, we were friends," Thomas replied slowly, showing no emotion.

"Did you have any inkling what was going to happen on Friday night?"

Thomas was silent for a moment before replying. "Sarah was full of life when she came to us. But in the last couple of weeks...

I wondered if it was all becoming too much for her. I think she was not coping well."

"Indeed? You are the first person to mention this," said Ramm. He noticed Thomas's knuckles were white as he knitted his fingers together.

"As you said, we were friends. Perhaps I saw things that others did not."

"And what did you see last Friday?"

"In the afternoon, when we were going over our lines, she seemed..." Thomas paused, staring blankly, apparently lost in his memories of Sarah.

"She was not her usual herself, she was distracted," he continued, regaining his composure. "I was worried, but I didn't have chance to speak to her. And I didn't see her again until she was found on the stage."

Ramm pressed for more details and Thomas told of other occasions in the recent past when Sarah had appeared confused or upset.

"But I never thought she was in any danger. Otherwise I would have done something about it," he added defensively.

Ramm told the actor he might have to give evidence when the inquest resumed. With the interview over, Thomas left and Ramm considered what he had just heard. The description of Sarah's mood could point to her eventual fate. On the other hand, the young man was used to playing a part and this could be another act. For that matter, others from the theatre might be doing the same.

By early afternoon Nathaniel Blake had printed out his photographs from the Horse Fair and, with his wire framed spectacles perched on his forehead, he was deciding which would make the best postcards. Cora came up beside him and began to pick up the large prints one by one.

"My, so much going on and so many people watching," she said.

"I think it's the busiest Horse Fair I have seen," Nathaniel replied.

"Some of those foals look frisky," Cora commented, then paused as she took a closer look at one of the prints. "Isn't that Signor Manfredi?" she said, pointing to a group of men near the horses.

Blake had not noticed who was in the crowd when he was taking the photographs, but could now see the tall thin figure of the dance teacher.

"I didn't know he was interested in horses. It looks like he's talking to one of the dealers," said Cora.

"Perhaps he's decided to have a horse and trap. He could probably afford one." Blake looked at the photograph again and could make out Manfredi next to a heavily bearded man with some sort of beret on his head, probably one of the gypsy traders.

Blake took up a magnifying glass and began to examine the other photographs, checking on the clarity and also seeing who else he could spot amongst the spectators. Sure enough, there was John Gibb and FJ. One or two farmers and shopkeepers he recognised, even some of the theatre company. And there was Manfredi again, this time in another part of the crowd.

"Signor Manfredi is in this one too," he told Cora. "It looks like he's talking to some of the theatre folk."

"Is he? Can I have a look, please?" His daughter put her hand out for the photograph and the magnifying glass. As she studied the picture Cora frowned. She was remembering how upset, angry even, the dance teacher had been when Sarah announced she was joining Professor Kilner's theatre. He had seemed far from friendly with the theatre that day.

"I wonder what's changed?" she thought.

Over at the *Leek Lion* office, FJ Finch was thinking about the tragedies his newspaper would report this week.

His mind went back to two years ago when two suspicious

deaths had also occurred within a matter of days. That affair had shocked the town and had finished up with the Blakes, himself, Oliver and even John Gibb involved. Surely it was impossible to have two more murders within a week.

He couldn't rid himself of the notion that James Broadhurst's death was somehow linked to his anti-German activities. It was just too suspicious to be a coincidence.

The volatile atmosphere at last night's meeting had unsettled him. Some folk had been desperate for John Bull to point the finger at the "infiltrators". But what if someone else wanted to silence him?

Only one or two of the older regulars were in the public bar of The Hare and Greyhound in Warslow early that Thursday evening. Many of the younger men were still at work on farms, taking advantage of the long hours of daylight.

The village had seen a flurry of activity that afternoon when the gypsy horse traders returned from Leek with their new stock. They had ridden along the main road into Warslow, each leading a string of lively colts and foals, their clattering hooves raising clouds of dust.

Old timer Walter had watched the spectacle from a chair on his doorstep. One or two of the gypsies nodded or tipped their hats as they rode past, but he pointedly ignored them.

"Be glad to see the back of ye," he had mumbled.

An hour later, Walter had seen that his wish was to be granted. The gypsy caravans were moving from their camp.

"They've gone then," he announced to his fellow drinkers that night.

"Looks like they did well at the 'orse fair, judgin' by what they brung back," said his mate Samuel.

"I bet they diddled a few folk out of 'ard earned money," Walter continued. "Never trust 'em, 'specially them Germans."

"Oh, give it a rest Wally. They only be tryin' make a livin'," Samuel replied.

"Lookin' at the gold rings and chains some of 'em have, they're doin' all right," said a third man.

Walter was not to be dissuaded. "Mark my words, these foreigners mean no good for any of us. I'm just glad they're out o' Warslow. Let's 'ope they're out o' the moorlands."

In fact, the waggon train with the dozens of young horses tethered behind was travelling barely six miles. By the time night had fallen the gypsies had set up a new camp, this time beside the track over the Mount, high ground on the edge of Leek.

As the travellers kindled new fires to cook pots of fresh rabbit stew, down in the town Inspector Albert Ramm was settling into his armchair to read. Tonight he was foregoing the exploits of Sherlock Holmes and instead he intended to study Sarah Hulme's diary, pursuing a mystery that was far from fiction.

He began to read through the final two months as the theatre toured towns in Staffordshire, skipping entries when he found the girlish language embarrassing. He picked up a notebook of his own and started to copy out the comments he thought were most relevant to his investigation:

June 3rd T is so kind and encouraging. It would be hard without his help. I think he likes me.

June 5th The strangest thing happened. Saw M sitting with Prof K. They both seemed angry when they realised I was there and K ordered me out of the tent.

June 15th He was here again, but ignored me. He used to be so friendly. I wonder if they were talking about me?

June 23rd We're going to Leek sooner than planned. K has changed the date. It is so exciting to be going home!

June 26th I'm sure something is going on between M and K. I mean to find out what it is although Lottie has warned me not to.

July 2nd Tried listening in again, can't stop myself. Could only make out some of the words.

July 4th Listened in. Positive they didn't see me.

July 6th Tomorrow we are on our way to Leek. Nervous about performing in front of people who know me. Must see C, so much to tell her. Hope she knows what to do.

Ramm snapped the book shut and sighed. The diary showed no sign that Sarah was not coping as Thomas Kilner had said. But it was clear there were things on her mind, something she wanted to tell "C" about, just as she had said in her last letter to Cora Blake.

What really puzzled Ramm was the "M" she mentioned so often. It must be Mulder, he decided. Quite why Miss Hulme was surprised to see the stage manager was odd.

Why was she preoccupied with listening in? Ramm's eyes closed and his head rocked from side to side as he weighed the possibilities.

Had Mulder made some approach to the young woman that had gone disastrously wrong? Then he had strangled her to silence her and cover his own tracks. He looked a rough character and was certainly big enough to lift Miss Hulme into the stage rigging.

But Ramm knew he could not rely on the diary alone. He needed hard evidence to make an arrest and, at the moment, he didn't have any.

CHAPTER ELEVEN

Giuseppe Manfredi stared at the cup of coffee he had let grow cold. It was Friday morning and he was on edge, his head aching from the whisky he had downed the previous night in the hope of getting to sleep.

Each day seemed to bring new challenges and Thursday had been no exception. The Horse Fair was not the sort of place he would ever be comfortable, but he had needed to be there. Then people had wanted to talk to him about Broadhurst's death. News like that did not take long to circulate in Leek, people passing on lurid details although they might know only half the story. He had struggled to keep his composure when mothers had wanted to gossip about it at their daughters' piano lessons. He knew there would be more speculation about Broadhurst – and Miss Hulme – once the *Leek Lion* came out on Saturday.

Sitting alone in his kitchen, Manfredi pondered what to do about his dance class planned for tomorrow. Could he face putting on an act for the young ladies? Last week had been bad enough with all the girls talking about Sarah. This week would be even worse. Of course Broadhurst's daughters no longer came to the class, but it would still be the chief topic of chatter. The young women would look at him with their sad eyes expecting sympathy which he would find hard to give.

"I should cancel the class," he thought. "I'll pin a notice on the door and then I won't have to see them at all."

His nerves were frayed. He was used to keeping secrets about his background and his private life, and sometimes he wondered whether a small town like Leek was really the right place for him.

Perhaps he would have done with it and leave.

"Calm yourself," he breathed. He could not just walk away and certainly not for at least a week.

Next Saturday he would conduct the hymns in the Market Place for the Sunday Schools Festival or Club Day as local people called it. It was one of Leek's biggest occasions and many hundreds of children and churchgoers would fill the streets with music and colour. He would be at the centre of it all, his musical skills recognised at last, he thought with pride. It had been worth attending the Catholic Church occasionally to prove he was as devout as the best of them, he smiled. Another act he had performed to perfection.

Manfredi took a sip of coffee, winced at the sour taste, then slammed the cup down. He was determined to see things through to Club Day, whatever happened in the days ahead.

When FJ Finch arrived at the police station that morning he was eager to discover what progress Inspector Ramm had made.

"Did you give any more thought to my theory, Inspector?" he asked as soon as he took the seat opposite the officer.

"The Germans, you mean? As yet, I have found nothing to indicate foul play in Mr Broadhurst's death," Ramm replied. Earlier he had received the post mortem report from Dr Handbridge, confirming that Broadhurst had drowned. Once the black dye was cleaned off, the surgeon had found bruises on the dead man's head and neck, but these could have resulted from his fall into the tank.

"You believe it was an accident, then?"

"Either that or self-inflicted, but I would not want that to appear in the *Lion* tomorrow."

"Self-inflicted, Good Lord!" Finch replied, his eyes widening, thinking of the implications of a well-known employer taking his own life. "Can we say that your investigations are continuing?"

"Yes, and I also want to make an appeal to find the person that Mr Broadhurst had arranged to see on the evening of his death. He was due to meet a prospective customer at the works, but I have yet to find out who it was."

Finch saw that the search for a mystery visitor would give his story a new angle.

"In fact," Ramm continued, warming to his idea, "I think we should ask for anyone to come forward if they were in Mill Street and saw someone entering or leaving the dye house. Let's say between half past six and half past seven on Wednesday evening. I'm sure you know the sort of thing we want to say."

Finch wrote quickly in shorthand in his notebook.

"So you have no idea who the person was that Mr Broadhurst was meeting?" he asked.

"Not at present," he said.

"What about Miss Hulme, Inspector. Is there any more to say on her case?"

"As I told your young man on Wednesday, I am still investigating."

"Foul play?"

"I cannot comment."

Finch closed his notebook, disappointed there was nothing new about Sarah.

"Before you go, Mr Finch, there is another important matter to tell you about. I have the honour to announce that His Royal Highness King Edward will motor through Leek and the moorlands on Friday of next week."

Finch was startled. He peered at Ramm to make sure the officer was serious, then opened his notebook and began to write furiously. The Inspector proceeded to give details of the King's route, estimated timings and planned road closures, adding what he had gleaned about who would make up the Royal party.

Finch took a moment to digest the surprising news.

"There will be huge interest in this, Inspector. How long have you known about it?"

"A matter of days, Mr Finch, but I can assure you that we are well prepared. We will ensure that both the public and His Majesty are safe," Ramm replied, anxious to give no hint of his own trepidation for the coming week.

As he made his way back to his office, Finch considered just how important the Royal announcement was to the town. This would be the first and only opportunity most people would have to see the King, even if it was a fleeting glimpse of his bearded jowls as his motor car rumbled past.

The crowds could be chaotic, he thought. He just hoped Inspector Ramm and his men really were ready for the occasion.

Cora Blake told her father she wanted to look in a millinery shop during her lunch break, but had no intention of doing so. She came out of the studio and walked quickly along the street, knowing she had to make full use of her time off work. She needed to speak to Thomas Kilner again and that meant going back to the rag-and-stick. She would have to put memories of Sarah's death to the back of her mind.

As she hurried along Derby Street she could see the shape of the theatre tent in the distance, its dusty canvas walls now representing something much more sinister than any sort of entertainment. Cora was about to cross into Sparrow Park she saw Signor Manfredi approaching. He seemed to be in a hurry too.

"Miss Blake," he said, nodding to Cora without breaking his stride.

"Signor Manfredi, I'm glad to see you," she said. Manfredi, forced to stop and engage in conversation, looked at Cora searchingly. He drummed his fingers nervously on his leather document case as if he was practising a piano exercise.

"I wanted to tell you that I will not be able to attend tomorrow's dance class," Cora went on.

"Dance class?" asked Manfredi, apparently interrupted from his train of thought. "Ah si, tomorrow, of course," he continued, in his usual mixture of Italian and broken English.

"I sorry to hear, but I cancel anyway. Too much... too much trouble." There were dark lines under his eyes, showing the same anxiety Cora had seen when he had addressed the dance class last Saturday.

On the spur of the moment, she decided to change the subject. "Did you have any luck at the Horse Fair yesterday?" she asked.

"Horse? Luck? Why you ask, Miss Blake?" Manfredi responded, his voice several tones higher.

"Because... I saw you there. Talking to someone." Cora thought it best not to say she had been scrutinising her father's photographs, nor that she had seen Manfredi with theatre folk.

"No, no horse. I there to look. No talking." With that he touched the peak of his hat and walked off.

Cora turned to watch Manfredi bustle away, catching a last whiff of his lavender cologne. He seemed more distracted than ever.

"He must have known Mr Broadhurst. It's no surprise he is so upset, the poor man," Cora thought.

But what he had said about the Horse Fair puzzled her. Perhaps the strain of the last few days had caused him to forget he had been talking to someone.

When she reached the theatre, Cora took a deep breath as she went through the canvas doorway. Parts of the tent walls had been folded back to let the light in, but the interior still conjured up the shadowy atmosphere she remembered from the fateful night. Her eyes were drawn to the stage, but instead of seeing a group of performers rehearsing their lines she saw vividly the scene from a week ago, Sarah's body gently swaying from the rigging.

Cora squeezed her eyes shut and when she opened them again managed to focus on the present rather than the tragic past. She was looking around to see if Thomas Kilner was there when an older man with long black hair and an elaborate black moustache approached her. Cora recognised him as Professor Kilner from her father's photographs.

"Can I be of assistance, Miss?" he asked, smiling and assessing her from head to foot as if she had arrived for an audition.

"I was looking for Thomas Kilner. Is he here?" Cora replied.

"And you are?"

"Blake, Cora Blake."

The smile momentarily left Kilner's face, but he quickly resumed an air of proprietorial authority.

"I'm afraid he's *much* too busy to speak to members of the public at the moment. In fact we are all very busy. We have a new production tonight, young lady," he said. He stared at Cora, his deep-set eyes glinting, and waited for her to leave.

Cora was disconcerted at coming face to face with the theatre owner. She was sure Professor Kilner was trying to bully her. Was he the person responsible for Sarah's troubles, she wondered.

"When might he be available? It's important that I speak to him," she said, standing her ground.

"If it's about the theatre, Miss Blake, then I am sure I can help," Kilner responded, although there was nothing helpful in his tone.

"No it's something else. Can you tell Thomas that I was asking for him, please?"

Kilner nodded brusquely and turned away to speak to a group of performers standing in a corner of the tent.

Cora had made her way out. Relieved to be in the open air again, she had paused just outside the tent when a dark skinned young woman darted after her. Cora recognised her as one of those she had seen tap dancing in the Market Place earlier in the week. She was about the same age as herself and had black curly hair.

"Are you Sarah's friend? I saw you talking to the Professor," the young woman said.

Cora nodded.

"My name's Lottie, I used to share a room with her," the performer went on, then lowered her voice. "I've got something to tell you... but not here," she said, glancing back towards the tent to check there was no one watching them. "Sunday afternoon is the only time I get off. Can we meet somewhere... somewhere more private?"

Cora realised this could be important and she quickly came up with a plan. "Have you seen the old church at the top of the Market Place? Go around the back, the side that faces away from the street. I'll meet you there on Sunday – at about three o'clock? – and then we can find somewhere quiet to talk."

The young woman hurried back into the tent. Cora walked away, intrigued about what she might learn from Lottie. Hopefully it would be more about Sarah's life ...and death... in the theatre.

Once he was sure Cora Blake was gone, Orlando Kilner went to find his son. Thomas was behind the main tent, helping Conrad Mulder to unload props from a cart for that night's production of *The Crimes of Sweeney Todd*.

"That young woman, the photographer's daughter, has just been looking for you," Kilner told his son.

Pushing his hand across his forehead, Thomas gave his father a worried look. "Cora Blake? Here?"

"I told her you were not available, but as you said yourself, she seems rather persistent," Orlando went on. His voice became harsher. "We can't have her snooping around. It would be best for you to see her and put her mind at rest once and for all."

"How am I going to do that?"

"By telling her just what you told the police officer," Orlando

120

replied, a little exasperated. "There's no reason why Miss Blake should not believe you, is there?"

"It might be more difficult than you think, Father. She knew Sarah well."

Conrad had stopped what he was doing and now joined in.

"Play your part, Thomas," he said.

Orlando nodded in agreement. "Go and find her. Today," he instructed.

Thomas took a deep breath. For the good of them all, he knew he would have to see Cora again, and the sooner the better. He went to fetch his jacket and cap.

Ten minutes later Cora gave a start when Thomas walked into her father's shop. Though she hardly dared admit it, she was excited to see him again, but at the same time she was anxious about what he had come to say.

"Miss Blake," Thomas greeted her in a formal tone. "I believe you wish to speak to me. About Sarah, I presume."

"I am only trying to find out what happened," she replied.

"What happened is that life in the theatre was too much for her," Thomas spoke quickly, as if delivering a speech he had learned. "She might have told you that she was happy, but in the end I don't think she was. She was gradually losing control. I think she... she just didn't know what to do."

Cora was taken aback. "But you were her friend, why didn't you help her?"

"Yes, I was friends with her, but we have all had difficult things to face in life..." Thomas halted as an image of his brother flashed through his mind, "and I was not able to save her."

Cora steeled herself to look into his eyes, trying to gauge if he was telling the truth. His expression gave nothing away.

"You will never know how sorry I am that it has turned out like this," he added. "But I have to move forward now, and so do you."

"If what you say is true..." Cora's voice trailed off. She felt deflated to think that Sarah had become so desperate.

Thomas bid a courteous goodbye, leaving Cora alone with her thoughts. She might have to learn to live with Sarah's death and her own guilt for encouraging her friend to join the theatre. But there was still someone else to speak to. Perhaps Lottie would have a different story to tell.

Inspector Ramm had faced more awkward questions from headquarters about the King's visit. Irrespective of mysterious deaths that needed to be investigated, his superiors would judge him on how well the Royal occasion was handled.

Ramm knew his force was too small to cope with the challenge and that afternoon had invited Major Wardle, commanding officer of the Leek Volunteers, to the station. The Volunteers' Band was always popular and the part time soldiers had earned new respect after being called up for the war against the Boers in South Africa. Smartly turned out, well drilled and ready to follow orders, they looked the ideal reinforcements for his officers on the Royal day.

He also decided to ask Leek Fire Brigade for their assistance in controlling the crowds. Next he would contact council officials to ensure the streets on the King's route were cleaned of horse manure and that potholes in the rural roads were filled with chippings.

Putting his list of duties for the visit to one side, Ramm returned to his file on James Broadhurst's death. He looked again at the photographs of the scene and considered what he had heard about trade declining. The list of names he had seen on the office desk could have been traders to whom the man owed money. Perhaps he had made his own death look like an accident, either for the sake of appearances or to claim an insurance policy.

Ramm put on his tunic and left to visit Mrs Broadhurst, hoping the widow might give some clue to her husband's mood and his finances.

Closed curtains and a black wreath fastened to the front door gave a mournful air to the Broadhursts' substantial house in Hugo Street, a neighbourhood popular with business owners. A maid in full uniform showed the Inspector wordlessly to a side room crammed with potted plants. As he waited he thought how, only days before, he had sat in the Hulmes' much humbler home, but one equally engulfed in sorrow.

Minutes ticked by and finally Constance Broadhurst entered with faltering steps, leaning on the arm of an aged woman whom Ramm took to be a relative. Mrs Broadhurst's face was deathly pale, her eyes cast downwards. The two women seated themselves on a small velvet chaise longue.

"Mrs Broadhurst, please accept my condolences," Ramm began, to which the widow gave a barely discernible nod.

"I am sorry to disturb you, but it is important we establish the circumstances of your husband's death. The sooner the matter is cleared up, the better for everyone," the Inspector continued.

The woman looked up, her head shaking slightly, a quizzical look on her face.

"A terrible accident, surely Inspector?" she said. Despite her distress, there was the hint of the superiority that came with wealth.

"That is something I wish to confirm, Mrs Broadhurst. Perhaps you could help me with a few details about Wednesday evening?" Receiving no response, Ramm went on. "I gather your husband had an appointment with someone at six thirty. He was due to meet a customer. Did he mention anything about that, I wonder?"

"No Inspector, I have no idea who he was meeting. James did not go into details about the business. He used to say that was the last thing I should worry my head about." Mrs Broadhurst looked wistfully across the room as she recalled her husband's voice.

"If that is the case, I presume he gave no impression of being concerned about the business or worried about money perhaps?"

"Money? He never discussed finances with me. He took care of all the bills and there was nothing amiss, as far as I am aware."

"Mrs Broadhurst, could I ask, did you notice him acting, how shall I say, differently in recent weeks?" Ramm wanted to raise the subject of James Broadhurst's mental state without offending the woman's sensibilities. He saw a flicker of recognition behind that far off look.

The older woman gave the widow's hand a sympathetic squeeze.

"Different? Well, I'm afraid James did start to behave a little differently." Mrs Broadhurst stopped and took a deep breath, summoning up her strength to continue. "Politics. He had become obsessed about the situation with Germany. He thought the country was in danger, all of us were. Sometimes it seemed that it was all he ever thought about."

Ramm remained silent, sensing there was more to come. He had known other occasions when a bereaved relative would seize the opportunity to unburden themselves.

"I think that was perhaps why he did one or two things that were a little unsettling. He started to cancel our accounts with some of the local tradespeople he didn't agree with. And stopped the girls' music and dance lessons."

"Music lessons?"

"I didn't know what to make of it. Signor Manfredi is such a sweet man. Lucy and her sisters were quite upset."

At the mention of her daughters, Mrs Broadhurst buried her face in a handkerchief and began to weep. The elderly relative gave Ramm a stern look and he realised he should leave before any more distress was caused.

He thanked the ladies for their time and walked back to the police station, thinking over what he had just heard. This obsession with Germany may have caused Broadhurst to neglect his business and his finances, he thought. Ramm felt sure that money, or the lack of it, had led to the man's demise.

Francis Cavendish was feeling more comfortable now that darkness had fallen and there were only the occasional pools of light from the town's gas lamps. It was past ten o'clock and the audience was streaming away from the rag-and-stick. A full house again. Last week's horror was soon forgotten, Cavendish thought grimly.

He had been scouting around the town for most of the day. He had seen Cora Blake go to the theatre tent and later watched as Thomas Kilner walked to the Blake studio. There must be something between those two, he thought.

Now he stood in the doorway of a shop near the bottom of Derby Street waiting for members of the theatre company to emerge.

He saw a constable on night patrol approaching and sank back further into the shadows and stood motionless. The policeman's attention was caught by something on the other side of the street and he walked past, taking no notice of where Cavendish lurked.

He watched him go by with a critical eye and mused on the quality of Leek's police. He knew that, like himself, many of the force had served in the army. They might be good at taking orders, but had no clue about crime, he thought. What would they make of the death at the dye house that people were gossiping about? How long before their inspector gave up his inquiries and took the easy way out?

He had little patience with the police. In fact there were few people he had any respect for. Always on the move, always on his guard, he had no time for friends. John Gibb came into his mind. In the old days, Gibb had been someone who could be relied on.

His thoughts were interrupted when he heard a familiar voice. Sure enough, Orlando Kilner was striding away from the tent, declaiming his usual nonsense, a couple of his fellows in tow.

When they had passed, Cavendish followed at a safe distance. It was no surprise when he saw the theatre owner go into The Cock Inn, just as he had done every night since coming to Leek. Through the front window he could see the theatre folk settling into the snug.

Cavendish decided against going into the inn. Instead he sat down in the porch of a church on the opposite side of the street and hunched over to make himself less conspicuous. He would wait until Kilner finally emerged and tottered off to his lodgings.

Down at Dieulacres Cottage Farm, in the outbuilding where John Gibb had his bed, the old soldier woke with a start. He had been having one of his all too familiar nightmares. He was back in a foreign land, surrounded by natives who wanted rid of him, dead or alive. He rarely talked about what he and his men had faced in Africa and Afghanistan; like most of the troops, he had tried to put it behind him.

Gibb lay staring into the blackness of the barn, thinking about the last few days and Francis Cavendish. Did he have nightmares? Had that driven him to behave like a different person? Gibb made up his mind. If he saw Cavendish again, he would speak to him and find out if he could help the fellow. It was the least he could do for an old comrade.

CHAPTER TWELVE

H.R.H. KING EDWARD VII TO VISIT LEEK.

It has been announced that H.R.H. King Edward VII will be in the moorlands on Friday next, July 22nd. This will be His Majesty's first official visit to our area since his ascent to the throne and is an occasion likely to attract great interest and patriotic celebration amongst the populace.

After spending the evening of Thursday July 21st at Swythamley Hall as guest of the 2nd Baronet Brocklehurst, the following day His Majesty and his accompanying party will proceed to Alton Towers where they will be entertained by the Earl and Countess of Shrewsbury at their country estate. There will be a procession of three motor cars, H.R.H. The King travelling in the 22 horsepower model recently presented to him by the Daimler Motor Company. The Royal party will enter Leek via the Macclesfield Road and Mill Street, arriving in Church Street at approximately midday. The motor cars will proceed via Stockwell Street, Ball Haye Street and thence into London Road and out of the town on the Ashbourne Road. The procession will continue through Bradnop to Bottomhouse Crossroads before travelling to Cauldon and thence en route to the final destination of Alton Towers. His Majesty has no engagements in Leek and it is not planned for the vehicles to halt in the town, however it is expected that large crowds will wish him well along the way.

Leek Constabulary have prepared plans to permit the smooth progress of the Royal entourage and will also be taking measures to ensure the safety of the public.

Inspector Albert Ramm stated: "This is a very special occasion for Leek and the moorlands and we expect large numbers of people along the route, especially within the town itself. My officers will maintain a full and vigilant presence to ensure safety and good order during the day so that the public can show their respect and affection for our dear Monarch."

The *Lion* understands that proposals are being considered for street closures, areas to accommodate the expected crowds and a variety of street decorations, although there will be insufficient time to erect the traditional celebratory arches.

MYSTERIOUS DEATH AT DYE HOUSE.

Leek Police are appealing for assistance from the public following the tragic death of a prominent businessman in the town.

Mr. James Broadhurst, proprietor of the Broadhurst & Co. dye works in Mill Street, was found dead at the premises on the evening of Wednesday last. The *Leek Lion* understands that Mr. Broadhurst died after falling into a vat of black dye following the cessation of work for the day. His body was found by two workers responsible for securing and guarding the premises overnight.

Inspector Albert Ramm, Head of Leek Police, told the Lion that investigations into the incident were continuing, but it that it was

SHOCKING DISCOVERY AT THEATRE.

Police investigations are continuing into the death of a young Leek woman, Miss Sarah Hulme, on the first night of a series of performances by Professor Kilner's Travelling Theatre in the town.

Miss Hulme, aged seventeen and the only daughter of Mr. and Mrs. Edgar Hulme of Grosvenor Street, was found to be deceased on stage as the opening production was about to commence on Friday last, July 8th.

An inquest was opened on Wednesday by H.M. Coroner, Mr. Herbert Evershed, and the hearing was immediately adjourned when Inspector Albert Ramm, Head of Leek Police, asked for additional time to carry out investigations into the death.

Speaking to the *Leek Lion*, Insp. Ramm declined to rule out foul

THE GERMAN THREAT REMAINS: The sad loss of our dear friend "John Bull" must prompt us to redouble our commitment to the cause to which his valiant efforts were dedicated.

His wise words have been taken from us, precisely at a time when he promised details of those we should treat with suspicion until it is proven otherwise.

Fellow townspeople we must continue to be vigilant to protect our great nation and be ever watchful for agents of the foe amongst us.

Yours in sorrow,
UNION JACK

The great iron press had clanked late into Friday night in the *Leek Lion* building on Market Street as the newspaper was printed, folded and stacked ready to be taken out to shops and vendors across the moorlands.

Next morning, the *Lion* was being studied closely in homes and on street corners as FJ Finch and his son Oliver sat in the news room reviewing their efforts. It had been a hectic week and the two journalists relished the thought of what the next seven days promised.

"Friday will be a day to be remembered, Oliver," said Finch. "We will need to clear our books by Thursday evening. The King's visit could fill half a page next week."

"I just hope Sarah Hulme's death is settled before then, if only to put Cora's mind at rest," said Oliver, as he leafed through his copy.

"And perhaps our James Broadhurst appeal will turn up something interesting. I must say, I'm troubled about the whole affair," his father added. His concerns had not prevented him from publishing yet another letter on Germany after he had seen just how many people were interested in the subject.

Finch went out to deliver a sheaf of newspapers to the public library in the nearby Nicholson Institute. The Institute's Reading Room was popular with those who could not afford their own newspapers. Its high wooden desks were occupied for much of the time, especially in winter when the cast iron radiators were a great comfort to poorer folk.

His next call was the Blake studio where he found Cora arranging postcards of the Horse Fair in the window.

"Good morning Miss Blake. Hard at work, I see," he said.

"Only for the morning, Mr Finch. I'm meeting a friend this afternoon," Cora replied.

"Is your father in?"

"He's in his darkroom. I can call him, if you wish."

"No, that's quite all right. I will go up and find him." Finch hoped he and Nathaniel would have a more privacy upstairs.

Tapping on the darkroom door, Finch asked if his friend could spare a few minutes. Blake replied he was developing a plate, but would be out forthwith.

When Nathaniel appeared from the gloomy red light of the workroom, sleeves rolled up and wiping developing solution from his fingers, Finch had settled himself in the armchair used for portrait sessions.

"My word FJ, the *Lion* has much to report this morning. A Royal visit, indeed!" said Blake, who had scanned the newspaper at the breakfast table.

"Yes, I've taken the liberty of promising photographs of the occasion. I presume you will be happy to supply?" asked Finch.

"Oh certainly, FJ, although it will be rather a rush. Will you be able to get the printing plates made in time?"

"We shall work all night if we need to, Nathaniel," Finch said confidently. He paused before continuing. "It is not His Majesty that I wanted to talk about, though. I would appreciate another word with you on these curious deaths."

Blake drew up a chair and looked earnestly at the editor. "Is Mr Broadhurst's death still on your mind?" he asked, lowering his voice so as not to be overheard downstairs.

"Exactly, Nathaniel. I still think it could be linked with his rants about Germany, even if the good Inspector does not agree."

"Are you saying you hold with this spy fever that's doing the rounds? German infiltrators and such. Surely the national rags have exaggerated it out of all proportion?"

"There is serious business afoot in Europe, Nathaniel. I don't know if there are foreign agents around here, but I do know that many folk believe it is true. If you had been at that meeting, you would have seen how high feelings are running even in our small town," Finch replied. "Broadhurst was stoking those fears and, for my sins, I gave him the space to do so."

Blake said nothing. He could see that his friend was feeling some responsibility for the tragic way things had turned out, hence his determination not to let the matter drop.

Finch went on: "You were at the dye works on Wednesday night. Let me ask you, honestly, did it look like an accident to you?"

Blake thought for a moment. "It was certainly a strange affair. A very odd way to die." He stood and turned towards to the darkroom. "I will show you the photographs, confidentially of course, and you can see for yourself."

Blake returned with copies of the pictures he had taken at the dye works. Finch shuffled through them quickly, as if eager to see the gruesome details. Then he considered each one individually, shaking his head from time to time. He looked up at Blake.

"Firstly, Nathaniel. I cannot see how Broadhurst could have fallen into that vat. It was no accident. He would have had to deliberately climb into it.

"Secondly, I struggle to believe that James Broadhurst would do away with himself an hour before the meeting at the Temperance Hall. This was going to be a big occasion for him. He was going to address his supporters, enjoy their approval and so on. More importantly he said he was going to reveal whom he suspected were foreign agents."

"And he had been here to have his portrait taken barely an hour before it happened," said Blake. "The man seemed totally assured, at ease with himself, you might say. He told me distinctly he wanted the photographs printing as soon as possible."

"No doubt he was planning to publicise his spy theories. He was ready to bask in the limelight," said Finch. "What sort of person plans such a public event and then decides to take their own life?"

Both men fell silent as they considered what now appeared to be obvious. Shocking as it seemed, James Broadhurst must have been murdered.

"A strange affair, as you say Nathaniel, and this very strangeness is something else that has been eating away at me." Finch continued. "A dye works owner drowning in a vat of his own dyestuffs? It's so melodramatic! Was Broadhurst's killer was making it look like the man had committed suicide in the most public way?"

"I hope our appeal comes up with something that will make Ramm change tack. Otherwise, I do not think he will pursue it. He has other things on his mind," Finch added.

"Made to look like suicide?" said Blake, thoughtfully. Finch's words had taken him back to the macabre scene he and Cora witnessed at the rag-and-stick. "Just like poor Sarah Hulme, perhaps," he murmured.

Finch focused keenly on his friend. "Miss Hulme?"

"Nothing could have been more dramatic, FJ. If she wasn't responsible herself, someone else certainly tried to make it appear that way," Blake replied.

The friends looked at each other grimly. Could these two shocking deaths be linked?

Carrying a basket that held a picnic for later, Cora met Ellen Simms at the railway station as arranged. After buying their tickets they went over the bridge and descended to the platform where they would catch the half past one train to Stockport.

Cora knew her friend earned less than ten shillings a week at the Great Mill and handed most of that to her mother to help feed the family. She was pleased when Ellen told her that Beatrice had offered her some money out of the campaign funds for the tickets.

There was a press of people on the platform, many of them armed with bags and baskets after visiting Leek's stalls and shops that morning, and the travellers surged forward as the train arrived in a cloud of smoke and steam. Cora and Ellen made their way

132

towards the rear and found seats in the third class carriage.

The two looked around at their fellow passengers. They hoped not to see anyone they knew as the journey was supposed to be a secret after all. A whistle sounded and they were jolted backwards on the hard bench seat as the train lurched forward. Almost immediately the carriage was plunged into darkness as they entered the tunnel under the western side of town. They were soon in the sunlight again and minutes later the train began to slow as it reached Rudyard, the first station on the route.

Several passengers got off and Cora guessed that most were visitors planning to spend the afternoon at Rudyard Lake. As the train rattled along beside the lake, she could see there were not as many people on its shore as on the previous Sunday, probably because most folk had only just finished their Saturday morning shifts.

Cora recognised the next stop as the village station in Rushton where she had been with her parents on a ramble, but soon they were in countryside that neither of them recognised. The landscape changed dramatically as the train pulled into Macclesfield which seemed much bigger than their home town. They could see large churches and mills on both sides of the line, with terraced houses crowded around the sloping streets.

Cora could tell from Ellen's expression that her initial excitement was a little shaken by this adventure into unfamiliar territory. In their seventeen years, this would be the longest railway journey that either of them had made on their own.

They both felt even less at ease when a new passenger sat down heavily on the bench opposite. Red in the face and smelling of beer and tobacco, the portly gentleman cast sidelong looks first at Cora and then Ellen. His mouth formed into a sly grin.

The friends did their best to ignore him. Ellen pulled her long skirt tight round her legs, Cora checked in her basket and then concentrated on the view through the window. Ellen shifted uncomfortably on her seat and reached for Cora's hand. She held it tightly until they arrived ad their destination.

Any thoughts that Macclesfield was a large town were banished as the train entered what they guessed was Stockport. They passed a succession of terraced streets, many criss-crossed with lines of washing. It seemed in every direction there were either mills or foundries with great chimneys. Leek could fit in a small corner of this place, Cora thought.

The train pulled into the station and, ignoring the leering man, the two got up and stepped down onto the busy platform, looking around warily. The station was much bigger than Leek with trains standing at three or four other platforms and passengers hurrying to and fro. Men in railway uniforms were shouting announcements and blowing whistles, porters were pushing carts stacked with luggage and mail sacks, some children were laughing, others were crying.

"What now?" asked Ellen.

"We wait and watch out for Miss Elliott. She must be here somewhere. If we walk off, we'll get lost and she'll never find us," Cora replied.

Just then someone called Ellen's name and they turned to see Beatrice coming towards them.

"I am so pleased to see the two of you. I'm sure you will find this afternoon very interesting. We need to go this way," said Beatrice, pointing along the platform.

Cora and Ellen followed closely as Beatrice walked quickly out of the station and then along pavements filled with people. They had to dart between a stream of horses and carts to cross a wide street. The two looked around at buildings which were grander than anything they had seen in Leek. They turned a corner and saw the most impressive one of all, its cast iron columns and high windows soaring above them. Market stalls were clustered on each side.

"We're here. This is the Market Place and that's the Market Hall.

It's impressive isn't it?" said Beatrice.

"It's like the pictures of the Crystal Palace!" Cora gasped, recalling one of her school books.

Beatrice led them between the stalls to a clear space near one of the entrances to the Market Hall. There were several well dressed women holding banners aloft. One banner read 'Votes For Women', another 'Women's Political and Social Union, Manchester branch', and a third declared 'Fairness For All'. Some of the campaigners were going up to customers at the market stalls, especially the women, and handing out pamphlets and engaging them in earnest conversation. One or two men looked on suspiciously.

Beatrice turned to Ellen and Cora. "We have to start things off quietly, so there's no trouble," she explained. "We try to make sure the police don't know that there's going to be a speech or a demonstration, otherwise they might stop it happening. They would say it's a breach of the peace or something."

At the mention of police Ellen and Cora exchanged a worried look, both concerned they might be getting involved in something that was against the law. Before they had chance to think any more about it, a man strode forward carrying a sturdy wooden chair which he set down on the pavement. He was joined by half a dozen other men who formed a rough circle with their backs to the chair.

Suddenly the women with the banners and the ones with the handbills began to chant "Votes for women. Deeds not words." Customers at the stalls drew closer, curious to see what was going on and the two young women from Leek soon found themselves surrounded by people.

A woman in her twenties, wearing a long grey dress and grey bonnet, came forward out of the crowd. One of the men gave her his hand as she climbed onto the chair. She was greeted by a great cheer from the campaigners as well as some onlookers who seemed pleased at the prospect of a spot of free entertainment.

Placing her hand on the back of the chair to steady herself, she looked around and began to speak in a strident tone, raising her voice to attract the attention of the folk in the crowd and those walking past.

"Good afternoon ladies and gentlemen. My name is Annie Kenney and today I want to speak to you about the great change that is coming to the country. It is a change that must happen. What am I talking about? Justice for women!"

Onlookers fell silent and crowded still closer.

"The great struggle has begun to secure a better life for the women of this country. We raise children, we make homes, we look after the sick. And we do long hours in mills and factories.

"I know what I'm talking about. When I was thirteen I was doing twelve-hour shifts in a cotton mill in Oldham. I still work in a mill, but I am also working for something else: Fairness for our womenfolk."

There were murmurs and nods from people in the crowd who themselves knew that life as a mill worker was a hard grind. Cora was transfixed by the woman's passion.

"We get less pay, we have fewer working rights and we don't even have the vote!" Annie Kenney's voice rose even higher.

"But let me tell you, ladies and gentlemen, a fight has begun, a fight for equality. It's a campaign that will bring together every class in the country, but our fight for equality is especially important to the working woman."

As the speech went on, the crowd grew even larger and shouts of encouragement grew louder. People at the back were jostling to get a better look at who was at the centre of it all.

"I am proud to be a member of the Women's Social and Political Union which our leader, Mrs Pankhurst, founded in Manchester last year," Annie went on. "Our motto is 'Deeds not Words'. We have pledged to fight until we have gained equal working rights for women and the right for every woman – yes, every woman, not just the well off – to have the vote. Deeds not Words!"

Cora felt her heart racing with the excitement of the occasion and what this woman was saying. She remembered feeling the same at a women's union rally in Leek Market Place a couple of years earlier, soon after she had met Ellen. That was also the day she had spoken to Oliver Finch for the first time.

Cora was so taken with the speaker that she hardly noticed anything else going on until Ellen gave her a sharp nudge with her elbow. She looked around and realised that the crowd was making more noise and not everyone was agreeing with the woman on the chair.

"Get back home where yer belong," a rough looking man shouted. More men followed suit.

"Vote? Yer don't deserve it."

"Who's looking after your kids?"

"Women don't get paid as much 'cause they never work as 'ard."

The angry comments seemed to be coming from all sides now and suddenly people were pushing towards the speaker. The men who circled Annie Kenney's chair linked arms and stared aggressively at the critics. Some of the crowd were waving walking sticks and umbrellas, reaching forward to try and hit Annie's protectors. The banners were being pulled to the ground.

Cora and Ellen found themselves caught up in the rowdy throng, jostled forward and then knocked from side to side. Both cried out as they struggled to stay on their feet. Cora felt her basket tip over and glanced down to see their sandwiches trampled.

Then the sound of a loud police whistle pierced the noise. The melée increased as several constables charged into the crowd, shouting and waving their truncheons. Cora saw that as well as trying to disperse people, the policemen were attempting to reach Annie Kenney. She remained standing on her chair, determined to face down her aggressors.

The two Leek friends were now truly frightened they might be attacked or arrested. Then they heard Beatrice's voice at their side.

"Come on girls, we must get you out of this," she shouted, pulling at Ellen's sleeve. She began to force her way out of the crowd with Ellen and Cora following.

The shouting turned to jeers and Cora looked back to see a policeman reach up and grasp Annie's wrist, pulling her roughly from the chair. Another officer took hold of the campaigner's other arm and she was led away, the two men towering over her.

Once they had pushed clear of the crowd, Beatrice led Ellen and Cora into a narrow side street where they stopped in the shadow of a tall building to catch their breath. The two friends looked around to see if they were out of danger.

"I'm sorry you had to get involved in that. Are you both all right?" Beatrice was clearly concerned for Ellen and Cora, as well as being shaken by the disturbance herself.

"I can't believe what happened. I thought it was going to be just a speech, not a fight," said Cora.

"Even if we want to be peaceful, there are plenty of folk out to make trouble when they see women campaigning. They hate what we're trying to do." Beatrice had an expression of grim resignation.

"Even the police?" asked Ellen, still obviously shocked.

"They will probably say it was Annie who caused the trouble in the first place. It's not fair, I know, but we won't let it stop us. We shall fight on."

Beatrice took the two to the railway station where they waited for the next train to Leek. Ellen repeatedly looked back and forth along the platform, convinced a policeman might recognise them. They spent much of the journey home in silence, their minds still on what they had seen and heard.

When they got off the train at Leek, Cora could not keep her feelings to herself any longer. "I don't know about you, but I'm angry," she said. "That speech was so inspiring. Then, when those people started shouting and pushing... and the police arrested her! It just makes me want to do something myself."

"But what can we do?" asked Ellen.

"Deeds not words – that's what she said," Cora replied defiantly.

As she walked home, Cora took deep breaths, trying to calm herself so her parents would have no hint of what had gone on that afternoon. Once in the house, she managed to invent convincing answers to her mother's questions about the walk with Ellen, but she found it hard to conceal what was really on her mind: Annie Kenney's call to action.

It was early evening when Francis Cavendish set off along London Road, the highway that led from the middle of town in the direction of Ashbourne. That day's copy of the *Leek Lion* had said this would be part of the King's route next Friday.

He thought about the *Lion* as he walked. The story on the Royal visit had been too detailed for his liking. All and sundry would now know exactly where and when the King's car would be travelling. Neither was he particularly happy with the reports on James Broadhurst. The newspaper seemed too keen to tell readers about Broadhurst's anti German mania. Did the editor not know he could be playing with fire, Cavendish wondered.

And if that wasn't enough, Cavendish had heard that gypsies had pitched camp close to town. He had seen some of their womenfolk on the streets with baskets of trinkets and charms. He heard the Mount mentioned and had asked the old fellow who owned his lodgings for directions.

After passing tall mill buildings, and a couple of terraced streets, Cavendish found the town soon dwindled to nothing more than scrubby fields and the occasional house. One cottage by the side of the road had a hand painted sign on the gate offering teas. He came upon what looked like a brickworks and then a large three storey institution, its sign stating it was the Leek Union Workhouse. On the opposite side of the road was an arrangement of smaller buildings which looked to be a fever hospital of some sort. Nearby, a group of men were standing outside an inn called The Flying Horse.

His landlord had told him to follow a small lane on the left and then to take a track which led over the Mount. Cavendish followed the directions and as the track climbed higher he gained a panoramic view of the town with the sun was sinking behind distant hills. Church towers and mills with tall chimneys rose above the roofs of terraced houses.

Cavendish halted when he spied the gypsy encampment in a field beside the lane, sheltered by a stand of tall fir trees. He could hear the sound of children playing and of wood being chopped for camp fires which were already sending smoke into the evening sky. From some distance he could make out the caravan shaped like a railway carriage which he had seen previously at Warslow.

Satisfied it was the same gypsies, Cavendish turned and started to walk back. The sun had set by now and he saw hardly anyone on the streets apart from one or two lads delivering baskets of groceries. He did not notice that he himself was being spied upon. A lone figure was tracking him back into town.

CHAPTER THIRTEEN

It was approaching three o'clock on Sunday and there appeared to be no one around St Edward's Church as Cora mounted the steps from Church Street. She knew that by the end of the afternoon the entrance would be crowded as parishioners gathered for evensong.

She followed the paving stones to the far side of the church and found Lottie standing close to the ancient building, in the shadow of the great tower. She tensed when Cora appeared around the corner, then relaxed as she recognised who it was.

"Thanks for meeting me. It's very quiet here," said Lottie.

The two young women threaded their way through the gravestones and sat down next to the wall that bordered the terraced cottages off Ball Lane. Cora thought the setting was perhaps a little macabre, but at least they had privacy.

"So, you wanted to tell me something about Sarah?" Cora began, her eyes roving over Lottie's dark features. She realised Lottie was the first black person she had ever actually spoken to. "I just can't believe she was so unhappy."

"That's just it, she wasn't!" Lottie replied quickly. "I could see she was really pleased about being on stage, and she was excited when she knew we were going to perform in Leek."

"Then what do you think went wrong?"

Lottie looked away, tears in her eyes.

"One night, we were both in our beds, talking about the show and things. Sarah said she had seen somebody with Professor Kilner that day. It was odd because she seemed to be really disturbed by it," Lottie continued. "A couple of days later, she said she had seen the same person with Professor Kilner again. She never told me who it was, but I'm sure it was someone she knew. I think she started to keep watch on the Professor, especially when he had his private meetings. She said she wanted to find out what was going on. I told her that was a bad idea because the Professor would be angry and might get rid of her or something."

"Why would she get into trouble?"

Lottie's eyes darted around the graveyard, making sure that no one was within earshot.

"We only put up with Professor Kilner because we love performing. I know he seems charming to some people," Lottie rolled her eyes, "but you need to keep on the right side of him, for sure. He can be nasty if we don't do exactly as he tells us. All he cares about is filling the tent. If there's not enough people in the audience, he pays us less money.

"And he's doesn't like mixing with most of us. We're all on strict orders to keep from under his feet, especially when he gets together with Thomas and Conrad. We're used to it and we just leave them to it, but Sarah was new and she was so curious, especially after she saw somebody else with them."

"She wrote to me and said she had something important to tell me," said Cora.

"She must have found out something when she was listening in."

They fell silent as they both thought about Sarah and the way she had died.

"If Professor Kilner is so bad, why don't you move somewhere else?" Cora asked finally.

"Sometimes I wish I could, Cora. But it's hard finding our kind of work and managers usually want a letter from where you worked before. Sometimes it feels like Professor Kilner's got us trapped." Lottie paused. "My Pa's spent his life singing and dancing, and most of the time it's in the street. They call him the Chocolate Coloured Minstrel. But people say cruel things sometimes and he's always struggled for money. I suppose I should count myself lucky. Things could be worse."

"Because of... the way you look?"

"My colour, that's right. At least I'm not a skivvy cleaning someone's house or doing their washing. And there's usually a part in the shows for somebody like me. Because I'm there, one of the others won't have to put on blackface make-up," Lottie replied ruefully.

"What's Thomas like? Is he the same as his father?" Cora asked cautiously.

"Good looking isn't he?" Lottie smiled, guessing what Cora was thinking. "He's good on stage, too, but Thomas has to do what his father tells him. We're always careful what we say when he's around in case he tells the Professor and gets us into trouble."

"But he was friends with Sarah, wasn't he?"

"Yes, she liked him, but that didn't help her in the end, did it?"

Cora waited until Lottie was out of sight before she set off herself, winding her way back through the churchyard. Her head was spinning. After what Thomas Kilner had told her on Friday she had been almost ready to accept that her friend couldn't cope with going on the stage. Now, after speaking to Lottie, all the hurt and anger came flooding back. She was sure something sinister had been going on at the theatre and that Sarah had been a victim.

Her next job was to see Ellen to talk about their plans for a protest. Cruso's Yard was close to the church and when she entered the courtyard Cora could see her friend was on her knees scouring the front doorstep with a donkey stone. These might be some of the poorest houses in town, but the folk who lived there – especially the womenfolk – tried to keep up some appearances.

Ellen looked up from her task and said she was helping Ma with housework, so Cora might have to wait a few minutes. Wiping her hands on her apron, Ellen hurried back into the house. As Cora waited she looked around the courtyard. In a corner, two small children were scraping the earth with a stick, watched by a thin dog. The privies smelled the same as a few days ago, so did the midden of rubbish. It reminded her how comfortable life was in her own home, especially since they'd moved to a new house after her mother remarried.

When Ellen appeared again she said she couldn't be spared for too long because one of her sisters had fallen ill and her mother needed help. "Let's go into Davenport's field," she said, leading Cora through a gap in the wall at the far end of Cruso's Yard and into the sloping field.

The wealthy family who lived nearby in the big house called Foxlowe grazed their horses on the field and children played hide and seek amongst the bushes. Ellen found a quiet spot in a corner and they sat down on the grass. Although they were supposed to be going to talk about Votes for Women, Cora immediately started to recount what Lottie had told her about Sarah and the rag-and-stick.

Ellen was doubtful. "It's horrible if something did happen to Sarah, but what can you do about it, Cora?"

"There must be a way to find out what Sarah was worried about," Cora replied, frowning.

"But are you going to have time for the Votes for Women campaign, as well?"

"Yes, I'm still keen, Ellen, certainly I am. In fact I've had an idea what we could do."

Ellen leaned forward, eager to hear the plan.

Cora took a deep breath. "Well, I think we need to do something here in Leek and try to draw people's attention to what women are fighting for."

"Call a meeting, you mean? I don't know how we can do that, unless Beatrice helps."

"No, I think we should make a banner, something simple saying 'Votes for Women'," Cora said, excited to share the idea that had struck her in the middle of the night.

"Then we can hang it somewhere it will get noticed... in Derby Street or the Market Place," said Ellen, picking up on Cora's enthusiasm.

"We could put it there eventually, but to start with I've thought of something else. You know the King's coming to Leek? Well, if we can make a banner before Friday we could put it somewhere the King will see it, where he can't miss it. Then it would be a message to the powerful people, not just local folk."

"But wouldn't that be breaking the law?" Ellen gasped. Two years ago someone had accused her of stealing, and although it had all turned out to be false and spiteful, the experience had left its mark.

"I don't know," Cora replied, then added hastily, "I mean, I don't think so."

"I just know it's something we have to do," she continued. "Remember what they said yesterday? Deeds not words."

"So where should we put the banner?"

"Well, in town there are bound to be crowds of people and someone might stop us hanging it out. What about somewhere on the edge of town, like Lowe Hill Bridge? The King would drive right underneath it and there should be no one about to stop us, especially policemen."

Ellen's heart beat faster as she imagined the scene. The words 'Votes for Women' stretched across the arched bridge over Ashbourne Road, the Royal cars rumbling beneath. She was thrilled by the idea. "I'll only be able to help if they give us time off from the mill on Friday. I suppose they might tell us tomorrow," she said.

"And I will probably have to help Father, but I'm sure we can sort something out," said Cora.

The two parted after deciding what to do next. Ellen would speak to workmates she knew she could trust and try to get her hands on enough waste cloth to make the banner. White for the background and something dark for the letters. Cutting and sewing would have to be done in secret, perhaps at someone else's house as her own home was too small. In the meantime, Cora would go to the bridge and try to gauge how big the banner should be.

When Cora arrived at Portland Street, her mother came out of the kitchen and told her that Oliver Finch was in the parlour. "He arrived about half an hour ago and said he would wait," said Edith.

"Oliver, I didn't expect to see you today," Cora said as she went into the front room.

Oliver looked up from the shorthand notebook he had been leafing through.

"I was on my way back from a job and thought you might be in. I haven't seen you for a few days and... I was worried about you," he said. He stood and took a step towards her, his expression a mixture of relief and concern.

"So much has happened," Cora sighed, gently closing the parlour door so her mother would not hear. She sat down. Was it time to be honest with him, she wondered.

She took a deep breath. "I know you said not to, but I spoke to Thomas Kilner again."

"Oh. Was that wise?"

"I really needed to find out more about Sarah."

"And did you?"

"Well, he told me she wasn't coping with the theatre. And I was beginning to think perhaps that was why it all happened. But when I was at the rag-and stick..."

"You went back there?" Oliver interrupted, surprised.

"I was looking for Thomas, wasn't I? Anyway, when I was there, one of the other dancers spoke to me and I met her again this afternoon." Cora explained what Lottie had told her.

"So who was this person that Sarah saw with Kilner?" asked Oliver.

Cora shook her head, her mouth tight with frustration. "I still don't know," she said.

"Honestly Cora, you need to tell Inspector Ramm about this," Oliver went on. "You cannot keep going to the rag-and-stick or seeing this Thomas fellow. What if there *was* something suspicious about Sarah's death? You might be in danger yourself!"

"I suppose you are right." Cora's tone softened as she reached for Oliver's hand and looked up at him. "I know you want to protect me."

Oliver put his arms around her and they were silent. A sound from the hallway made them draw away from each other. Young William had poked his head around the parlour door, grinning at them. He dodged out of sight and slammed the door.

Oliver cleared his throat. "Your mother tells me you had another walk with Ellen yesterday."

"Yes... we did go out together," Cora replied slowly. She was torn between keeping another secret from him and sharing her new passion for the women's campaign.

"What is it? Did something happen?" Sensing her hesitation he thought there was more worrying news to come.

"Well, Ellen and I didn't go into the countryside. We caught the

147

train to Stockport instead."

"Stockport? Whatever for?"

"There was a demonstration about why women should get the vote, and we went to watch," Cora explained. She thought it best to leave out details of the disturbance they had got caught up in. Glancing towards the door, she added hastily: "Mother and Father know nothing about it, so please don't say anything."

"You are full of surprises, Cora!" he smiled.

Encouraged by Oliver's reaction, Cora decided to tell him about her plan for a protest in Leek, once more swearing him to secrecy. This time he blew out his cheeks.

"*Please* be careful. From what I've read, not everyone agrees with women getting the vote and making these protests. And is anyone in Leek really interested?"

"That's exactly why we need to do something."

"But what if the banner came loose and fell onto the King's car or something? You and Ellen could be in trouble!"

"It's worth the risk, Oliver. Things have to change, women must get the vote and stop being arrested for speaking their minds."

Much as he was concerned about Cora's plan, Oliver could not help admiring her as well as seeing that it would make a good story. "Well, I shall pretend to know nothing about this banner for the time being. But if you succeed, I'll try to make sure it's in next week's *Lion*."

Cora gave a small smile. She was doing this to make people aware and Oliver would help her to do so.

CHAPTER FOURTEEN

As soon as Nathaniel Blake arrived at the studio on the Monday morning he was anxious to talk to Cora about the Royal visit.

"I need to decide the best place to stand," he said. "Looking down from Overton Bank perhaps, or it may be better from outside Foxlowe. I do hope we will be able to see His Majesty in his motor car. It should be travelling slowly enough," he went on, but he saw Cora's mind was on other things.

"I shall want you beside me, Cora. I need your help to change plates quickly and take as many photographs as we can. There will be no time to spare. I also want to capture the crowds, the flags, the banners and such."

"Banners?" The word had startled Cora had from her thoughts.

"God Save the King, that manner of thing. I'm sure there will be plenty of those."

"Oh, I see," Cora said flatly. She was starting to feel disappointed. If Father expected her at his side in the middle of town she would have to leave Ellen to take care of the banner at Lowe Hill.

"You seem preoccupied this morning, my dear. Is it Sarah? Are you thinking about the funeral tomorrow?"

"I don't know whether I can face going to the service, Father. It will be too upsetting," she replied.

"Not still blaming yourself, are you?"

"Father, can you speak to Inspector Ramm again? He has to find out what really happened! Someone's told me Sarah was spying on Professor Kilner and that might have got her into trouble."

"Spying on him? Why was that?"

"I think Sarah saw someone she knew... talking to Professor Kilner... and she decided to find out what was going on. I think that's why she had a 'secret' to tell me."

Blake was ill at ease to hear Cora was still trying to find out about Sarah's death. However he had his own misgivings about the affair, especially since talking with Finch. Dabbling in amateur detection had almost landed him and his daughter in trouble in the past, but the details were still niggling him. He decided to raise the subject with Inspector Ramm again, but first he would speak to Finch.

The Inspector began the week in usual fashion by gathering his team together.

"I want you all in fine fettle for the King's visit. Those with medals must wear them," Ramm told his officers.

"Your duties should be straightforward. Keep the crowds in order and prevent folk from walking in front of the motor cars, especially the King's. The Territorials and the Fire Brigade will assist. Of course, there may be some thieving and a few folk toasting the King's health a little too heartily. No doubt someone will fall from the railings, that sort of thing, but I'm sure there will be nothing we cannot handle."

He turned to Sergeant Reynolds who proceeded to report on recent incidents.

"A couple of drunks, Sir, spot of fighting, nothing serious," the portly Sergeant said matter-of-factly, running his finger down his ledger. "Someone came in to say they were concerned about the gypsies on the Mount. No real sign of trouble, but we'll keep an eye on them. And we've finally heard what was stolen from the sheds at Cauldon Lowe last week. Nothing particularly interesting, just tools and a crate of stuff they use for blasting in the quarry."

"There's no limit to what people will thieve. Keep an ear out in case they try selling it," Ramm commented before moving on briskly. "Now, as regards our two unresolved deaths, I expect Mr Evershed will want to hold the inquests as soon as possible. We need to press on with inquiries," Ramm continued.

"Concerning Mr Broadhurst, we must try to identify this business visitor. I want one of you to knock on doors in Mill Street today and ask if any neighbours saw someone near the dye house last Wednesday evening. As for the unfortunate Miss Hulme, I want to talk to that fellow Mulder again. Constable Knowles, can you bring him in from the rag-and-stick?"

Ramm was interrupted by the sound of the telephone ringing in the front office. Reynolds went to answer it and hurried back a minute later.

"Headquarters, Sir. They want you down there. A meeting about the King's visit. They say they want to know what you've arranged for Friday."

Ramm tried to suppress a groan. This put his plans for the rest of the day into disarray. A visit to Police Headquarters was a drawn out affair because the train journey from Leek took the best part of two hours. Checking his pocket watch he saw he had already missed the first train to Stafford. The next would be half past eleven.

"Knowles, make haste now. I want to see Mulder before I leave."

Meanwhile FJ Finch was at his desk, sifting through the morning's post. A pile of council notices, handwritten text for advertisements and another letter about Germany which he was about to open when Blake appeared at the top of the stairs.

The photographer had a folder under his arm. It contained the notes and photographs he had drawn together on Sarah Hulme's death. Before leaving the studio he had also added copies of the pictures taken at the dye works and a few scribbled thoughts about James Broadhurst. At the last minute he had included photographs of the Horse Fair, he wasn't sure why except that Cora had been so curious about them.

Finch looked up quizzically. "Nathaniel! What can I do for you?"

"A word about what we discussed on Saturday, if you will. I cannot rid my mind of these awful deaths, FJ. The way the two of them looked will stay with me for a long time," said Blake. "It's enough to make me wonder if this police work is worth doing."

"What you do for the Inspector is important to the town, Nathaniel, but I quite understand how troubling it must be sometimes."

Blake told him what Cora had found out about the theatre and why she thought Sarah might have been in danger.

"So there may be a mystery man involved at the rag-and-stick? James Broadhurst also had a mystery visitor, didn't he?" said Finch thoughtfully. "There are certainly some rum characters in town at the moment. What with Kilner and his fellows, those gypsies at the Horse Fair. And there is that old comrade of John Gibb's."

"Gibb? I've heard nothing about this."

"It's decidedly odd. Gibb is convinced he served with the chap in Africa. Cavendish is his name, something of a hero apparently. But when John approached him, the fellow threatened him and claimed to be someone else. John's worried the man has become unhinged.

"This Cavendish keeps appearing around town. Gibb spotted him first at the rag-and-stick and then coming out of The Cock. I noticed him at the Post Office, arguing with the telegraph boy. The next day he was at Broadhurst's meeting about Germany and then we both saw him at the Horse Fair."

"The Horse Fair? Can you spot him on any of these?" Blake asked, fishing out the photographs he took on the day.

Finch leafed through the pictures, pulled a magnifying glass from a drawer and peered at one in particular before pointing out Cavendish.

"I've got to tell you, Nathaniel, I think there's something suspicious about that fellow. I cannot imagine what he's up to in Leek."

"He can't be this 'mystery man', surely?" Blake replied.

"I wouldn't like to say. He could have been at the dye house before he came to the Temperance Hall. As for the rag-and-stick, he seems to have come to town around the same time they did."

"But Sarah Hulme couldn't have known him. How could he be the person she was so interested in?"

"I'm just airing my thoughts, Nathaniel. If I knew the answers I would be giving them to the Inspector."

When Constable Knowles arrived at the travelling theatre he found Conrad Mulder with hammer in hand, assembling wooden scenery for that night's performance. Having summoned the man from the stage, the officer was about to lead him away when Orlando Kilner hurried towards them.

"What is going on? Can I be of assistance, officer?" he asked breathlessly.

"Mr Mulder is wanted for questioning, Sir."

Kilner stared first at Knowles and then Mulder. The stage manager, towering over the constable, made no attempt to speak and stood impassively, dusting his hands on his breeches.

"Perhaps it would be best if I came too," said Kilner, adopting a tone of authority.

Before the officer could reply, Kilner continued. "Mr Mulder has very poor English, as I am sure your Inspector is aware, and I will be able to help your good selves by acting as... er... an interpreter."

This was a new situation for Knowles and he took a moment to respond as he considered what his superior might say.

"You can come with us if you wish, Mr Kilner, but it will be up to the Inspector to decide whether you are allowed into the interview," he said.

Kilner nodded his thanks and then said something quietly to Mulder in a language Knowles did not understand. This sort of secrecy set him on edge, he wondered if the two were planning something. He reacted brusquely. "Come along, gentlemen," he ordered, "we have no time to waste."

On the short walk from the theatre tent Knowles watched the other two in case any more passed between them. Nothing was said, however, and when they arrived at the station, the constable asked them to wait by the entrance counter.

Knowles went to tell Ramm why Kilner was with Mulder. The Inspector did not like the idea of Kilner being involved. Admittedly, it had been hard to squeeze an answer from Mulder previously, but Ramm distrusted the theatre owner's motives. However, if the Belgian did not understand the questions it could make the interview pointless. With a sigh he told his constable to show the men in.

Ramm looked at the two striking figures before him. One was huge and unkempt, the other colourfully dressed and excessively groomed, and yet in some ways they were similar with deep set eyes and prominent noses.

"Where possible I want to hear the responses from Mr Mulder," the Inspector began. "You, Mr Kilner, should only intervene if it's obvious your colleague does not understand what I have asked. Is that clear?"

Kilner nodded and said something to Mulder who looked stonily at the officer.

Ramm had only a rudimentary grasp of languages, but Kilner's words had sounded more like German than French.

"What language was that?"

"A dialect, Inspector. Belgium has many of them and this is spoken in the region where Conrad comes from."

"How do you know this *dialect*?"

"I worked in theatres on the Continent for many years, Inspector. I was adept at learning other tongues. I first met Conrad in Belgium."

Ramm turned to Mulder. "How well did you know Sarah Hulme?" he asked.

"I know her little," Mulder replied with an implacable expression.

Orlando Kilner said something to his stage manager in what the Inspector presumed was the dialect. Mulder responded gruffly.

"Conrad says he had hardly spoken to Miss Hulme. Before her... er... death, he did not even know her name," Kilner explained.

Ramm pressed on. "Mr Mulder, did you desire some sort of relationship with Miss Hulme?"

Mulder looked uncomprehendingly and turned to Kilner whose eyebrows had shot up at the question. Words were exchanged between them again, before Mulder replied.

"I not want her. I do nothing," he said.

Although he was the one being questioned, Mulder looked calmer than Kilner, who now sat forward in his seat and glanced rapidly between the other two. "Surely you can see, Inspector, that Conrad had nothing to do with Miss Hulme," he said, waving his hands for emphasis.

The Inspector was not to be deflected.

"What intrigues me, Mr Mulder, is that Miss Hulme made entries in her diary which appear to refer to you on numerous occasions. She was disturbed about something. I believe she may have been frightened of you."

Kilner appeared startled at the mention of a diary while the Belgian replied angrily: "No, no, you wrong!"

From the swiftness of Mulder's response Ramm realised the Belgian had understood him perfectly and Kilner's foreign language antics were probably a ruse. These two might even be covering for each other, he thought. He was angry and frustrated, but equally he knew that evidence against Mulder, or anyone else, was pitifully thin. He was relying on initials in a diary.

The Inspector asked again if either had seen Sarah Hulme on stage before her death, hoping to spot a difference with their earlier statements, and he pressed Mulder on how much he knew Miss Hulme, what he may have said to her. Their responses involved much head shaking and denial.

Ramm was exasperated. He felt he was never going to get a straight answer from Mulder and suspected that Kilner was just as slippery. He also knew that time was against him this morning: he had a train to catch. He told the two they could leave, but warned that he intended get to the bottom of what happened to Miss Hulme.

"Hopefully we have clarified matters for you, Inspector. No doubt you have more important things to address," Kilner said with a smile as he left.

There was something sarcastic in Kilner's attitude, Ramm thought. He wondered whether he would ever get the truth from the man.

It was late afternoon when Inspector Ramm returned to Leek. The grilling by his superiors had felt more like being called in front of his old headmaster, but they seemed satisfied with his arrangements for the Royal occasion. The County Constabulary was anxious things should go smoothly and Ramm would not be surprised to see one or two "higher ups", even the Chief Constable himself, in town hoping to see His Majesty.

The weather had turned hot and the railway carriage on the

journey back from Stafford had been uncomfortably stuffy. He struggled not to doze off, keeping himself awake by thinking about the Sarah Hulme case. The interview with Conrad Mulder had been unsatisfactory. He felt he had still not grasped everything that had gone on at the theatre that night.

In the yard outside the railway station the air was thick with smoke and fumes drifting from the nearby gas works. Ramm glanced across at the towering buildings and his mind went back to the time he and Blake had pursued a murderer into the hellish interior of the works. That was an experience he did not want to repeat!

Ramm coughed into his handkerchief as he climbed into the wagonette that ferried train passengers to the middle of town. Once at the police station, Ramm was informed that inquiries on Mill Street close to the dye works had produced no new leads, but Sergeant Reynolds announced with some satisfaction that James Broadhurst's secretary had got in touch. Miss Grindey had found the letter from the mystery visitor.

Ramm imagined the secretary had lost no time in sifting through documents in her late employer's office, acquainting herself with matters he had not told her about when he was alive.

"Excellent news, Sergeant. We must send someone to collect it," he said.

"I have done so already, Sir," Reynolds replied. He flourished a sheet of notepaper.

Ramm looked at the typewritten sheet. He was surprised to see that it was not on a company's headed paper, but when he saw the content he realised the reason and also why Broadhurst was so keen to meet this person.

Dear Mr Broadhurst,

I am aware that these are difficult times for trade and it has come to my attention that Broadhurst & Co may have an urgent requirement for new business.

I am in possession of documentation relating to a highly lucrative dyeing contract. Another local firm was approached but is unable to undertake the work due to a lack of capacity and an absence of suitable equipment. I am in that other firm's employment and so would ask most earnestly that you treat this correspondence as confidential.

I am willing to meet and furnish you with fullest information in order that Broadhurst & Co could secure this important contract. This situation would, I believe, be to our mutual benefit..

As I am not at liberty during business hours, I would propose attending your Mill Street premises at 6.30 p.m. on the 13th inst.

Yours most sincerely,

A Fellow Dyer"

"It's a puzzler, isn't it, Sir," said Reynolds as he saw the Inspector's frown.

"Well, it's proof of the appointment, but as to who Broadhurst met we are no wiser," said Ramm.

John Gibb rarely came into town of an evening. He had never been one for visiting the local pubs. He had never been welcome there when he was tramping the roads and since starting to work for Rosa Carter he preferred the quiet life on the farm.

The last time he had walked into Leek after a day's work had been the evening when he spotted Francis Cavendish at the rag-and-stick. His old comrade was still on his mind and Gibb decided to stroll around the streets for an hour before it went dark. If Cavendish was still in the town, there was a chance that they may come upon each other again.

Gibb was ambling down St Edward Street, his steady pace unchanged from the days when he carried his possessions on his back, when he was nearly upended by wheelbarrow emerging from Strangman's Walks next to The Black Lion Inn. A boy and a girl each held a handle and were straining to push the barrow which was loaded with coal. Gibb remembered there was coal depot just along the alley where folk could collect their own fuel. Normally he would have helped them home with their burden, but as he looked down the street he realised he had more important matters to deal with.

Francis Cavendish was approaching on the opposite pavement. He seemed to be looking idly into the shop windows, some of which were already hung with patriotic decorations in readiness for the King's visit. Gibb crossed the street and Cavendish stopped in his tracks outside the Co-op drapery and boot shop. He realised he could not avoid another confrontation with the Scotsman.

"Major Cavendish, we must talk," Gibb said firmly when he reached the other man. "Can I help ye at all?"

Cavendish was silent for a few moments as he considered his options. Gibb had obviously decided to ignore his warning and, in a town as small as Leek, there was a good chance they would run into each other again. He also sensed that the old Sergeant Major he might be of some use to him.

"Not here," Cavendish replied. "Follow me and keep a safe distance. I'm in Albion Street."

Saying no more, he turned around and marched back down the street. Gibb followed some paces behind. Cavendish turned into Broad Street and then walked along King Street before reaching the terraced house where he was rooming. He let himself in at the front door and waited for Gibb. The two made their way quietly upstairs.

"Be seated Gibb," said Cavendish, pointing to the only chair before sitting down on the edge of the bed.

Gibb was relieved Cavendish had finally acknowledged that he knew him, but he was still concerned what may happen if the other man turned aggressive again. In a room as small as this there was no escape.

"Major, I want nae trouble with ye," he said.

"Gibb, I have no wish to tangle with you, either. And let me apologise for last week. I am in a ticklish situation and had no desire to involve you."

"Major, we were comrades. Just tell me if I can help."

Cavendish held up his hand. "You can start by dropping the 'Major'. You can call me Francis."

"So you're out of the army then, Major... er... Francis?"

"I will come to that, John. But first I must ask you to treat everything I say in the strictest confidence. If you divulge anything to anyone else, it could turn out badly for you. Do you understand?"

Gibb would have liked to reminisce about their service days, but he could see that Cavendish had something more serious to discuss. "So what brings ye to Leek? What is this 'ticklish situation'?" he asked.

Cavendish looked out of the window towards St Mary's Church, one side of its pale stone tower glowing golden in the sunset. Over the past few days he had been wondering if he could trust anyone in this town. Perhaps he should take a chance with Gibb, a stalwart from the old days.

"It's a rather twisted tale," said Cavendish as he began to reveal what had brought him to Leek. As he talked, he had an uncompromising look that Gibb had seen in conflict years ago. The man was older, thinner and greyer, but as zealous as ever. He would do whatever it took to achieve his goals.

Cavendish spoke for ten minutes and Gibb was sorely troubled by what he heard. "What about the police?" he asked.

"I steer clear of them, John. Sometimes I have to do things they would frown upon, shall we say." A hard smile passed across Cavendish's lips, but Gibb saw this was no joking matter.

"This town of yours has become a dangerous place, John," Cavendish continued, "and I am going to need the support of someone I can trust, totally. Are you game? Even if there's a risk to life and limb?"

"Aye, I am," Gibb nodded, although he was still not sure what he was letting himself in for.

Darkness had fallen by the time he made his way back to Dieulacres Cottage Farm. His head ached. He could barely believe what his old comrade had talked about. It could be the truth, or it could be the ravings of a deranged man, a danger to himself and to others.

John felt he had no alternative but to become involved, if only to keep a watch on Francis. Duty and friendship were calling.

CHAPTER FIFTEEN

The following morning FJ Finch could see from Albert Ramm's expression that the officer would have little time for him.

"Apologies for disturbing you, Inspector, I simply wanted to check if you had made any progress with the Broadhurst case. Did our appeal yield any clues?"

Finch had been pursuing his own inquiries, determined that the *Leek Lion* would be the first with the story if it proved James Broadhurst's death was connected with his political activities. He had spoken to some townspeople who he knew shared Broadhurst's theories about the German threat, but it seemed there had been no inkling about who 'John Bull' suspected were foreign agents. He had also called at a couple of the hostelries on Mill Street to sound out the gossip.

"I was in The Spread Eagle last evening," Finch went on, "and the landlord, Mr Fisher, mentioned that some of the theatre folk were in The Square on Mill Street last Wednesday evening drumming up business. I thought there was a chance they may have seen something."

"I admit we are still trying to establish the identity of Mr Broadhurst's visitor. However, I still believe there was no foul play involved."

"If that's the case then I expect the matter will be settled," Finch conceded, although he still had Broadhurst's claims about foreign infiltrators on his mind. "By the way, you did not happen to see a list of names amongst Mr Broadhurst's papers?" he added casually.

Ramm guessed the editor was digging for a better story and felt he should try to quell Finch's conspiracy theories.

"Names? Well, as a matter of fact there was a list and I think they were all connected with Mr Broadhurst's financial dealings. Nothing sinister at all. I do not wish this to be spread across the *Lion*, but I believe that the man may have had business worries."

Finch raised his eyebrows as he was unaware that the Broadhurst dye works had problems, but he was not prepared to let the matter drop.

"These were names that you recognised? People you think he owed money to? Only Broadhurst promised to reveal who he suspected were foreign agents and..."

"Mr Finch, enough! You know my opinion of this German business and I do not intend to divulge the poor man's debts. We should leave it there, I think."

After Finch left, Ramm pondered again the anonymous letter which Broadhurst had received. He could see why the dye works owner might be intrigued by the possibility of a valuable new contract and was prepared to go ahead with the meeting. But could this letter have had something to do with Broadhurst's death, Ramm wondered.

Finding out who had written the letter would be almost impossible. They could not start questioning everyone who worked at other dye houses in the town. Their only hope was that someone had seen the visitor last Wednesday evening.

However, any thought of prolonging the investigation was banished by a telephone call he received soon afterwards. It was the Coroner's secretary informing him that Mr Evershed intended to proceed with inquests into the deaths of Sarah Hulme and James Broadhurst the following day, Wednesday, at eleven o'clock. The Coroner wished no further delay.

For Ramm, the rest of the day would be spent preparing evidence to present at both the inquests. Further inquiries, if there were to be any, would have to wait.

Cora gripped her mother's hand tightly as they walked down Fountain Street towards the Primitive Methodist Chapel that afternoon. Despite the sun, one side of the narrow street was in an ominous gloom cast by the four storey Hope Mill and the towering chapel next door. As they went inside, Cora felt the air was surprisingly cool and she took a sharp breath, stealing herself for what lay ahead: Sarah Hulme's funeral.

When she got up that morning, Cora had thought she would not be able to face the service. Then her mother had said she owed it to her friend to attend. It would be an opportunity to say farewell to Sarah in a more peaceful setting than the horror of that night at the rag-and-stick, her mother told her.

But as Cora sat in the chapel she was finding it hard to rid her mind of what had happened on stage, especially as the tent was just around the corner in Sparrow Park. Glancing around the chapel she saw that nearly all the pews were full. How many of these people actually knew Sarah, she wondered. How many felt the loss as deeply as she did? They had been friends since childhood, then companions at the dance school, and finally... finally Cora had been there perhaps moments after Sarah died.

For much of the service, Cora kept her head down, staring at the polished parquet floor, her hands fiddling with the black cardigan she was wearing. Two hymns were sung, the minister saying they were Sarah's favourites. In his eulogy, he referred to Sarah's love of performing and it brought sobs from various parts of the congregation. Cora realised some of the girls from the dance school must be there. She looked up and saw that one of those crying was Lottie, the young woman who had shared a bedroom with Sarah. She was the only person Cora recognised from the theatre. There was no sign of Professor Kilner, nor his son; so much for Thomas being Sarah's friend, she thought.

Then she caught sight of Signor Manfredi. He was gazing upwards, his eyes moving distractedly as if searching for something amongst the beams of the chapel roof. He didn't appear to be listening to what was going on. She thought again how deeply Sarah's death seemed to have affected him.

After the service, Cora went home while her mother collected eight year old William from St Luke's School. Although it was summer, the kitchen stove was lit and she put a kettle on the hob to make tea for when Mother returned. Then she flopped down on a chair feeling drained. The service had brought back so many painful memories and not only of Sarah, but also her little sister's funeral a year earlier. That had been a tiny affair, like so many during the scarlet fever epidemic, but her parents had looked just as Mr and Mrs Hulme did in the chapel.

They hadn't been able to visit poor Emily in her last days in the Fever Hospital. When Cora and her mother walked there with one of Emily's favourite toys, they had been told to leave it at the door. She remembered seeing people standing outside the wards, peering through the windows, hoping to catch a glimpse of their children inside. Cora's mother could not face that, seeing her child but not being able to comfort her. No wonder Mother had been so upset in the chapel this afternoon, she thought.

She realised she needed to try and pull herself together. Cora had promised to see Ellen again that evening. Her friend would be relying on her to help with the banner. Though she had to cope with her feelings about Sarah's death, preparing for the protest was still important.

At the Blake house late that evening, the kitchen table was spread with notes and photographs. Nathaniel was hoping to make sense of the tragic deaths, or at least of his own theories.

He expected not to be disturbed. William had gone to bed long ago and Edith was in the parlour reading a magazine. Cora had gone directly to her room after returning from a ride. It was unusual for her to go out on her bicycle in the evening, even in summer, and this had been her second jaunt in two days. When he and Edith had asked her where she had been, she had told them only that she had been "around the town" and thought the exercise would be good for her. They were both quietly relieved Cora was getting out in the fresh air, especially after the trial of attending Sarah's funeral that afternoon.

Cora's welfare was one of the reasons he was poring over his papers. By reaching some conclusion himself he hoped to be able to persuade his daughter to give up her own delving. But he had a growing conviction there was no simple explanation for either Sarah's death or James Broadhurst's.

He had managed to secure a few words with Inspector Ramm during the afternoon, even though the officer seemed rather abrupt.

After explaining what Cora had found out about Sarah listening into Professor Kilner's conversations, he was surprised to find the Inspector knew about it from the young woman's diary. Blake was intrigued to hear that Sarah appeared to have been preoccupied with the stage manager, Conrad Mulder.

"He and Kilner are close as can be," Ramm had told him. "But I'm afraid suspicions are not enough, Mr Blake. I still have no real evidence against the man."

Blake did not intend to tell Cora what Ramm thought about Mulder. The last thing he wanted was his daughter going back to the rag-and-stick to seek out that man or anyone else.

Now looking over the notes he had made about the deaths, he considered how best to organise his ideas. He began to sketch a diagram, putting the two victims at the centre and drawing lines to people and places they were connected to. He saw that even though their lives – and deaths – had been very different, Sarah Hulme and James Broadhurst had things in common. The person with most connections to the victims might be the one he should concentrate on, he thought.

He was sitting back assessing the pattern of lines and circles when Edith came into the kitchen.

"What is this all about, Nathaniel?" she asked, looking over his shoulder. As she recognised the names she added: "Oh, I see. You can't stop yourself dabbling in such things, can you?"

"Edith..." Nathaniel began wearily.

"Please don't try to fob me off! You are forever puzzling over matters that you should leave to the police. Look what happened with that affair at the Abbey? You were lucky to get out of that and so was Cora."

"Edith, I know you are concerned, but I have been thinking about the way Sarah and James Broadhurst died for days, and I simply cannot let it rest."

"But why, Nathaniel? You're a photographer not a detective."

"Why? Because I've come to the conclusion that neither of them took their own lives, no matter what Inspector Ramm thinks," Blake replied, becoming more animated. Edith sat on one of the kitchen chairs and prepared to be patient as her husband tried to justify himself.

"Let's begin with Miss Hulme. We both know that Sarah loved performing. Isn't it strange she would take her own life after such a short time with the theatre? It's what she dreamed of. And why do such a thing when she was back in her home town? If she was so upset she could have left the theatre and been back home in a few minutes.

"But above all, Edith, I was there that night. I've thought about what we saw on stage a dozen times. There was no sign of anything – a chair, a bale, nothing – that she could have used to reach into those ropes. It's horrible to think about, but someone else may have put her there."

Edith nodded and tried not to look at the photographs on the table. She was well aware what her husband sometimes faced in his police work and she had witnessed his dark moods afterwards, but she chose not to see the gruesome scenes herself. She felt sick at the thought of what Cora saw in the theatre that night.

Nathaniel was in full flow now. "As for James Broadhurst," he continued, "I was talking to the man last Wednesday afternoon and he seemed full of vigour. I admit I'm no expert, but there was not the slightest hint he would be in a state to take his own life barely an hour later.

"I was called to the dye works," he gestured towards the photographs, "and I simply cannot see how he came to fall into that vat of dye by accident. It must have been deliberate, either by his own hand or someone else's. Finch agrees. He thinks the whole affair is simply too suspicious."

"Oh, of course Finch agrees! He's looking for a better story, isn't he? But what does the Inspector think?"

"Honestly, Edith, Inspector Ramm has too much to cope with at the moment. I think he will be relieved to have the inquests done and dusted before this Royal visit takes place."

Edith stood up. "I can see I shall not be able to persuade you to cease this searching," she said with a sigh. "But promise me one thing, Nathaniel. Please keep our Cora out of this. It was brave of her to go to the funeral today, but now I'm hoping she can start to put Sarah's death behind her."

John Gibb met Cavendish again that night, once more in the tiny bedroom in Albion Street. They kept their voices low in case the old clockmaker could hear them. Cavendish delivered the sort of briefing a commanding officer would give before battle.

What his comrade had said gave Gibb much to think about as he left the house an hour later and he paid no attention to a figure leaning in the shadow of Ward's Mill further along Albion Street.

He knew he had to be prepared to trust his old comrade, just as Francis was putting his faith in him by sharing his secrets. However he had no way of knowing the truth of Cavendish's story, a tale as wild as the look in the fellow's eyes. John would dearly appreciate a word of advice from Finch or Blake, but Cavendish had sworn him to secrecy. He had said lives depended on it.

Above all Gibb feared what Francis had said about acting outside the law. Was the man prepared to kill to achieve his plan, John wondered. By agreeing to help, would he himself be drawn into something illegal?

"I'm an old fool," he said to himself. He knew he was somehow being attracted to the risks that Francis had described. He relished the challenge of getting involved in real action again. Since his army days had ended he had felt cast adrift. Working on the farm was satisfying enough, but John had to admit to himself that he had missed the excitement that came from being in a life or death situation.

If Francis was telling the truth, John thought, in the next few days he might find out just how dangerous things had become in Leek.

Cavendish gave John Gibb enough time to be well clear of the house before going out himself. He wanted to check the middle of town in case any of his targets were still at large.

He stepped cautiously down the creaking stairs and went out into Albion Street. It was dark now and as he turned the corner into King Street he noticed that none of the gas lamps were lit. There was no one else about, John was long gone, but he could just make out the shapes of equipment and piles of earth where some kind of work was going on. Lights still flickered in some of the front rooms, although most people were now in bed, ready for their usual early start the following morning.

Halfway along the street, the tall Georgian terraces were separated by a school and a large house associated with the

Catholic Church that stood at its rear. As Cavendish walked past the school, a figure sprang from the deeper darkness of its entrance.

Sensing danger Cavendish instinctively reached for the small knife he kept in a scabbard on his belt. At the same time he whirled round to face who was behind him. But his opponent was on him before he could complete the turn. Strong hands gripped his throat from behind and then he was wrenched back as some kind of ligature was whipped over his head and around his neck.

Cavendish struck backwards with his knife and heard a cry of pain from his assailant. Before he could strike again he dropped his knife to the ground so that he could reach up to free the noose from around his neck. But it was growing tighter by the second and, try as he might, he could not force his fingers under smooth, hard surface of whatever gripped his throat.

He began to flail his arms, hoping to reach back to his attacker, but he only managed to grab a fleeting fistful of the person's jacket before his hand was knocked away. Cavendish heard the man grunt from the effort of holding the ligature in place while keeping his victim at arm's length.

The noose became ever tighter, biting into the skin of his neck and choking off the precious supply of air. He felt himself losing consciousness and slumped backwards onto the paving stones. He tried to shout out, but his voice, like his breath, was cut off. The last thing he remembered before blacking out was a smell of cologne.

CHAPTER SIXTEEN

Inspector Ramm had not begun his breakfast of toast and treacle when there was a knock on the front door. It was barely seven o'clock on Wednesday morning and the knock told him there was another emergency requiring his immediate attention. This was the fourth time he had been summoned at home in less than a fortnight.

"There's been an incident, Sir," said Constable Phillips, his tone managing to convey both the urgency of his mission and his hesitancy at his superior's likely reaction to being disturbed.

"Incident? Spit it out man!" Ramm replied.

"A man was found in King Street. Throttled."

Ramm was shocked to the core. More violence on his patch and just days before the King was due! Where was this going to end?

"Throttled? Good Lord!" Ramm exclaimed. "Lead on, Phillips," he added, reaching for his tunic, peaked cap and the slice of the bread that Edna was toasting in front of the range.

"Sister Benedict found him first thing this morning. Still alive but only just. We've had him taken to the Cottage Hospital," Phillips explained breathlessly as they hurried along Queen Street.

"The fellow was on the steps to the Loreto convent. Looked like he'd been there all night," he added.

"A brawl after closing time, no doubt. Why such urgency, Phillips?"

"Well, it looks a bit more serious than the usual fisticuffs. Certainly more unusual, Sir. And we've no idea who he is."

"All right. First show me where it happened and then I'll go round to the hospital to have a look at him."

The two men made their way to King Street and Constable Phillips pointed out the spot where the man had been found. It was a flight of stone steps to the Loreto Convent which stood higher than the street.

Ramm looked around at the disarray in the street. Paving stones had been removed and there were several large wooden reels. Workmen were taking picks and shovels from a handcart. "What's going on here?" he asked.

"It seems they're laying the new electricity cables, Sir."

Ramm nodded, he remembered now. He had been invited to the opening of the town's Electricity Works a month before. A council official had told him King Street would be one of the first streets to get a mains supply. The gas lamps were going to be fitted with electric bulbs, some sort of trial for the new equipment.

"See that wire, Sir," Phillips continued, indicating the black cable which was wound around one of the reels. "The attacker used a length of that around the chap's neck. Fair strangled him. Miracle he survived, although he doesn't look too good."

"A miracle. Perhaps we should be thankful for some things," said Ramm, glancing at a painted statue of the Virgin Mary which stood in an alcove beside the convent. "Have a good look around on the pavement. Then find out if anyone along the street saw or heard anything, I'm going to have a word with the nun who found him." he added.

Ramm walked up the path to Loreto Convent. It was more like

the home of a wealthy mill owner than a religious sanctuary. Built of red brick, it had substantial bay windows, both upstairs and down, on either side of the double entrance doors. He tugged the bell-pull and heard a faint sound from within.

A young nun opened one of the doors. Ramm introduced himself, inquired of Sister Benedict and was asked to wait in the entrance hall. The hallway was of substantial proportions with an impressive staircase at the far end. Its whitewashed walls were bare except for a crucifix. The house was completely silent save for the sound of his own boots squeaking on the Minton tiled floor.

Sister Benedict, who was tall and walked with the confidence of someone in charge of her domain, emerged from a side room.

"Will you come this way, Inspector?" she said in a lilting Irish accent. Ramm had seen Sister Benedict around town in her flowing habit before, but had never heard her speak.

She led him into a room furnished with a long table surrounded by about a dozen chairs. She indicated Ramm to take a chair and seated herself opposite, resting her clasped hands on the highly polished table top. He looked at her large hands and thought how often they must be held together in prayer.

"I expect you would be wanting to speak about the... incident... outside, Inspector. An awful affair, so it is," the nun began.

"Indeed, Sister Benedict. I gather you were the person who found the injured man."

"I did and a terrible sight it was," Sister Benedict replied. "He was lying right in our gateway, the poor man! He was stretched out on the steps."

The nun paused as she pictured the scene. "At first I thought it was someone asleep, a tramp perhaps. They come to us for succour, you know, Inspector? Then I saw the black stuff, the cable, around his neck and thought it might be some sort of accident, what with this work going on in the street.

"I knelt down and could see there was still some breath in him.

173

I've worked in hospitals, Inspector, so I didn't panic. First I tried to get that horrible stuff from around his throat, but it was *so* tight. I managed to loosen it a little and then came back inside and told Sister Teresa to run up to the police station. She's young and can move a bit quicker than us old ones. Some of the other sisters came outside, we put a pillow under his head and tried to make him comfortable while we waited – and said a prayer."

"What time was it when you found him?"

"We're early risers here you know, Inspector. It was coming light, so it would be around five o'clock. I was going to the church to get ready for morning prayers." Her eyes fell as she thought how their daily routine had been disrupted.

"And you did not see or hear anything last night?" Ramm asked.

"I heard nothing, but I can ask the others. I looked out of the window last thing and it was pitch dark out there. The gas lamps have been turned off, you see, while they do the work for this new electricity."

Ramm thanked the nun and was rising from his chair when she added: "We're going through bad times, are we not, Inspector?"

Ramm nodded solemnly and Sister Benedict went on, wringing her smooth hands. "Our little town has seen some tragedy these last few days, so it has. Now this, on our own doorstep. May God preserve us from any more calamities."

As the Inspector took his leave he reflected how the "calamities" he was grappling with were seeping through the community. Even into the peaceful confines of the convent.

It was market day and the streets were becoming busy, especially around the livestock pens which were filling up with beasts, bringing the sounds of the country to that part of town. Making his way to the Cottage Hospital, Ramm was forced to step out of the way of a herd of sheep being urged along Ball Haye Street by a

174

farm boy shouting and waving a stick. When he arrived at the hospital, the matron told him they were anxious to continue treating the victim's injuries, however she would allow him to take a brief look at the man.

He lay unconscious, his gasping breath making a rattling sound in his throat. His features were disfigured with purplish bruises. Deep indentations around his neck, now black and swollen, showed where the electricity cable had cut into his skin.

Ramm's mind went back to the rag-and-stick. How Sarah Hulme had looked as she lay on the stage that tragic night. He had no idea who this man was, although even someone who knew him might have difficulty recognising him this morning.

He considered whether to call Blake to take a photograph. Should he summon the photographer for yet another gruesome assignment? By how the man looked, this stood every chance of becoming a murder investigation and photographs of the injuries might be useful.

Matron was hovering in the background, keen to see the officer leave. Ramm asked if he could check the man's clothes and she drew them out of a cabinet beside the bed. He could see from the label that the jacket was of high quality – its owner was no ordinary working man. In the pockets he found a watch that looked to be a better make than his own and a wallet containing a quantity of cash but no means of identification. This had not been a robbery, he thought. There was a single door key on a piece of string.

He felt something heavy in an inside pocket, put in his hand and pulled out a small brass telescope. Like the watch it was of high quality. He turned it over looking for an engraved name or initials, but saw only a coat of arms. For Ramm it stirred a memory of his army days, it was the sort of thing an officer or a battlefield scout might use. Perhaps it was a memento of this man's time in the services, he thought. Strange to carry it around in the town, though, unless he was watching something or somebody.

Ramm set off back to the police station. He was appalled by the attack, and not only its severity, but its timing. Yet another mystery to deal with.

Nathaniel Blake felt a sense of dread when Cora came up to the darkroom to tell him a police officer wanted him downstairs. He had stayed up late going over his notes and photographs last night and when he finally went to bed his fitful sleep had been haunted by images of Sarah Hulme and James Broadhurst. The last thing he needed this Wednesday morning was to have to face another scene of death. Therefore he was a little relieved when Constable Knowles informed him he was needed at the Cottage Hospital to photograph a patient. Not a body then, thought Blake.

But when he reached the injured man's bed he realised his relief had been misplaced. Obviously it was something grim, otherwise Inspector Ramm would not have asked him to take photographs. At first he wondered whether the poor man had tried to hang himself and memories of poor Sarah Hulme flashed into his mind. However if this was a suicide attempt, it was unlikely that the police would spend much time investigating nor want photographs.

The man lay with his eyes closed and was showing little sign of life. His neck was swathed in bandages through which blood had begun to seep. Another bandage was wound around the top of his head and the only part of his face which Blake could see revealed little but a greying moustache and an array of bruises. A nurse stood beside him and he asked whether she could move the head bandage slightly so that he could see more of the man's face. She agreed reluctantly and Blake took his photographs as quickly as possible with his portable camera.

"I used to think Leek was a peaceful town," he said to himself, "so what is behind all this violence?"

Back at the studio, he hurried upstairs not giving Cora chance to ask what had gone on. He immediately started to process the glass plates. It wasn't until the injured man's image began to emerge on the photographic paper in the developing tray that Blake sensed a glimmer of recognition. There was something about the victim's thin nose and his moustache that was vaguely familiar.

As he hung the prints up to dry, he puzzled over where he had he seen the man before. Then he remembered and went to search through the pictures he had taken at the Horse Fair. He found the one that Finch had commented on and took a closer look with his magnifying glass. Yes, it was John Gibb's old comrade, Cavendish.

This was the fellow that Finch thought was suspicious, the one that Gibb thought was in some sort of trouble. Now it looked like someone had tried to kill him.

Blake gently lifted a corner of the print pegged above workbench and peered at the injured man's face. He shook his head and heaved a despairing sigh. Yet more proof, he thought, that something sinister was going on in Leek.

When Blake delivered the prints to the police station he told Inspector Ramm he might know the injured man's identity.

"I think it's a fellow by the name of Cavendish who is visiting the town. He's an old comrade of John Gibb apparently. Gibb might give you a positive identification," said Blake. He could not contain his curiosity, and added: "How did he get those injuries?"

"He was found strangled with a length of electric cable. Why and by whom we have yet to discover."

"You don't think there could be a link, Inspector?"

"A link, with what?"

"The deaths of Miss Hulme and Mr Broadhurst."

"As far as I'm concerned, the only thing connecting these unfortunate incidents is that they have all occurred at the worst possible moment for the Leek Constabulary."

"But surely, if..."

"Mr Blake," Ramm interrupted, "I simply do not have time for idle speculation this morning."

Blake knew there was no point in trying to argue his case when all he had himself were suspicions. After all, it was only Finch's vague surmise that Cavendish, a stranger in town, could be somehow involved.

Half an hour later, John Gibb feared the worst when he saw a constable striding towards him across Rosa Carter's field beside the River Churnet. He was needed by Inspector Ramm, the officer said. Gibb did not ask why, his thoughts had been filled with Francis Cavendish since he had woken. He felt sure this visit from the police must be something to do with the man and the mysterious things he had talked about.

However John was not prepared to be escorted to the Cottage Hospital, nor for what he saw there. His old comrade was bandaged and barely alive.

Last evening Cavendish had been full of energy, appearing to almost relish the challenges and the dangers that might lie ahead. But those dangers had come sooner than either of them had expected and Gibb was aghast at what this meant not only for his old friend, but for what was happening in Leek. This could be as brutal as anything that fuelled his nightmares of his army days.

John stood and stared at the injured man, at first lost for words. He asked the officer how it had happened, but the constable said Inspector Ramm would explain and proceeded to take Gibb to the police station. Seated in front of Ramm, John confirmed that the injured man was indeed Francis Cavendish.

"Do you know what he was doing in Leek, Mr Gibb? Where he was staying?"

Walking from the hospital, John had been considering how much he should divulge, given that Cavendish had sworn him to secrecy and had shown little faith in the police. He decided on caution until he had found out more what had happened to Francis.

"I know him from the old days in the army, Inspector. He was a brave man."

Ramm nodded, but looked quizzically at Gibb. He sensed something evasive in the man's delayed response. However he had doubted John's honesty once in the past, only to find out the Scotsman was utterly dependable.

"It's a bad business, Inspector. How on earth did he finish up like that?" Gibb asked.

"It appears he was attacked last night in King Street. You wouldn't know why he should be there, would you?"

Gibb replied he knew nothing more. The Inspector considered questioning him further, but with two inquests to attend, he was pressed for time and he told Gibb he could leave.

John was newly shocked to hear that Francis had been set upon so close to his lodgings. He had been in King Street himself last night. Had the attacker seen him too? Gibb realised he would have to take great care. He might be the next victim.

Nathaniel was in a state of nervous tension when he hurried through the town busy with market day visitors. He reached the *Leek Lion* building and ran up the stairs to the top floor.

"Have you heard, FJ? About Cavendish?" he blurted out as he entered the news room.

The editor's eyes widened as he fixed Blake with the full force of his newsman's curiosity.

"What has he done? Tell me!"

"It's not what he's done. The fellow has been strangled. He's barely alive!"

Finch gave a low whistle and reached for a pencil to start making notes.

"This complicates things," said Finch. The man he had

considered a suspect had now also become a victim.

"As far as I'm concerned it shows just how dire things are," Nathaniel went on. "Two suspicious deaths and now an attempted murder. And once again the circumstances are quite bizarre. Cavendish was throttled with an electricity cable on the steps of the convent."

"He was in King Street? I thought Cavendish might be up to something, but I never expected this to happen!" said Finch. "This will be a shock for John Gibb, too."

"What do you think it might mean, FJ? If some madman attacked Miss Hulme and even James Broadhurst then perhaps the same person may be responsible for this."

"The inquests on the other two are this morning. Oliver is at the courtroom now, although I doubt we will find out much more than we already know. Inspector Ramm might stop digging once the inquests are done."

"But surely this can't be the end of it?" Nathaniel replied. He unfolded the chart he had drawn the previous evening and smoothed it out on Finch's desk. "Look FJ, I've been trying to put our thoughts together on paper. Now Cavendish has been attacked, I shall need to make some changes."

The editor looked at the sheet. He puzzled over the lines, arrows and circles, then his expression changed as he saw its significance.

"Ah, I see what you're getting at, Nathaniel. There are so many connections between these people, one way or another," he said.

"I'm sure someone at the rag-and-stick is mixed up in this. These tragedies started after they arrived in town," said Blake. "Ramm suspects the fellow named Mulder was involved with Miss Hulme in some way, but I have no idea what he could have to do with Broadhurst or Cavendish."

"Mulder? Which one is he? I've found out that Kilner's people were in Mill Street around the time Broadhurst died. I told Ramm, but he didn't seem particularly interested. If the theatre really is involved, we have no time to lose. Their last show is on Thursday night and then they will be gone from town."

Both decided they should continue their investigations, before it was too late.

Orlando Kilner was considering the days ahead with some satisfaction as he sat in the Coffee Tavern across the street from his theatre. The tea and coffee shop had opened years earlier as an alternative to Leek's many inns and ale houses. Temperance campaigners saw it as a place where folk could gather safe from the demon drink.

A cup of coffee in the middle of the morning was part of Kilner's routine, although the beverage offered here bore little resemblance to what he had enjoyed during his years on the Continent.

Today, with the livestock market busy nearby, the Coffee Tavern was crowded with country folk, although Kilner and his son had managed to squeeze into a corner. Orlando's boldly checked suit attracted curious looks from other customers, but the general hubbub made it difficult for the Kilners' conversation to be overheard.

Orlando leaned in towards his son and fixed him with a serious expression, his deep-set eyes unblinking.

"So Thomas, is everything ready?"

"Yes, Conrad and I will have it all in hand tomorrow evening."

"You will have to stay up all night if necessary, because we must be gone from here by daybreak. I want to be out of the area before His Royal Highness arrives. Then we shall have three nights in Hartington before we move on to Bakewell, although I don't know what the audiences will be like. It's a small place and there may be no appetite for entertainment!"

"Are we free from interruptions now?" Thomas asked.

"Conrad answered all the police questions and I expect no

interference from anyone else. I suspect that Inspector fellow has plenty on his hands without bothering us again. He will probably be glad to see the back of us!"

Kilner's last remark was followed by a guffaw that attracted the attention of several of the farmers sitting nearby. Orlando noticed them looking at him and stood up.

"Good day to you, ladies and gentlemen! Have you been to the Kilner Travelling Theatre yet? We have only two more nights in Leek. Not to be missed!" He made the announcement with dramatic wave of his hand before bowing ceremoniously. Now everyone in the room turned and there was a ripple of laughter.

Thomas smiled too, happy to see his father relax a little. It reminded him of happier times before his brother, Edward, had died in South Africa. After that their lives had changed.

Barely a day went by without Thomas thinking about his brother and he knew his father was the same. Thomas believed that sometimes when his father looked at him, he was really seeing Edward, the son who had made the sacrifice.

If only his brother had not gone to the Boer War, things would be so very different, he thought.

"Thomas? Are you listening?" Orlando could see that his son's attention was elsewhere. "I was asking about tomorrow night." As usual, Orlando was fretting about the details, everything had to be perfect.

"Don't worry, Father. It is all arranged," Thomas sighed. He knew he owed it to his father, and to Edward, to do what was expected of him.

As soon as the inquests were over, Oliver Finch hurried out of the courtroom. He needed to type up his notes without delay so that he could be back in time for the police cases that afternoon, but first he intended to call in at the Blake studio. He wanted to tell

Cora about the verdict on Sarah Hulme.

She looked up expectantly when Oliver bustled in, but she could see from his expression that he had something serious to tell her.

"The Coroner has just held the inquest on Sarah. His verdict was suicide," he said.

Cora felt like the breath had been knocked out of her. "So that's it? No one's going to find out why it happened, or who's to blame?"

"Well, it doesn't necessarily stop an investigation, but it appears Inspector Ramm has no proof that anyone else was involved."

"But this is so wrong! There was something else going on. Everyone knows Sarah would never have... done that. "

"Well, the Inspector said he had heard from some of the other theatre people, including Thomas Kilner, who said Sarah wasn't coping too well. It looks like she didn't leave any sort of note, but Inspector Ramm said he had seen her diary and..."

"Sarah's diary?" Cora interrupted, her voice rising with indignation. "He's been reading Sarah's diary?"

"Yes, and..." Oliver flicked open his notebook, "...he said it 'indicated a confused state of mind' ."

"Confused? She was worried, not confused. Frightened of someone at the theatre."

"I'm sorry Cora, but unless something new comes to light, this could be the end of it." Oliver tried to be sympathetic, but he could not help thinking the verdict might settle the unfortunate affair once and for all, and deter his friend from her own investigations.

"What about Lucy Broadhurst's father, has that been decided too? They don't waste any time, do they?" There was no hiding Cora's bitterness.

"Well, yes actually. The Coroner ruled it was accidental death," Oliver responded. "By the sound of it, no one will ever know quite what happened."

Cora said nothing. Perhaps no one would ever know the truth

of Sarah's death either, she thought. But was there any more she could do? She was jolted from her thoughts when Oliver spoke again.

"Are you still planning to make this banner for Friday?" he asked, hoping the change of subject might improve Cora's mood.

On her bicycle excursions of the last two evenings, Cora had taken measurements at Lowe Hill Bridge and visited the house where Ellen was cutting and sewing scrap cloth that she and two workmates had found. The protest was progressing well.

"Oh yes. No one is going to stop us doing that," she said defiantly.

Inspector Ramm knew he should be relieved now the inquests were over, but he still felt there was unfinished business to be settled.

There was no convincing evidence that Sarah Hulme's death was anything other than suicide. However he suspected that Kilner and his people, especially Mulder, had not been truthful.

He owed it to Sarah's parents to see that a crime, if there had been one, did not go unpunished. He had seen their anguish as they sat through the inquest. How much harder for them if it turned out that a killer had escaped justice.

As for James Broadhurst, the circumstances were baffling, but an accident had been the Coroner's only option. However, the anonymous letter was worrying Ramm. Was it genuine or had it been some sort of trap?

At times like these Ramm had appreciated passing ideas back and forth with Nathaniel Blake. Unfortunately with these current matters, Blake's imagination was perhaps becoming a little overheated and he was seeing conspiracies where there were none.

Finch's suggestion that Broadhurst's list of names could be connected with this German nonsense was also troubling him. Perhaps he should take another look, he thought, just to be safe.

He telephoned the dye works and spoke to Miss Grindey. She promised to locate the list amongst Broadhurst's papers and said she would send an office boy to the police station with it.

Next he asked Phillips what progress was being made with their inquiries in King Street.

"The Sisters were closest and they heard nothing, neither did anyone else living nearby," the constable reported. "A couple of folk say they saw a tall stranger on the street a few times during the last week. It might be that the man is living around there."

"I also found this in the gutter," he added, holding up the knife that Cavendish had dropped in the struggle.

Ramm examined the knife. It was unremarkable, although well sharpened. It could have belonged to the victim or his attacker.

"I need to see if I can get anything from the man himself," said Ramm.

When he reached the Cottage Hospital he was relieved to find the victim still alive, but disappointed when a nurse told him that the man was unable to speak.

He moved closer to the victim's bandaged face and said: "I believe your name is Francis Cavendish. Can you nod if that is correct."

The injured man's eyes were fixed blankly on the ceiling. Ramm was unsure whether he could hear or even understand what was going on. Were his senses damaged, he wondered, or was he ignoring him?

Ramm tried again. "Can you remember what happened, Mr Cavendish?"

Still no response.

The Inspector stared at the figure lying prone in the bed. It was a mystery equal to any he had faced in the past fortnight. A stranger to the town, brutally attacked and left for dead. No sign of robbery. No address, no proper identification, no reason why he should be there.

Ramm thought again about John Gibb, at present the only person who knew the victim. He could not help thinking the Scotsman knew more than he was admitting. Was there something going on between Gibb and Cavendish? He decided he would call him to the station again.

Ramm gave a sigh as he turned away. If Cavendish could not – or would not – speak, this investigation was going to take a very long time.

CHAPTER SEVENTEEN

Giuseppe Manfredi had heard about the inquest verdicts when he was making his round of piano lessons earlier on Wednesday evening. News like this spread quickly in Leek, particularly amongst people who had known either Sarah Hulme or the Broadhursts and their daughters. The tragedies were a nightmare for the mothers of his pupils, but now the inquests were over they would want to move on and think about happier things. It was a relief for Manfredi, too. The deaths had hung heavily over him and now the gossip would subside.

When he arrived home that night, he reached for the whisky decanter, poured a glass and slumped into his armchair. He gazed into the amber liquid, glowing in the light of an oil lamp. As the warmth of the alcohol hit his stomach he felt his confidence oozing back.

Yesterday had been challenging, but all things considered, it had gone well, he told himself. He had even managed to endure Sarah's funeral after realising it was important he should be seen there.

He put down the glass and flexed his hands. His wrists ached and so did one of his arms. It had been painful playing the piano this evening so he had made his pupils do most of the work. Perhaps another whisky might ease his muscles, help him to find sleep and rid him of the awful nightmares of struggle and death?

He swept a hand over his thinning hair as he thought of all the planning and preparation ahead. It would mean another late night. There was so much going on, first the King's visit and then his crowning glory, the Club Day singing in the Market Place.

There was always a slight chance the procession could be

cancelled, of course, as it had been when a thunderstorm washed it out a few years ago, but if so he would have to live with the disappointment. His life's work would continue regardless. If not here, he would start afresh somewhere else. He might even go back to the old country. Yes, perhaps he should leave Leek on a high note.

Nathaniel Blake stayed at the studio late that evening. He had sent Cora home early when he saw how upset she was after Oliver Finch had brought with news of the inquests. She was furious at the injustice she believed had been done to Sarah Hulme.

Once his work was done he had returned to his notes and his chart of victims, suspects and so on. After Edith's reaction the previous evening, he thought it best not to take his detective work home again. Looking at his papers he was baffled how Francis Cavendish could be connected to the two deaths. However the bizarre nature of the attack in King Street made him think there must be some link.

It was past supper time when he opened the front door in Portland Street.

"Nathaniel, I was starting to worry where you might be," Edith said.

"There were things I needed to finish," he replied. Seeing his wife's anxious expression it was obvious she suspected he had been doing something other than photographic work and he regretted not telling her the truth.

"Police work was it? Cora mentioned that they had called for you again this morning."

Nathaniel was surprised. Edith usually preferred not to know about the more troubling assignments he carried out for the police.

"Well, yes, there has been ...an incident. Someone was injured, I'm afraid."

"I think you mean strangled," Edith replied. "Don't look so shocked, Nathaniel. I do hear what's going on, you know. Someone was talking about it at the grocer's. The Sisters found a man and managed to save his life. That's the story, isn't it?"

Before Nathaniel could say anything, Edith pressed on. "I hope this is nothing to do with those other awful affairs you're involving yourself with. Have you thought you could be putting yourself in danger? And what about Cora and the rest of us?"

Much as he found his detective work fascinating, Nathaniel realised that Edith had a point. If his suspicions were correct and there was a murderer at large in Leek, he himself could be at risk and so could his family.

"Where is Cora now? In her room?" he asked with new concern for his daughter.

"She went out again. She said she was going around to Ellen's house."

"Out again? And she's not back yet? It's nearly dark!" Edith's warning had made him think he should be doing more to protect Cora, especially after what may have happened to Sarah. He was considering whether he should go to the Simms' house straight away when there was a light tap on the front door. Cora had returned safe.

From the awkward silence in the kitchen, Cora sensed her parents had been having a serious conversation.

"Is anything wrong?" she asked.

"We were just concerned about you being out again and coming home after dark," Nathaniel replied.

Cora knew that she could not expect to go out every evening without them being curious. She needed a convincing story.

"I've been helping Ellen and her friends. She's making a banner to greet the King on Friday," she said.

"Well that's as it may be, but with all that's going on at the moment, I think it would be safer if you were not out after dark.

At least until things have been cleared up," Nathaniel said.

"But the banner isn't finished yet. I might need to help her tomorrow evening too," Cora went on, preparing her excuses in advance.

"This banner sounds a good idea," said Edith, trying to diffuse a disagreement between father and daughter. "It's just that we don't like the thought of you being out on your own."

"Yes, very enterprising," Nathaniel conceded, seeing that Cora perhaps deserved encouragement to do something other than fret about Sarah Hulme. "Is Ellen going to wave it or will you hang it somewhere?"

Cora realised that the more she said the more inventive she would need to become.

"We are still talking about that. It's quite large, so I may have to help her to put it up somewhere in town on Friday."

"Well don't forget I shall need your assistance when the King drives past, but I certainly wouldn't wish to stop you helping your friend."

Cora had eaten before she went out, so when her mother began to serve her father his belated supper, she said she would go to her room to read. The truth was that she needed to collect her thoughts about how she and Ellen would manage with the banner.

Earlier that evening she had seen the sewing was nearly finished. She had helped a little, although Ellen and a workmate had done most of the work. It was more than a dozen feet long with 'VOTES FOR WOMEN' spelled out in bold black letters on thick white cloth. Pieces of cord had been fastened to each end so that it could be tied in place.

"That should catch the King's eye," she had told Ellen.

The size of the banner meant it would take the two of them to carry it to Lowe Hill. They decided to do that on Thursday evening when there was less chance of them being seen, and then find a place near the bridge to hide it until the next day.

Their plans for Friday depended on having enough time to hang out the banner. Thankfully the patriotic owners of the Great Mill had announced that the dinner break would be two hours long rather than one so their workers could join in the celebrations. Ellen and Cora planned to tie the banner in place and then Cora would cycle back into town to help her father.

Although she felt a little guilty about keeping her plans from her parents, Cora knew her father had his own secrets. She had seen him making notes and had tried to listen in to his conversations with Oliver's father, which she was sure were about Sarah and Mr Broadhurst. She was peeved to be left out, especially when it seemed the police had given up their own inquiries. On Thursday, she decided, she would try to find out what progress her father had made.

That evening FJ Finch paid another visit to Mill Street to speak to Bill Fisher, landlord of The Spread Eagle, the inn nearest to the Broadhurst dye works.

After ordering a pint, FJ had casually asked Fisher to tell him again what happened the evening James Broadhurst died. In particular when members of the Kilner Theatre gathered in the street near the pub.

"It was quiet in the pub, so I stood outside to watch what was going on," said Fisher. "Some of 'em were singing songs and another was telling jokes and things. There was a juggler and a couple were lifting each other up doing, what d'you call it, acrobatics."

He added: "It was about seven o'clock when they packed up and went up the street pretty sharpish. One of 'em said they had to get back to the rag-and-stick."

"Who else was around? Did you recognise anyone?" Finch asked him.

"Some of the locals. Folk came out of their houses and one or two were walking home after work. And that skinny Italian that runs the dance school was talking to some of the theatre folk. I suppose he has a bit to do with these music and dance types, don't he?"

Their conversation moved on to when Charlie, the dye house worker, had dashed in saying there had been an accident.

"Sorry affair. Mr Broadhurst was a real gentleman," Fisher concluded, shaking his head dolefully.

FJ finished his ale and left, promising to give The Spread Eagle a mention in the *Lion*. He decided that while he was in that part of town he would speak to John Gibb about Cavendish. The attack in King Street had made Finch more suspicious than ever.

Walking along Abbey Green Road, Finch crossed a small stone bridge and was soon in the verdant countryside where monks had lived centuries ago. Dieulacres Cottage Farm, where Gibb worked for widow Rosa Carter, was down a track close to the ruins of the old Abbey from which it took its name. Two years earlier the farm had been the scene of a mysterious death, but that evening everything appeared peaceful.

Gibb was sitting on a stool outside the barn. He appeared to be mending a spade in the twilight, but kept glancing towards the track for any unexpected visitors. At the sound of footsteps he looked up sharply, then relaxed when he recognised the approaching figure was the newspaper editor.

"A good evening to ye, Mr Finch."

"And to you, John." Finch paused, trying to gauge the Scotsman's mood. "I am truly sorry to hear what happened to your old comrade Cavendish. I take it the police came to see you?"

Gibb laid down the spade and heaved a great sigh. "Oh aye. They took me to the hospital to see the poor fellow and then the Inspector had some questions. I expect it was you who told 'em I knew Cavendish?"

"Well, I happened to mention it to Nathaniel and it was he who told Ramm. Blake thought it might assist the investigation."

"I suppose it was meant well," Gibb replied, although the way he sighed again gave the impression he thought otherwise. He looked away across the fields, apparently unwilling to say more.

"Had you seen anything more of Cavendish in town? I know you were concerned about him."

Gibb was silent while he thought how to respond. As with Inspector Ramm that morning, he was in a quandary about how much to reveal about Francis. He was sworn to secrecy, but on the other hand, he might need friends like Finch and Blake in the days ahead, especially after what had happened to his old comrade.

"As a matter of fact I did see him again and we made our peace. We'd had a misunderstanding, you might say."

"Did he tell you why he was in Leek?"

There was another long pause, Gibb still avoiding looking Finch in the eye.

"His business here, Mr Finch, is a private matter, I believe."

Finch continued to press for information. "Some kind of dispute, was it? Perhaps that was why he was attacked."

"Mr Finch, Francis Cavendish was... is... a hero," Gibb replied. "And if I can do anything to find who did that terrible thing to him, then I will."

Finch heard grim resignation in the Scotsman's tone. He had given little away about Cavendish, but those long silences told their own story. FJ had the distinct impression he was more closely involved with his old comrade than he was admitting.

CHAPTER EIGHTEEN

When he arrived at the police station on the Thursday morning, Albert Ramm was pleased to see an envelope containing the list James Broadhurst had written. There were a dozen or more names ranging from a tailor to the dance teacher. The handwriting was a little erratic and Ramm could picture a troubled Broadhurst anxiously writing the names of suppliers with whom he was cancelling his accounts.

He rubbed the paper gently between his finger and thumb as he pondered on what Finch had said about foreign agents. He decided he should speak to some of those on the list about their dealings with the dye works owner. The conversations would have to wait, however, as preparations for the King would have to come first.

He asked Constable Knowles to take the paper to Nathaniel Blake and have it photographed. If the list did prove to be important evidence, then it would be useful to have a copy.

FJ Finch went around to Nathaniel Blake's studio early to report how his investigations were progressing. Once again he and Blake were in the upstairs room, out of earshot of Cora.

Finch recounted what the landlord of The Spread Eagle had told him about the visit by the travelling theatre on the night that James Broadhurst died. "Apart from Mill Street locals he could only recall seeing Giuseppe Manfredi."

Nathaniel remembered the Italian had been talking with someone from the theatre at the Horse Fair.

"I also went along to have a word with John Gibb," Finch

continued. "I know John was worried about Cavendish last week and I thought he might appreciate someone to talk to."

"Did he have much to say?"

"Very little. The two of them had settled their differences, apparently. I could tell John was keeping something back, though. He said Cavendish was in town on private business, but John would not say what it was. He certainly looked shaken and I don't think he's going to let the matter drop."

Their conversation was interrupted when Cora came upstairs with rapid steps.

"Constable Knowles is here, Father. Inspector Ramm has something he wants you to photograph. The constable's going to wait while you do it and then take it back," she said, handing an envelope to Nathaniel.

"Very well, tell him I shall deal with it right away," he said.

When Cora had gone back downstairs, he opened the envelope and carefully withdrew the handwritten sheet. Finch could not hide his curiosity and was craning his neck to see what Nathaniel was holding. Blake realised it would be impossible to conceal the paper, or ask his friend to leave without offending him. After examining the sheet he handed it to FJ.

Finch frowned as he studied the writing, then his eyebrows shot up in surprise.

"Good heavens! This must be James Broadhurst's list. There are some interesting names on there!" he said, his voice dropping to a whisper so that officer downstairs would not hear.

Finch secreted himself in the darkroom in case Constable Knowles decided to come upstairs and Blake mounted the document on a board and set about photographing it. When he was satisfied he took the paper back to Knowles who left hastily.

Finch stayed in the darkroom, anxious to talk to Blake while he processed the plates and printed the images.

FJ's eagerness worried Blake. If Inspector Ramm discovered he had shown the paper to the editor it would be embarrassing. He might even lose his work with the police, although after what had gone on in the last two weeks, he wondered if that might not be a bas thing.

"I wouldn't be surprised if Broadhurst had made a list of folk he suspected were siding with Germany, Nathaniel," Finch enthused. "I expect Ramm thinks they are connected with the man's business worries, but I've always believed his death had some connection to that dashed public meeting. I know it sounds crazy, but this list could be the reason he was killed!"

In the glowing red light of the darkroom, they both looked down at Blake's photograph of the list.

"Let's face it, FJ, these people might simply be his creditors," Nathaniel said.

"Mark my words, Nathaniel, this list is more sinister than that. Why else is Ramm having it copied?"

"Perhaps he is having second thoughts, in spite of the inquest verdict," Blake replied.

Finch announced that he had to get back to the office and reminded Blake that he would need prints from the King's visit as soon as possible on Friday afternoon. As for himself, there were stories to finish and proofs to check so that he and Oliver could concentrate on the Royal event the following day.

Blake sat down to consider what his friend had said about the list of names. Could one of these people, respectable local business people and such, really have something to do with Broadhurst's death? He knew from past experience that a murderous plot could develop in the most unlikely places.

A shiver of fear passed through him as he recalled Edith's warning. If the person capable of drowning James Broadhurst was still at large, then was it safe for him, a simple photographer, to go in pursuit?

John Gibb had spent a restless night. Every time he heard a movement in the yard outside he imagined Francis Cavendish's attacker had tracked him down to the farm. As soon as it was light, he was relieved to be out and about again. Once his morning tasks were done he asked Rosa if he could go into town. He had told her the previous day that a friend had been injured – he did not go into details – and now he said that he wanted to see how the person was faring in hospital.

Forty minutes later Gibb was back at the Cottage Hospital, begging the matron to allow him a moment with Francis. Standing beside the bed again, he saw Cavendish was little different from the day before. He was heavily bandaged, there were bruises on the parts of his face that were visible and he still appeared to be unconscious.

Gibb clenched his fists in frustration. His anger at what had befallen his comrade was mixed with a feeling of helplessness. What could he do to put this right?

As if in answer to the unspoken question, Cavendish opened his eyes a crack. He slowly scanned his surroundings before his gaze settled on Gibb. His breathing quickened and there was a choking sound from deep in his throat. He was trying to speak, but no words would come. John wondered if he would ever hear Francis's voice again.

"Take it easy, old chap," Gibb said softly.

Cavendish's hand, with cuts and broken fingernails from the desperate struggle with his attacker, rose an inch from the counterpane and made a shaky movement. Gibb understood and went to find a nurse. After some persuasion and a little Scottish charm, a piece of paper and a pencil were found for him.

"After this you must go," the nurse said firmly.

It was a painfully slow process. Gibb held the paper and helped wrap Cavendish's fingers around the pencil. He managed to scrawl a single word before his hand dropped and his head sank back on the pillow.

After what seemed an age, Cavendish moved his hand again. He wanted to write more. This time, with Gibb's help, he traced three more ragged words before dropping the pencil and falling back with a groan.

Gibb studied Cavendish's shaky writing. "Carry out the plan," he read.

John knew what his comrade was referring to and realised he had no choice. The mission that had brought Cavendish to Leek had now become his own.

Cora had stood at the bottom of the stairs to try to listen to what her father and FJ Finch had been talking about that morning, but had only caught the odd word. By the time the editor left she could contain her curiosity no longer.

"Father, what is going on?" she asked when Nathaniel came downstairs.

"Whatever do you mean, my dear?"

"Have you and Oliver's father found out something about Sarah? Because if you have, then don't you think I should know about it, too?"

Before Nathaniel could answer, Cora pressed on, becoming more agitated. "After all, I was the one she wanted to tell about her secret. It was me who found out about her spying on Professor Kilner. And it was..."

"Steady on, Cora," Nathaniel interrupted, raising his palms in submission. "It's not just about Sarah. There has been a lot of nasty business in the town and FJ and I were trying to think how... how we can all keep safe."

"Did you know the police had read her diary?" Cora blurted out.

Nathaniel was taken aback. "Well, yes, Inspector Ramm did mention it, but..."

"I don't think it was very fair to read something private like that and then tell everyone about it. Oliver said it was mentioned at the inquest."

"The Inspector is only doing his job. I think the diary helped him to find out what has been going on."

"But he came to the wrong conclusion, according to what Oliver told me."

Cora's feelings were divided. Although she believed the diary was private, she couldn't help wondering what Sarah might have written, especially about Thomas Kilner.

"Did she mention other people, like Professor Kilner's son?" she asked.

Nathaniel tried to be as vague as possible, he didn't want Cora involved any further, even if the deaths were occupying his own thoughts.

"I do not know the details. The Inspector simply said that Sarah used lots of initials. T, M, things like that. I think it's best if we keep out of it. The inquest has been held and that might be an end to it," he said.

With that he went back to his darkroom leaving his daughter to frame a photograph. But work was the last thing on her mind. Ever since that terrible night at the rag-and-stick she had been determined to find someone to blame and she still wasn't certain who that would be.

Back at the farm, John Gibb and Rosa Carter were having the simple meal they took around the middle of the working day when he announced he needed that afternoon and the whole of the following day off work. He was sorry for the short notice, he said, but his injured friend was in dire straits and needed his help.

He went out to the farm building where he slept and opened the old wooden chest where he kept his few belongings. He took out the ragged coat he had worn in his years on the road. "What adventures that coat has seen," he thought as he batted dust off the grey tweed. The weather was too warm for a heavy coat, but he wanted to return to his days as a tramp, if only for the next twenty-four hours.

Then he pulled out the battered hat he used to wear, his knapsack and finally his dirk, his treasured knife. His heart fluttered a little as he saw the stag's head engraved on its handle, the symbol of his old Highland regiment. He had not needed its razor sharp blade for the past couple of years, but now things may be different. He might have to defend himself at some point. That impending danger was another reason he could not share his secret, the secret Cavendish had passed on to him, with anyone else. Rosa, Nathaniel, FJ – none of them could be dragged into this.

Adding a crust of bread and a couple of apples to his knapsack, he sauntered off along the farm track. His destination was the Mount where he intended to find a comfortable spot to spend the rest of the day and the night. He did not know what he was going to see, or what he would have to do, but he expected to get little sleep before tomorrow.

Walking up the Ashbourne Road out of town, Gibb felt memories of his previous life flood back as he passed the Union Workhouse. He looked up at the four stone columns at its entrance and thought about the times he had gone through that imposing doorway to seek shelter for the night. The Workhouse was not the sort of place to spend more than the occasional night because the master expected a payment and the vagrants ward could attract some grim characters, but it had been a winter refuge when it was too bitterly cold for his usual moorland haunts.

He reached the track that led over the Mount and, after passing a tall stone farmhouse, found what Cavendish had told him about, a gypsy encampment encircled by a stand of fir trees. As he neared the camp, he noticed something unexpected. Four men stood on the track on opposite sides of the field where the caravans stood. In his years wandering the countryside, John had come across gypsies many times and they were usually friendly to fellow travellers like himself. But he had never seen a camp with guards on duty.

The two men nearest were talking idly, but when they saw Gibb walking towards them, they straightened their shoulders and stood to block his way. As he drew closer he could see that each held a sizeable cudgel partly hidden by their long coats.

"A good day to ye," said Gibb in the relaxed manner common to many men of the road. He hoped to make light of the situation by acting as if he hadn't seen their weapons.

The gypsies eyed him coldly and said nothing. They made no attempt to move out of his way.

Gibb took another casual step forward, trying to avoid eye contact with the guards and pretending to admire the scenery. The two men swiftly hefted their cudgels towards him.

"Be off. This no place for you," said one of the gypsies menacingly a thick foreign accent.

All his life John had taken exception to being bullied and now he looked from one to the other, weighing his chances if a fight broke out. Cavendish had warned him that the German gypsies were tough characters and these two, who were younger than himself, looked like they could handle themselves. It was more than likely he would come off worst. He might finish up in hospital like Cavendish, he thought. And his comrade's mission would be a failure.

Gibb wanted to give no hint he was anything other than a tramp, someone who would take the easy way out. Slowly he turned and walked back along the track. At a safe distance he glanced over his shoulder and saw the two guards were still watching him.

At their last meeting, Francis had said he planned to keep watch on the gypsy camp. Gibb realised his spying skills were probably no match for Cavendish's and he wished he had the pocket telescope that Francis had shown him. Neither was he sure how to act if he did see anything suspicious. He would just have to trust to his instincts.

He spotted a clump of bushes that would keep him out of the guards' view and slumped down into the thick grass at the edge of the track. He decided he would wait, until it was dark if necessary, and then move into the field closer to the camp. He pulled his crumpled hat down over his eyes and pretended to doze.

Inspector Ramm was relieved that there was no crime reported in the moorlands that afternoon because at precisely two o'clock all the district's constabulary were crammed into the mess room at the police station. As well as his Leek officers, he had summoned half a dozen of the constables based in villages near the King's route. He had also called in the Captain of the town Fire Brigade, Major Wardle from the Territorials, the Clerks of the Urban and Rural District Councils, the Station Master, the Postmaster and Matron from the Cottage Hospital.

Ramm had tried to consider every eventuality they might face during Friday's Royal visit. This afternoon he wanted to impress upon key personnel what was expected of them.

He had just begun to run through his priorities when there was the distant sound of the bell in the reception office. Ramm nodded to Constable Phillips who hastily went to see who was there.

Nathaniel Blake couldn't get James Broadhurst's death and Finch's theories out of his mind, and was now waiting impatiently at the front desk. He needed to speak to Inspector Ramm, he said.

"I'm afraid that's impossible. The Inspector is in a meeting and says he's not to be disturbed," Phillips announced.

"But this is important, Constable! I would not be here if it wasn't."

"So is his meeting, Mr Blake. Do you wish to report a crime or some sort of incident?"

"Well, not exactly. It's something I need to talk to Inspector Ramm about," Blake replied.

"So it's not what you would call an emergency, then? In that case, I'm afraid you will have to come back."

"When would you suggest?" asked Blake, becoming a little exasperated.

"This meeting could go on all afternoon, so perhaps you should try in the morning, Mr Blake." Phillips had a new thought. "No, hang on, not the morning. The Inspector will be even busier then, what with His Majesty and everything."

"Yes, yes, I do appreciate that," said Blake with a sigh, trying not to show his irritation. He turned on his heel and left the station.

When Phillips returned to the mess room, Ramm looked across at his constable and raised his eyebrows questioningly. Phillips gave a slight shake of the head to indicate it had been nothing of importance.

The meeting ground on for another hour until interrupted by the reception office bell again and Phillips went out once more. This time he was gone for a longer time and when he came back he indicated to Ramm that there was something he needed to tell him.

"Excuse me one moment, gentlemen and... er... Matron," Ramm announced, "I need to deal with something."

Out in the corridor, Phillips explained that the latest caller had been Will Adams, an old clockmaker who lived in Albion Street. Adams had heard about the attack in King Street and said the injured person might be the man who was lodging in his spare room. He hadn't seen the fellow since Tuesday.

"Ah, perhaps we have a lead at last," said Ramm.

"It might not be the same person, Sir. I know John Gibb

identified the victim as Francis Cavendish, but Mr Adams says that his lodger gave another name. Arthur Westbridge."

Ramm frowned.

"What is going on in this town? Nothing is straightforward anymore." Ramm paused to think. "What number Albion Street? When this blessed meeting is over, I shall go round and speak to Mr Adams myself."

As it turned out, the discussions over the Royal visit occupied the whole of the afternoon. By the time they finished Inspector Ramm's stomach was rumbling and on his way to Albion Street he called at a baker's shop for a slice of meat pie. Fortified, he had found the house in question and waited rather impatiently for Adams to descend the steep stairs from his attic workshop to answer the door.

Ramm asked the clockmaker if he could check his lodger's room and was shown upstairs. He was struck by how small the bedroom was, not the accommodation he had expected after seeing the quality of Cavendish's jacket and pocket watch at the hospital. Adams watched from the landing until Ramm said he would call him when he was done and gently shut the bedroom door.

There was little to see: a narrow single bed, a bentwood chair and, standing in one corner, a small, well-polished leather suitcase. Ramm opened it and rummaged through the clothes inside but found nothing that gave any clue as to the owner. The only document was a folded map of the Leek moorlands.

On one wall was small cast iron grate that contained a pile of ashes. Ramm bent down to take a closer look and saw that Cavendish, or Westbridge, had been burning papers. He could just make out the words *Post Office Telegraphs* on one of the charred sheets, but nothing more.

"Surely there must be something else," Ramm said to himself.

He looked at the bed, removed the pillow and lifted the thin mattress. On the metal springs was a brown envelope which the Inspector extracted before letting the mattress drop down again.

Inside the envelope he found three sheets which he carefully unfolded. Each carried the lion and unicorn of the British coat of arms and was printed in flowing script apart from where names and dates had been written in. Official looking seals, some in foreign text, had been stamped around the sides. Although he didn't have one himself, Ramm recognised that these were passports. He peered at the writing and saw that each was made out in a different name: Francis James Cavendish, Arthur Westbridge and Peter Alfred Gainsford.

Either the man had stolen these or he was some sort of confidence trickster, Ramm thought. And by the number of times they had been stamped, he travelled abroad a lot.

When he had lifted the mattress, the Inspector had spotted something else through the bed springs. Now he lay on the floor, looked under the bed and then groped towards the far corner. There was a small cloth bag which, as he pulled it towards him, Ramm realised contained something hard and heavy.

"Good heavens!" he puffed as he struggled to his feet and emptied the bag onto the bed cover. He recognised the weapon immediately. It was a Webley Mark I, the powerful revolver that had been issued to British military since his own service days. It was a favourite with army officers, as well as with members of the criminal fraternity.

"Well now, I wonder why he needed this?" Ramm said out loud. He examined the firearm as he passed it from one hand to another, it was oiled and ready for action. He broke open the top and saw cartridges in all six chambers.

"The more I find out about this man, the less I like the look of him," he thought.

Satisfied there was nothing more to find in the room, Ramm

called to Will Adams and found him waiting at the foot of the stairs.

"Tell me Mr Adams, did your lodger.. er Mr Westbridge... give you any idea where he was from or why he was here in Leek?"

"No, Inspector, nothing. Kept himself to himself."

"Did he do anything that made you suspicious?"

"Well, I sometimes heard the floorboards creaking very late on. He seemed to be out at all hours of the night. Not that it's any of my business, of course." Adams did not want to give the impression he had been spying on his lodger.

"Any visitors?"

"Funnily enough, I think he did bring somebody back this week. Monday and Tuesday it would be. He was very quiet, but I thought I heard talking."

"You didn't see who it was?"

"No, just voices. Westbridge's very well spoken, you know. I think the other one might have been Scottish."

Ramm thanked Adams and made his way to the police station deep in thought. He suspected exactly who Cavendish's visitor had been. When he got back to the station, he was pleased to see Constable Phillips was still on duty.

"Go to the hospital to see if this man has had anything to say yet. Then find Mr Gibb, he should be at Abbey Green, and tell him I want to speak to him straight away, straight away! I shall be here until late tonight."

Soon afterwards the telephone rang in the front office. It was Sir Philip Brocklehurst's estate manager ringing to say that the Royal party had arrived safely at Swythamley Hall and had settled down to their evening meal.

"I'm happy for them," Ramm replied with some irony. He knew he would not see his own supper yet.

He was in his office when Phillips came back an hour later. He was alone.

"Where's Gibb?" Ramm shot out the question.

"Not at the farm, Sir. Mrs Carter says he's gone to help an injured friend and won't be back until at least tomorrow."

"And Cavendish?"

"No change, Sir. The nurse says he hasn't stirred and it doesn't look as if he can speak."

Ramm threw his pencil down in frustration. He was determined to get to the bottom of this business with Cavendish, but the mystery would now have to wait until after the King had safely passed through the town.

CHAPTER NINETEEN

John Gibb had no pocket watch and relied on the distant chiming of St Edward's Church bells to keep track of time as he lay in the undergrowth. There was little activity. A cart had been to the farm with a load of hay and a couple of gypsies had ridden to the camp on horses. Two gypsy women had strolled past heaving baskets of pheasant and rabbit, no doubt intending to sell them door to door.

In contrast to the confrontation with the camp guards, he felt surprisingly at peace. Birds were hopping around in the bushes behind him, a peewit called from the higher ground and he could hear occasional shrieks from children playing around the caravans.

When Gibb heard the faint sound of seven o'clock being struck he decided to move. Peering out from his hiding place he could see no sign of the men who had been guarding the camp entrance. He scrambled to his feet and crossed the track, stepping through a gateway and into a rough field. He quickly crouched down and surveyed his options. In one direction the field stretched away to a hawthorn hedge beyond which the gypsy caravans were grouped.

It was too risky to move closer until it was dark, he thought. Instead he chose the opposite end of the field. Gibb sat in the corner with drystone walls on two sides and a substantial patch of nettles in front of him. Soon he heard footsteps on the lane from town and what sounded like two young women in conversation. He was sure he recognised one of the voices.

Cora and Ellen had found the walk from town took longer than expected because of the awkward weight of the rolled-up banner they were carrying. They were starting to worry that they would not be back home before dark. Cora was still convinced there might be a killer at large and she knew her parents would be anxious if she returned late. At least she was not on her own.

After leaving the Ashbourne Road they felt more isolated on the quiet lane that led to towards the Mount and Lowe Hill Bridge. A sudden breeze caused a great rushing sound in the line of huge trees that shaded the lane and Cora wondered whether it had been a good idea to come here in the evening. But it was now only a short way to the bridge and they quickened their steps.

"We're nearly there, thank goodness," said Cora, a little breathless. Her arms were beginning to ache because she was less used to the sort of physical exertion that Ellen faced every day at the mill.

"As soon as we've hidden the banner we must to start for home," she continued. "We might have to run back to town."

"I'm just glad I didn't have to carry it on my own," said Ellen.

"Don't worry, Ellen, I wouldn't have left you to do that. This is something we are doing together," Cora replied.

As they rounded a bend by a farmstead a noise in the undergrowth stopped them in their tracks. They laughed as a piglet ran out of the grass and into the farm on the other side of the lane.

Seconds later they heard the crunch of stones and thought it was another animal, before they realise someone was walking behind them. They stopped again and looked back. Cora could see the figure of a man in a long coat and a battered hat.

"Oh no, a gypsy, or might it be a tramp? Don't speak to him if he comes up to us," she said to Ellen, keeping her voice low.

They were nearly at the bridge and Cora simply wanted to finish their mission and get away from there. "Come on, hurry!" she said, dragging Ellen forward and doing her best to ignore the man, who seemed to be getting closer.

It was a long time since Ellen had been on the top of Lowe Hill Bridge and when she looked over the low brick parapet she was surprised how high they were. Below them, the main road was deserted at this time in the evening. Tomorrow, she thought, she would see the Royal motor car go under the bridge and, at the same moment, the King would look up and see their banner.

"Quickly now," said Cora, glancing again in the direction of the man. "Let's find a place to hide it."

She spotted a pile of fence stakes on the far side of the bridge. "We can put the banner underneath those pieces of wood. It should be safe there."

The two were busy hiding the precious roll of cloth when Cora sensed a movement frighteningly close by. The stranger had followed them onto the bridge and was watching them.

"What on earth are ye up to?"

Cora swivelled round in surprise. She knew the accent straight away, it was John Gibb.

After the two young women had walked past his hiding place minutes' earlier, Gibb had peeped over the wall and seen that it was Miss Blake. He could not help being concerned for their safety, especially as he knew how Cora's adventurousness had landed her in trouble in the past. He had decided to follow them as stealthily as his heavy boots would allow. He was now bemused to see them rearranging the fence stakes.

"Mr Gibb! How very... unusual to see you here," Cora stammered.

"I could say the same thing of you, Miss Blake. Is it safe for ye to be this far out of town at this time of an evening? And whatever are you two doing with that wood?"

Cora and Ellen looked down at the pile of stakes that hid the banner, then at each other and then at Gibb. Ellen was dumbstruck and Cora realised she needed to think of something fast.

"Ellen and I were out for a walk and... we thought we saw something in here. A hedgehog, I think it was. Wasn't it, Ellen?"

Ellen nodded vigorously.

Gibb did not believe a word of it, but neither was it his place to interrogate the young women, nor did he wish to keep them any longer than was absolutely necessary.

"Well, I think it best if you both make for your homes. And don't stop to look for any more hedgehogs," he said.

"Thank you, Mr Gibb. Good evening to you," said Cora as she and Ellen hurried past him. Although she was relieved the banner had not been discovered, Cora could not help being puzzled why John Gibb was at Lowe Hill himself and why he was wearing those ragged old clothes.

Blake was pretending to read a magazine as he and Edith sat in the parlour, waiting for Cora to return. They were both on edge, wondering where she had got to. Nathaniel's mind was swirling with ideas about the tragic deaths. Was Cavendish involved? What had Conrad Mulder done? Was Broadhurst murdered? Who else was involved?

He was bitterly frustrated to have been turned away from the police station that afternoon, but knew it was folly to try to take the law into his own hands. He might be endangering his family as well as himself. He resolved to go back to the police station first thing in the morning and speak to the Inspector again.

Edith had been watching her husband and guessed he was

preoccupied with something far removed from his photography magazine. She was about to speak when there was a sound at the front door and Nathaniel leapt from his chair. She saw that he had been just as concerned about Cora as she was.

From their daughter's pink cheeks and wild hair it was obvious she had been running.

"Cora, thank goodness you are back safe," said Nathaniel. "You didn't see anyone while you were out, did you?"

"No, no one except Ellen." Cora replied quickly. She knew she could not mention John Gibb without revealing where she and Ellen had been. She just hoped Gibb didn't talk to her father before she had chance to hang the banner from the bridge. Eventually she would have a lot of explaining to do.

Orlando Kilner had chosen well for their final performance in Leek that Thursday evening. He had advertised *The Two Little Vagabonds* as 'A Powerful and Emotional Drama of Intense Human Interest' and the audience was delighted with the tale of youth overcoming adversity.

When the Professor stepped forward to acknowledge the applause at the end of the evening, those seated closest to the stage might have detected a tear in his eye. Despite his uncompromising attitude, Kilner was an emotional person and he loved the acclaim of his audience.

The last night in a town was often an occasion for the company to celebrate, although this time many of them were more muted, remembering their tragic opening night in Leek. And tonight there was to be little chance to relax. Once the last of the spectators had drifted away, Professor Kilner called for attention. He announced that instead of dismantling the theatre the next morning, as was usual, the work would begin immediately and all the equipment would be loaded onto the carts. Everyone would have to give a hand, he said. There were groans from some of the performers, though most were wary of showing dissent.

"And we will make an early start tomorrow because I want to leave by first light. Be sure to be back here by five o'clock," Kilner continued.

"Five o'clock! Why the rush?" asked one of the actors incredulously.

"With the Royal visit tomorrow there is no telling what will happen on the roads later in the day. I want nothing to delay our departure," Kilner replied.

The performers, many still in their costumes, began to move seats, untie ropes and shift scenery. The stage hands would load the equipment onto the carts and, before dawn, collect the dray horses from the field where they had been tethered for the last fortnight.

Kilner drew his son and Conrad Mulder outside, away from the bustle of activity. "Be as quick as you can tonight," he said before turning back to the tent and shouting more instructions to the crew.

"I be happy when we leave this town," said Conrad quietly.

Gibb had returned to his hiding place in the field. The moon was out when he next heard footsteps approaching. He lay perfectly still and tried to picture how many were on the stony track.

Two or three men were talking in voices too low for Gibb to tell what was being said. When they had passed, he eased himself to his feet and looked over the wall. The dark figures were moving towards the gypsy camp, one of them was carrying a paraffin lantern which cast a pool of light on the track. All three appeared to be tall and one was even bigger with broad shoulders.

When he was sure it was safe, Gibb made his way slowly across the field in the direction of the caravans. He took care not to make any noise, although could not help disturbing half a dozen sheep.

They scampered away, their ghostly shapes moving silently in the moonlight.

Nearing the camp, Gibb dropped to a crouch and kept perfectly still, alert to any sign of alarm from the gypsies. The situation stirred memories of creeping up on the enemy when he was in the army, though the terrain had been much different then. Satisfied that he had not been seen, Gibb sank to the ground and began to crawl forward, inching his way towards where smoke was rising from the camp fire.

When he reached the hawthorn hedge he sat up and cautiously raised his head so that he could see over the top. He could make out four men on their haunches around the fire, their faces orange in the glow of burning logs.

One of them was a heavily bearded fellow with a black beret that John had seen haggling at the Horse Fair the previous week. A watch chain across his belly glinted gold in the firelight. John guessed the other three were the new arrivals. One was the huge fellow, another was someone he thought he had seen in town, but did not know his name.

Gibb watched as the bearded gypsy lit two more paraffin lamps with a taper, then fetched a bucket of water which he used to douse the camp fire, sending up a cloud of smoke and steam. The man turned and disappeared behind one of the caravans. He came back with a wooden crate which he set down carefully on the ground. They gathered round the crate and one reached inside, gently pulling out what John thought was a short piece of metal pipe.

John could not get a good view of what was going on until someone moved one of the lamps and illuminated the side of the crate. It was marked in bold black type. John could make out only two words but they were enough to send a shiver of fear through him. *Nobel, Glasgow.*

From his army days he knew the Scottish factory was famous for one thing only, dynamite. And it looked like the shadowy figures on the other side of the hedge had a crate of the stuff.

The huddled conversation continued as the men examined what Gibb now assumed were sticks of dynamite. He saw the big fellow give a nod of approval.

After they had carefully returned the dynamite to the crate and replaced the lid, the four left the camp. Gibb saw the light of their lamps swinging back and forth as they walked along the track.

He sank onto the ground beside the hedge, filled with apprehension. He had imagined that if he confronted the gypsies he might face weapons – cudgels like the guards wielded, knives or even guns. But dynamite was another matter altogether. What could he do about that on his own?

Gibb saw the dark figures were now further along the track. He started to walk quietly across the field, maintaining a safe distance. When he lost sight of them he realised they had reached the lane and turned towards the bridge, not back to town.

With great care, he clambered over the wall and into the lane, trying to make no sound as he too walked towards Lowe Hill Bridge, just as he had followed Cora and Ellen earlier that evening.

When he reached the bend in the lane he crept slower, leaning forwards as he peered ahead. He could make out shadowy figures and spots of lamplight moving around on the bridge. Then he saw that the lamps were coming back towards him and he looked around wildly for a place to hide.

At his side was a row of farm buildings with a yard in front, a hay cart standing in one corner. Gibb darted into the yard and dropped to the ground behind the cart. He dearly hoped the farm dogs were asleep, otherwise their barks could give him away. He held his breath as the four men walked past and by the time he dared to emerge onto the lane they had disappeared into the night.

CHAPTER TWENTY

The streets were busy as Albert Ramm made his way to the police station this historic Friday morning. The last of the workers whose shifts started at six o'clock were jostling through the great entrances to the mills, knowing they had only five minutes' grace or their wages would be docked.

Ramm had resolved to make an early start on a day that he was both relishing and dreading in equal measure. At the end of Queen Street he saw that the street cleaner was out early too, tackling the horse manure that had accumulated on the cobbles the previous day. The bowler hatted workman sloshed water on the street from a tank on his cart before wielding a hefty brush. His horse waited patiently, head down. There was a flurry of movement when three young children, all barefoot, came out of a terraced house nearby and shrieked as they ran to watch. One of them couldn't resist splashing a foot in the pool of dirty water.

As Ramm neared Sparrow Park, the paved area seemed strangely empty. Then he realised what was different – the travelling theatre had gone. The previous evening, when he was finally on his way home, he had heard the performers' voices, the audience laughter and a little accordion music coming from the tent. Now, the only sign that the rag-and stick had ever been there were a few crumpled posters on the ground.

In some ways it was a relief, the theatre's departure drawing a line under the tragedy of two weeks' ago. However, if he did decide to probe Sarah Hulme's death any further, his task would be that much harder now that Professor Kilner and his band of entertainers had moved on.

On arriving at the police station he was pleased to see that all his officers were present. It looked like all had brushed their uniforms and polished their boots, and those who had done military service were, like himself, were wearing medals.

The two constables on night patrol reported nothing unusual. Ramm told them to take a rest in the mess room before joining the day shift. He then dispatched another officer on the station bicycle to check the streets on the King's planned route through the town. He wanted nothing to delay the Royal progress.

Inspector Ramm found himself looking at the clock on the office wall every few minutes, counting down until the Royal arrival. It had just passed eight o'clock when he was informed that Nathaniel Blake wanted to speak to him.

"He says he's not going to leave until he's seen you," said Sergeant Reynolds rather wearily.

"All right, send him in," Ramm replied.

Blake did not wait for a greeting when he reached Ramm's office. "I know you are a busy man, Inspector, but there is something I must tell you," he said.

"Please be brief, Mr Blake."

"Cora is still convinced Miss Hulme was in some sort of danger. To be honest, I think she may be right," Blake explained.

"I appreciate Miss Blake's concern, but I have spoken to these people from the rag-and-stick and got nowhere. And now, unfortunately, they have left town," Ramm replied.

"What about James Broadhurst? Finch suspects it wasn't an accident and, quite frankly, so do I. It might very well be connected with this German business. Perhaps Cavendish has been involved in it all, too."

Blake expected Ramm to be sceptical, but he could see the officer was taking him seriously.

"I do intend to speak to some of those on Mr Broadhurst's list, people he probably owed money to. But as for this morning, Mr Blake, we have other pressing matters to deal with."

The Inspector paused, then asked: "Have you seen anything of John Gibb? I need to speak to him about a matter of some importance."

"If I see him today I will be sure to let him know. He may well come into town to watch out for the King."

After Blake left Ramm felt ill at ease. Blake and Finch's persistent theories made him worry that he might have missed something. Perhaps he should have spoken to Broadhurst's contacts sooner, perhaps he should have made another visit to the rag-and-stick. Once the Royal visit was out of the way he would start his investigation afresh, he would speak to Gibb and try to find out more about the mysterious Cavendish.

John Gibb had woken with a start. The sun was up, birds were singing and he realised he must have dropped off to sleep in the middle of the night.

After the mysterious visitors had walked off into the darkness, he had returned to his hiding place in the field. He had lain staring up into the stars, brooding over whether he should go to the police. Would they take him seriously? What could he tell them? Men huddled around a crate that might have contained dynamite.

That was the point he must have fallen asleep. Now when he looked across to the gypsy camp he saw that something had changed. Some of the caravans had been moved. Women were taking down the muddied sheets that had screened the far side of the camp. Men were rounding up the horses that were grazing nearby, slapping the hindquarters of ponies. They were getting ready to move on.

He dared not go any closer in broad daylight and so remained crouched down, hidden by the wall and the nettle patch. An hour passed and he grew impatient of skulking in the field. He decided he must tell the police. He would not break the confidences Cavendish had shared, but simply say that something suspicious was going on at the gypsy camp. He set off at a brisk pace.

His mission turned out to be a waste of time, however. He reached the police station to find Constable Knowles was the only officer there. Knowles was curious why Gibb had been at the gypsy camp and made a note his concerns, but he made it clear no officer could go to the Mount until after His Royal Highness had passed through.

Gibb had argued to no avail and so he had strode out of the station determined to get back to the Mount without delay. He drew disgruntled comments as he barged his way through folk who were beginning to gather on the pavements, but that was the least of his concerns. He was worried he had made a fatal mistake in leaving his hiding place. He may have missed something important.

While Gibb had been walking from the Mount, Inspector Ramm had gone out to see for himself what was going on and found that a transformation had taken place in the past few hours.

The Cattle Market was now full of horse drawn vehicles of every shape and size. Shooting brakes, wagonettes, milk carts, traps, in fact anything with wheels had been pressed into service to bring visitors into town. Derby Street was lined with wagons belonging to carters from far off villages. There were even a couple of gleaming motor cars, guarded by their chauffeurs.

Ramm realised he had failed to take into account this vast influx of people for this special day. Folk from all parts of the moorlands were determined to see their Monarch and had come to Leek to join in the occasion. As well as those who had arrived by horse drawn transport, many others had caught trains into the town. It was becoming a day out for the whole district.

It seemed that on every street there were men up ladders stringing bunting from the lamp posts. Leek was built on the silk industry, so there was no shortage of material for the decorations, although Ramm could only surmise how much had been donated by mill owners and how much smuggled out by their workers.

Union Flags were poking out of nearly every upstairs window. There were banners of all shapes and sizes, either homemade or bought for the day.

From Overton Bank, Ramm looked down onto Mill Street and saw flags and bunting fluttering outside every terraced house, no matter how humble the dwellings that crowded both sides of the street. In the distance a huge Union Flag flapped in the breeze from the tower of Leek's tallest mill. On Clerk Bank opposite, pupils of Leek Church High School were lined up for a photograph in front of the ancient stone building which was festooned with garlands and flags.

As he made his way towards the Market Place, he noticed some of the special displays in shop windows. Milliners and dress shops concentrated on hats, scarves and blouses of red, white and blue. Grocers had piled tins and packets of anything that had a tenuous Royal connection or a crown on the packaging. Ramm paid particular attention to the public houses which, as usual, had already been open for several hours and sounded as if they were doing brisk trade. He was horrified at the thought of a drunken celebration spilling out onto the street, offending His Majesty, and he had told his constables to be vigilant for such unruliness.

Most children had been given the day off school and were gathering in groups on street corners. Many were in their Sunday best, especially those from better off families. The girls in floral dresses, straw boaters and polished ankle boots; boys were in dark knickerbockers and tightly fitting jackets with wide white collars over the top, and all wore caps.

In the Market Place a team of council carpenters worked furiously to finish a podium to be used by dignitaries to watch the Royal party go past. The sound of hammering and sawing could be heard in the background as Inspector Ramm addressed his army of reinforcements who had gathered in the cobbled square. The Leek Volunteers and the town Fire Brigade were resplendent in immaculate uniform, the sun glinting off the firemen's polished helmets and the soldiers' medals. After making certain that all knew what they needed to do, he left it to their commanders to dispatch the men along the Royal route.

When he returned to the station he found the Chief Constable and half a dozen other senior officers crowded into his office. All heads turned towards him as he entered.

"Good morning gentlemen. I have been to inspect our reinforcements and all is in order," said Ramm. Before anyone could respond, Sergeant Reynolds hurried from the front office and announced: "They have just telephoned from Swythamley Hall to say His Royal Highness will be setting off in the next half hour."

Ramm looked at the clock and saw it was nearly eleven which meant everything was running to schedule. He had little knowledge of motor cars himself, but he had been told the King's Daimler would take about thirty minutes to reach Leek from Swythamley.

"Gentlemen, perhaps we should make our way into the town to observe the celebrations and to await His Majesty," said Ramm, anxious to avoid any questions from his superiors.

When he saw the size of the crowds filling the Market Place and Derby Street, Nathaniel Blake wished he had set out from the studio sooner. Cora had already gone to meet Ellen outside the Great Mill and he had told her to be sure to be back before midday to help him. She had been evasive when he asked where they were going to put the banner. He was surprised the two friends had not

221

already decided, given how his daughter liked to organise things.

With equipment in both hands, he edged through the good-natured throng to the top of the Market Place. He had planned to set up his tripod outside the big Georgian house that some people still called 'No.1 Leek' although the new owners, the Davenports, had renamed it Foxlowe. But Nathaniel could see that spectators were already three or four deep along both sides of street, children squeezing to the front to see what was going on. An aged mill owner was being pushed up Stockwell Street in his bath chair by a manservant who proceeded to park the three-wheeled contraption in a prominent position.

Blake was looking around for the best place for his camera when he saw Inspector Ramm and what appeared to be a group of high ranking officers near the platform opposite Foxlowe. He approached Ramm and asked if he could put his tripod on the edge of the street, in front of the crowds. Ramm agreed, on the understanding it would not interfere with the Royal cars. The Inspector turned to the officer at his side and introduced Nathaniel.

"Mr Blake is the photographer who assists us, Chief Constable. His work has proved most valuable."

"Indeed. A most enterprising idea, Inspector. Progress, that's what we like to see," the police chief replied, before spotting an opportunity for self-advancement. "Perhaps Mr Blake can take a photograph of ourselves on the platform before the King arrives," he suggested.

"Oh certainly, Chief Constable," Blake interjected, happy to oblige Ramm's superior.

Nathaniel set up his tripod in the street, mounted the camera and proceeded to photograph the police officers looking suitably serious. He then took pictures of the waiting crowds waving their flags.

Before going to the mill to find Ellen, Cora had dashed home to grab her bicycle from the back yard. Her mother and William had already left to join the crowds. Her young brother had been running around the house waving his Union Flag since breakfast time.

At exactly eleven o'clock the steam whistle had sounded across the Great Mill's complex of tall buildings. Hundreds of workers had poured out of its doorways, men pulling on jackets and caps, women lifting long skirts with one hand while holding their bonnets on with the other. Some went to the middle of town to claim a good spot to spectate, others wanted to go home to collect family members and enjoy the occasion together.

Ellen Simms left the packing room, made her way through a series of winding corridors and hurried out onto London Road. Weaving between groups of people on the pavement she looked around anxiously for Cora, then spotted her waving excitedly. She went over to her and the two set off up the road. Ellen, who was several inches taller, was striding ahead whilst Cora leaned onto her handlebars, straining to push the heavy bicycle and keep up.

"Perhaps I should have chosen somewhere closer to hang the banner?" she said to Ellen, breathlessly. "But at least it will be easier riding down the hill and back into town."

As they passed the Workhouse, Cora looked at the pendant watch she had pinned to her blouse. The small silver timepiece had become her's when her grandmother died and she only wore it for special occasions. Today was not only special, it was an occasion when every minute counted and Cora was constantly checking the time. After they had secured the banner, she intended to ride back as fast as possible to help her father, while Ellen would stay behind to guard the banner and make sure it didn't fall down before the King passed under the bridge.

"There's no time to lose," said Cora as they finally reached the lane which led across Lowe Hill Bridge. Although she had always said that she and Ellen were doing this together, Cora felt she was the one responsible for making the protest happen.

"I know, I know," Ellen replied, her voice high with excitement and anticipation. She was used to Cora being a little bossy and, even if it had been Cora's idea in the first place, Ellen knew that she herself had been the one to actually make the banner.

Minutes later they were on the bridge. Cora threw her bicycle on the ground and the two ran forward and pitched into frantic activity. They pulled the banner from the pile of wood and then scrabbled round to find rocks to hold the ropes in place. They panted and groaned as, between them, they heaved walling stones to secure the ropes behind the parapet. Then they draped the banner over the side of the bridge. It was a perfect fit, spanning the arch over the Ashbourne Road.

Cora gave a great sigh and wiped the sweat from her forehead. "Finished at last! Now..." She stopped abruptly when someone walked onto the bridge. It was someone she recognised.

Thomas Kilner was as shocked as she was. "Miss Blake!" he said.

"What are you doing here? I thought you had left town," Cora asked. She had seen that the rag-and-stick tent was no longer at Sparrow Park when she walked to work that morning.

Young Kilner ignored the question. "You must leave immediately," he said forcefully.

She began to reply but Thomas interrupted angrily. "Go now! Both of you!"

Four burly men, bearded and wearing long black coats, were now standing behind him. One of them stepped forward and looked menacingly first at Cora and then at Ellen. He growled something to Thomas in a foreign language.

Ellen reached across and grasped Cora's arm. "Perhaps we had better go," she said, her voice filled with fear. She tried to pull her friend away, but Cora stood firm. She was bewildered why the young actor should be there, but at the same time she sensed that something was very wrong. All her suspicions about the Kilner Theatre came flooding back.

"We're not moving until you tell me what's going on," she said defiantly, although the shakiness of her voice betrayed that she was just as frightened as Ellen.

Two of the men lunged forward, seized Ellen and Cora by the arms and started to drag them roughly to the far side of the bridge. Both young women screamed and tried to wrestle themselves free, but stood no chance against the much stronger men.

"Stop, you're hurting me!" Cora cried out as she struggled frantically in the man's grip. Ellen managed to twist round and kick her captor on the shin, but he held her fast.

"Shut up, both of you!" Thomas shouted loud enough to shock them into silence.

Ellen began to whimper while Cora glared at Thomas, her cheeks burning with resentment and streaked with tears. She had wondered before whether he had told her the truth about Sarah, whether he could be trusted. Now she knew the answer. He might be a killer.

CHAPTER TWENTY ONE

It was quarter to twelve by St Edward's Church clock and Nathaniel Blake was irritated that his daughter had failed to return to the Market Place. "Where is the girl? She knows I need her," he said to himself.

Cora had promised to return after helping Ellen, but there was no sign of her and the King was getting closer. Inspector Ramm, who was standing nearby with a group of dignitaries, had told Blake that His Royal Highness was on schedule and so the Royal visitor was due to pass by in the next fifteen minutes.

"I shall just have to manage on my own," Blake muttered.

He loaded his camera with a new glass plate and ducked under the cloth hood to take another photograph of the crowds lining the street. The pavements were more crowded than ever, many of the women holding parasols and umbrellas to shade themselves from the sun. People were becoming increasingly excited and were happy to wave their Union Flags when they saw Blake's camera pointing their way.

After taking the photograph, he pulled out his spare camera, a more modern portable model that used celluloid film. He decided he would take his first picture of the Royal procession using his big plate camera on the tripod and then, if he was quick enough, take more images with the portable one. Things would be so much easier if Cora got back in time to help, he thought.

Blake didn't know it, but there was no chance his daughter would be joining him in the Market Place.

Cora and Ellen were slumped on the track over Lowe Hill Bridge, their hands tied behind their backs. One of the men who had seized them stood close by, making sure they didn't move. Both young women were dishevelled and covered in dust. Ellen had a cut on her cheek and was sobbing, Cora was gasping in frustration as she tried to free her hands, but the rope wouldn't budge. The man guarding them took a kick at Cora's foot. "Be still," he growled.

Thomas Kilner looked over the low parapet of the bridge and saw the banner draped across the stonework.

"So this is why you are here. Some kind of protest, is it?" he said with a hint of sarcasm.

"And why is it that you are here?" Cora replied, managing to keep a challenging tone in her voice. She was now convinced that Thomas must have been involved in Sarah's death and she was angry at herself for having been taken in by the good-looking young actor.

"You might call it a protest, Miss Blake, but something a little more... dramatic... than yours."

Cora could not imagine what Thomas and these rough looking men wanted to protest about, but from the way she and Ellen had been treated she knew there was nothing peaceful about it. "Is this why Sarah died?" she shouted back.

Her comment seemed to catch young Kilner off guard and he looked at her sharply. "That had nothing to do with me," he said, then his voice dropped so low that Cora could barely hear what he said. "I begged him not to do it. I knew we shouldn't have got involved with that man."

He raised his voice again. "I'm sorry, Miss Blake, but there are things that I must do and then... and then we will decide what to do with you two." He cast a glance at his companion who mumbled something Cora didn't understand.

"You, your father, you're evil, all of you!" Cora wailed.

"Quiet!" Thomas barked before calling to one of the men: "Gag them both." The man drew a length of rag from his coat pocket, tore it in half and set about wrapping a piece first across Ellen's mouth and then Cora's. They thrashed their heads about to resist as best they could, but the struggle was to no avail. The ruffian pulled the rag firmly across each of their mouths and knotted it at the back of their heads.

Ellen slumped forward, shocked and exhausted. Cora tried to stand but was roughly pushed back down. Her cries were muffled, but the fierceness in her eyes as she glared at Thomas was undimmed.

He took out a watch and checked the time, then looked across at Cora again and shook his head. "You don't understand. I'm not evil. I'm doing this for Edward, my brother."

Thomas was serious now, rather than angry. He wanted Cora to understand. "Edward was killed by the British in South Africa. My family is from Germany, so your people think we're the enemy."

Cora had stopped moaning and frowned as she concentrated on what he was saying.

Thomas stared out from the bridge, seemingly lost in thought.

"Father blamed this country for Edward's death, he said it was British greed for South African gold. But today he will have his revenge." He looked at his pocket watch again. "Not long to go now."

He had an air of resignation. He had not slept the previous night because he knew that even if his father's mad plan succeeded, he himself had little chance of escaping. Orlando had plotted and schemed for years, but he was miles away by now. Like his brother before him, Thomas had to do his duty and, just like Edward, he might pay the ultimate price.

Cora watched as Thomas opened a sack by his feet and pulled something out, his hand shaking. At first she was puzzled, then she thought she recognised what it was. She nearly choked on her gag as she realised it was a stick of dynamite.

A great wave of sound swept up Mill Street and narrow Church Street as the King approached.

The vehicles, the latest models supplied by Daimler, were painted in gleaming maroon and black. The roofs were down, so spectators had a clear view of the King in the rear of the leading car. The blue leather seats were a snug fit for a man who had enjoyed decades of lavish living.

The bearded King, in a fawn suit and one of his favourite Homburg hats, looked from side to side, smiling and raising a practised hand to greet the crowds. In contrast to the Monarch, who was enjoying the attention of his people, most of the dark-suited occupants of the other two cars were unsmiling.

As the procession came closer, crowds on either side surged forward to get a better look, one or two young women even reaching towards the King's car as if to touch him.

"Keep back. Keep back!" shouted the army Volunteers given the job of keeping this particular section of the route clear.

Town dignitaries who had crowded onto the platform at the top of the Market Place stood to attention, those in uniform raising a smart salute. There was no room on there for Inspector Ramm, so he saluted from street level.

The Royal cars slowed to a halt outside Foxlowe and, at the same moment, the Volunteers' band struck up the National Anthem. The King returned the salute and then swivelled in his seat to acknowledge the spectators who filled the pavements, leaned from upstairs windows, and clung onto railings and lamp-posts.

Nathaniel Blake didn't have time to cheer, but he was relieved that the procession's unexpected halt gave him precious time to take a series of photographs from just feet away.

The great cheers and flurry of flag-waving carried on as the procession continued through the town. The sounds of excitement drifted into the normally quiet corners of the Cottage Hospital where Francis Cavendish lay.

Many patients had been taken outside – some on crutches, others in wheelchairs, some even in their beds – to watch the King pass right in front of the hospital on Stockwell Street before the Royal cars turned into Ball Haye Street.

Although Cavendish was still in the ward, he knew exactly what was going on. He thrashed his head from side to side in frustration, but the sudden movement only succeeded in sending a searing pain through his neck. He tried to get up, but fell back in dizziness. He tried to shout a nurse, but could only manage a feeble croak. He might have survived the murderous attack, but at that moment he felt powerless.

He had started to fret whether John Gibb had really understood what was going on. Did he grasp what he needed to do? Cavendish groaned. The King was here and there was nothing he could do about it now.

In fact, after his wasted visit to the police station, John Gibb had now returned to the Mount. Looking across the field he saw immediately that the gypsies had left. The only signs of the camp were trampled grass, broken branches and a blackened patch where the fire had been.

Gibb turned and strode towards Lowe Hill Bridge. His heart was pounding after his dash from town and from a growing sense of dread. Rounding the bend before the bridge, he stopped dead. He crouched down as he tried to fathom what the figures on the bridge were doing. Then he gasped in horror at the scene.

Cora's scream at seeing the dynamite was muffled by the gag, but it was clear enough for Thomas to glance across at her.

"I'm afraid it has to be done," he said, although the look on his face was more of sadness than satisfaction. He produced another stick of the explosive from the sack. He looked over the parapet where he would drop the dynamite into the King's motor car.

Cora started to struggle again. Her cries roused Ellen who had been staring at the ground as if trying to blank out the reality of their predicament. Now she tried to get to her feet, ready to run for freedom. The men standing nearest seized Ellen and Cora by the shoulders and forced them to sit still. The two other men guarding the track behind Thomas looked at each other uneasily and exchanged comments in their own language. They were obviously unhappy with the unexpected complication that the young women presented.

Then Thomas and all four men went still because in the distance came the sound of car engines. It was sure to be the King and his companions approaching.

The rumbling grew louder and a cloud of dust was being raised in the distance, although a bend in the main road meant they could not see the cars yet.

Thomas knelt down and took out a tin of vesta matches, ready to light the fuses on the dynamite.

But then came another sound. A bloodcurdling roar that harked back to the days of savage highland battles. John Gibb had chosen his moment to come charging onto the bridge, his regimental dagger glinting in his right hand, a wooden fence post held aloft in his left. He launched a double attack on the two men nearest, stabbing one through the coat with his dagger and swinging the wooden shaft at the other man's head. Caught by surprise, neither had time to retaliate. One sank to the ground clutching the knife wound in his side, his hands covered in blood. The other staggered back dazed by the blow.

The two men who had been holding Cora and Ellen sprang to tackle Gibb, but the Scotsman was on them immediately. This time he wielded the fence post in both hands, swinging it in a murderous arc at their heads. One was knocked unconscious, but the other managed to ward off the blow with his arm and dived forward to wrestle Gibb to the ground. It was a desperate struggle in the dust as he tried to throttle John.

On the main road below, the Royal cars were getting closer. Thomas Kilner had escaped the mayhem of Gibb's attack and now struck a match to light the fuse of one of the sticks of explosive. He would wait until the last second to drop it into the King's open-top Daimler. The fuse hissed and his hand shook with the tension of the moment.

John Gibb had managed to get his fingers around a rock and smashed it into his opponent's head. The man's hands fell away and John hauled himself to his feet. To his horror he saw Thomas's arm raised, about to pitch the dynamite from the bridge.

With a desperate cry, Gibb threw himself forward onto Kilner, crushing him against the stone parapet. Thomas let go of the dynamite and it fell onto the ground at their side. Gibb stamped his boot onto the fuse with barely an inch left to burn. From below came the sound of the Royal cars passing under the bridge, their passengers unaware of the drama above.

John looked across to where Ellen and Cora cowered on the ground, their faces showing their shock at what they had just witnessed. He bent down towards them, but stopped when he glimpsed another movement.

Kilner was back on his feet, snatching up a second stick of dynamite and striking a match, the fuse starting to glow. Before Gibb could grab him, Thomas ran from the far side of the bridge and into a field. The ground sloped towards the main road where the Royal cars were rumbling away. It was a last crazed attempt to reach the procession and to kill the King. John started to give chase, but knew he would not catch up with the younger man.

Thomas was holding the explosive aloft as he ran, bracing himself to launch it towards the motor cars. He was about to make the throw when he suddenly pitched forward and went sprawling as his foot caught in a rabbit hole. Thomas lay winded on the steeply sloping ground. He lifted his head in time to see the last of the fuse burn through, inches from his head.

The explosion sent up a dark cloud of smoke, soil and stones.

At the sound of the blast, a look of consternation passed across the King's face and he sank a little lower in his seat. The vehicles ground to a halt and passengers turned to stare in amazement and trepidation across the field, trying to make out what had happened as smoke drifted towards them.

"Some of these women are getting out of hand. Did you see that banner, Your Majesty?" commented a Royal equerry.

The King nodded brusquely and then barked an order to his chauffeur. The man stamped on the accelerator pedal, sending the powerful Daimler on its way. The Royal party had seen enough of Leek.

John Gibb had been knocked backwards by the explosion. Rubbing grit from his face, he watched in dismay as debris fell back into a crater where Kilner had fallen. For a moment he stood silent, looking for any sign of life in the field, then he was relieved to see the Royal cars moving away in the distance. The King must be safe.

He heaved a sigh as he turned back to Lowe Hill Bridge to free Cora and Ellen from their bonds.

Chapter Twenty Two

Nathaniel Blake paused outside his studio when he heard an unusual sound in the distance, but he had no time to dwell on the matter. He was under pressure to develop and print the photographs he had taken of the King and the exuberant spectators.

Although he was still disappointed that Cora had not returned in time to help him, he could not deny it had been a memorable occasion and he was confident his photographs would be good enough to sell. His first priority were the prints he had promised FJ Finch for the *Leek Lion*.

Nearby, Inspector Ramm was being congratulated by the Chief Constable on his handling of the Royal visit when he heard the muffled sound. He gave a slight shudder. His officers, and the men of the Fire Brigade, were scattered across the town, so the last thing he wanted was a new emergency.

It was not until they reached the police station that Ramm realised that something serious may indeed have happened. Constable Knowles, on the front desk, was in a state of some agitation having just answered a call from the Workhouse which had been recently equipped with a telephone.

"Apparently a lad ran in to say there had been some sort of big bang up near Lowe Hill," said Knowles.

"Is His Majesty safe?" the Chief Constable thundered.

Knowles looked fear-stricken. "I don't know, Sir. The King, er, wasn't mentioned," he stammered, before suggesting: "Perhaps it was something to do with the gypsies."

"The gypsies? Why?" asked Ramm, horrified by the sudden turn from celebration to likely catastrophe.

"Well, John Gibb came in earlier to say he was worried what the gypsies were up to on the Mount. I told him there was no one available and we..."

"Find out what's going on immediately, Inspector," ordered the Chief Constable, but Ramm was already running out of the door. He dashed across to Haywood Street, climbed aboard a trap and ordered the startled driver to take him to Lowe Hill without delay. As they pulled away Knowles came running up behind and Ramm managed to haul the breathless constable into the trap too.

The driver, urged on by an anxious Ramm, needed all his skill to avoid good-natured spectators who were now milling about the streets, many making their way back to work. Once on the Ashbourne Road the trap picked up speed and soon they were at Lowe Hill.

"What on earth?" the Inspector breathed as he saw Cora and Ellen's banner strung across the narrow arched bridge. Was the blast part of some sort of political protest, he wondered. Had the King's visit been marred? Should he have posted reinforcements on the edge of town? All his earlier pride and satisfaction was draining away.

"Drive on!" he shouted as he sensed the man with the reins hesitating. Ramm had to be sure that the King was safely clear of the town, that there was no fresh horror on the road ahead.

After rounding the sharp bend beyond the bridge, Ramm immediately spotted a pile of debris in the neighbouring field, but was relieved there was no sign of disruption on the road. They continued closer to Bradnop before Ramm was satisfied the Royal party had gone on its way.

Going back towards Leek, the Inspector halted the trap near to where an explosion had apparently occurred. He and Knowles got out, clambered over a low stone wall and walked across to the patch of blackened earth, from which a little smoke was still rising. Ramm peered at the crater and the soil and stones scattered around its edge, then his eyes narrowed as he focused on something else amongst the debris. It was a torn forearm with the hand still attached.

"This is a grim affair, Knowles, and no mistake," he said. The constable flinched as he too saw the gruesome remains.

At that moment there was a shout and Ramm turned to see John Gibb beckoning from the edge of the field near the bridge. Knowles breathed in sharply, already regretting how he had dealt with the Scotsman.

After the explosion, John Gibb had gone back to the bridge to find Cora and Ellen sitting dazed and alone. The men who had been their captors had managed to escape, despite the injuries that Gibb had inflicted.

The young friends winced as Gibb had untied their gags and the ropes that bound their hands. They were both covered in dust and dirt, their faces streaked with tears. Ellen, rubbed her arms to bring some feeling back into them. Cora had red marks across her face left by the gag. She looked up at Gibb.

"What happened to Thomas?" she asked in her wavering voice. She still could not quite believe what had happened in the last hour and how cruel the young actor had appeared. The shattering sound of the blast had brought an ominous end to the episode.

Gibb shook his head. "Dead, Miss Blake, and good riddance if ye ask me."

"Did he, did he...?" Cora could not bring herself to ask whether Kilner had succeeded in his attack on the King.

"The only person that man blew up was himself, Miss Blake. His Majesty escaped and there was no harm to him, as far as I could see."

Cora slumped forward. She was exhausted now that their ordeal was over. She was relieved the King was safe but horrified at the fight she had witnessed and at the way Thomas Kilner had died.

Cora and Ellen sat with their backs against the bridge parapet, holding hands and comforting each other quietly. John Gibb could see that they were in no condition to return home without help. He needed transport of some kind to take them to town and considered going to ask at the nearby farm. However he did not want to risk leaving the two on their own in case the ruffians returned. He had decided to wait, sure that the sound of the explosion would bring someone to their aid.

The first on the scene had been a farm lad who Gibb dispatched to raise the alarm. Next, the farmer and his wife came running, the woman returning home to fetch water and a cloth so she could tend to Cora and Ellen. The farmer had gone to hitch a waggon when John saw Inspector Ramm pass under the bridge. Minutes later he had managed to attract the officer's attention.

Now Ramm stood on the bridge and felt sick as he surveyed the scene. The young women had been victims of some manner of assault. John Gibb bore the cuts and bruises of a fight and there was a patch of blood on his coat. To top it all, a body had been blown to pieces just across the field. Such violence while the rest of the town was enjoying the Royal visit!

"I cannot imagine what has been going on here, but you young ladies need to see a doctor," the Inspector said. "Who were the culprits? Was it the gypsies? Quick Constable, go to that camp on the Mount and make sure none of them leaves."

"Don't waste ye time. They're are long gone, Inspector," said Gibb. "They struck camp ages ago and those four who were here must have joined them, although one was in a bad way. But there were other folk involved in this affair as well as the gypsies."

"It's the theatre people," Cora interrupted, finding her voice. "They were behind it all."

Ramm looked first at Cora and then at Gibb. "Do you have any idea who it was that was blown up?"

"Thomas Kilner!" Cora cried angrily. "He was trying to kill the King with dynamite! I saw him!" There were tears in her eyes again. "And that's not all. He was involved in what happened to Sarah, I'm sure of it!"

Ramm was rocked by this new twist. A plot to kill the King on the day he came to Leek? It was the stuff of nightmares. And by the looks of the scene at Lowe Hill, it had so nearly succeeded.

His mind was racing. Was His Majesty still in danger? Who else was involved? Would Leek Police, or more likely he himself, get the blame? How in heaven was he going to sort this out, he thought.

"We must act quickly. Let's get you three back to town as soon as possible," Ramm said. "Then I need to find out exactly what happened."

John Gibb helped Ellen and Cora into the farmer's cart and then got in himself while Inspector Ramm and Constable Knowles boarded the trap. "We've no time to waste," Ramm told the driver.

The trap had barely come to a halt in Leonard Street when Inspector Ramm jumped down and hurried into the police station. He immediately began to fire instructions at Sergeant Reynolds.

"Put a call through to Alton Towers and ask if His Majesty has arrived. If he's not there yet, find out who else might have a telephone along the route. I want to know that he is definitely on his way. We might need to borrow a motor car from someone."

Before Reynolds could reply John Gibb, Ellen and Cora came through the door. The Sergeant looked at the battered and bruised newcomers in surprise while Ramm ploughed on with his orders.

"Ring Dr Brunt and ask him to come round straight away to examine these young ladies. Then we need to find the gypsies who have been on the Mount. It looks like they set off up the Buxton Road, but who knows where they might be heading? Get one of the men out on a bicycle and send a telegram to the Constable

Mellor at Longnor and tell him to keep a look out."

Reynolds puffed out his checks before asking: "Did you find out what that blast was?"

"Yes and no, Sergeant. It's rather complicated. Send someone up to Lowe Hill. There's a great hole in the ground just past the bridge and I want it guarded. No one is to go near it until we've investigated properly."

Ramm produced his handkerchief and wiped sweat from his brow as his marched down the corridor to his office. The Chief Constable was waiting for him.

"Well, what's going on? I trust there was no interruption to the King's progress?" the officer asked. His tone conveyed that he was only prepared to accept positive news from the Inspector.

"There was an explosion, Sir, in a field. It appears that at least one man was killed. As far as I can tell, His Majesty's motor car was not affected in any way."

"As far as you can tell?" the Chief Constable rasped back. "You mean you don't know for certain? Good God man, we're talking about the King of England!"

"We are confirming His Majesty's arrival at Alton as we speak, Sir," Ramm replied.

"And do you know the cause of this explosion, Inspector?"

Ramm thought quickly. He had no wish to create panic amongst his superiors or be the target of recriminations.

"At first sight it would seem that a culprit blew himself up while handling stolen explosive." Ramm felt his reply contained enough truth not to be misleading. It also left him scope to revise the story when all the facts were known.

The Chief Constable seemed pacified. "A very unfortunate coincidence, to say the least, Inspector," he said in more measured tones. "But as long as His Majesty is safe, we can all breathe easily. I'm sure you will be submitting a full report when the matter is cleared up."

Ramm dispatched one of his constables to fetch Nathaniel Blake to the station. He asked Reynolds for news of His Majesty and was told that the King had passed Cotton crossroads and was expected to arrive at Alton Towers soon.

"Tell our colleagues at Cheadle and Uttoxeter they will need every man guarding the King's route tomorrow until he catches his train. Say there's been rumour of a threat," Ramm told his sergeant. "I shall be glad when he's back at the Palace," he added.

In the interview room he found Dr Brunt was attending to Cora, Ellen and John Gibb's cuts and bruises. Ramm was desperate to hear details of the Lowe Hill incident and was glad when the police surgeon closed his leather bag and left. To save time he decided to speak to Gibb and the young women together.

It was now past one o'clock and back at the studio Blake was busy in his darkroom. He was growing increasingly concerned by his daughter's absence. The King was long gone and the crowds had dispersed so there was no reason why she should be delayed in returning from helping Ellen. He hoped there was no problem, that she hadn't been knocked over in the rush or something.

When he heard the distant tinkle of the bell above the shop door, he first thought Cora had finally returned. On hearing a man's voice call from below, he heaved a frustrated sigh. He snatched up a cloth to dry his hands and hurried downstairs. He was surprised to see one of the Leek constables.

"You're wanted at the station, Mr Blake," said the officer.

"But I'm in the middle of printing some important photographs! I simply cannot leave now," came Nathaniel's exasperated reply.

"The Inspector says you must come immediately. It's about your daughter, Sir."

Nathaniel threw down the cloth and ran back upstairs to fetch his jacket.

At about the same time, FJ Finch was joining his son in the *Leek Lion* newsroom. They had spent the last two hours on the streets, observing the spectacle, interviewing dignitaries and taking precise note of the King's journey through the town. Now they had many words to type and precious little time to do so.

But before he could begin, the editor had something else to tell Oliver. One of his contacts had told him of some sort of incident at Lowe Hill.

"Someone said a great hole has been blown in the field near the bridge," said FJ.

"Lowe Hill Bridge?" Oliver replied sharply.

Finch sensed real concern in his son's voice. "What's the matter?" he asked.

"It's just that I heard there was going to be some kind of, er, protest on the bridge today."

"Protest? In front of the King, do you mean?" FJ pounced upon a potential story for the *Lion*.

"Well..." Oliver began cautiously. If something had happened at Lowe Hill, he was worried Cora might be involved. This was no time to keep things to himself. "Well, Cora and her friend Miss Simms were going to hang a banner for the King to see. They're campaigning for women to get the vote," he explained.

"Miss Blake? A protest? Does Nathaniel know about this?"

"I doubt it."

"If there has been an incident we must have it in tomorrow's *Lion*. You need to go up there straight away. See what's gone on. But waste no time, we have much to do before we go to press."

Oliver stuffed his notebook in his jacket pocket and dashed downstairs to get his bicycle from a corner of the press room on the ground floor. Concern for Cora, as much as desire for a news story, forced his feet round on the pedals.

Inspector Ramm could not hide his surprise when Cora revealed why she and Ellen had been at Lowe Hill Bridge.

"You're telling me that the two of you hung that banner across the bridge? I can barely believe it, Miss Blake," said Ramm. He leaned on the table, firing rapid questions as the two friends and John Gibb sat opposite. Cora and Ellen exchanged sheepish looks.

"What about you, Mr Gibb? Why were you at Lowe Hill?"

"Well, like I told yer man this morning, I'd been watching the gypsies and..." John began.

"Wait a minute," Ramm interrupted. "Exactly why were you doing that? It wouldn't be connected with your friend Cavendish, would it? A rum fellow and I wouldn't be surprised to find out he's mixed up in this mess."

Gibb hesitated before deciding that as the assassination plot had failed, there would be no harm in telling the truth.

"Actually, Francis was trying to stop all this," Gibb began, determined to defend his friend's honour. "He's an agent of the government and he asked me to keep an eye on yon gypsy camp."

Gibb saw that Cora and Ellen's eyes had widened in surprise and Ramm was sitting rigid, totally focused on what he was saying.

"I was up there on the Mount last night. I saw the gypsies and some other fellows – that young Kilner might have been one of them – with a case of dynamite," the Scotsman continued.

"And why didn't you tell us about this? Or about what Cavendish was doing?" Ramm asked.

Before Gibb could answer there was a commotion in the corridor and Nathaniel Blake burst in.

"Cora! My dear, are you hurt? What's this all about?" he cried, taking his daughter in his arms. He was shocked to see the state of her dress, the marks on her face, her eyes still red from crying.

"Mr Blake, calm yourself! This is official business," said Ramm.

"But she's been injured, Inspector, and so has Ellen. You can't hold them here. What was it, some sort of accident?" Nathaniel looked from face to face, bewildered by the turn of events. He frowned as he saw that John Gibb had been hurt, too.

"It's all right, Father. We're feeling a little better now," said Cora. Ellen nodded in mute agreement, unable to hide her discomfort at being in the police station and reliving the horror of Lowe Hill Bridge.

"Mr Blake, you can sit with us and see that we're treating the young ladies properly, as long as you promise not to interrupt," said Ramm.

"But..." Blake began. Ramm held up his hand to silence the photographer, then returned his attention to John Gibb. "You were saying, Mr Gibb?"

"I was sworn to secrecy, Inspector," Gibb said confidently. Ramm looked unimpressed, but said nothing and the Scotsman continued with his story. "Anyway, I came down here to try to get help this morning, but got nowhere. So I went back and saw men on the bridge. Miss Blake and Miss Simms were prisoners."

Blake gasped as he heard this.

"I surprised the ruffians and set about knocking heads together."

"You were marvellous, Mr Gibb," Cora interjected, her eyes shining.

"You fought five men?" said Ramm, incredulously.

"Well, first two of them and then another two," Gibb replied modestly. "But that young devil Kilner managed to get away. That's when he blew hisself up."

"And Kilner was definitely planning to kill the King?" asked Ramm.

Blake gave another gasp.

Cora decided it was time to speak. "Oh yes!" she said. "He held up a stick of dynamite and said it was revenge for his brother who died in the Boer War. But Mr Gibb pounced on him and stopped him throwing it off the bridge. Then he ran off," Cora fell silent as she thought of the young actor's fate.

There was silence in the room as all of them thought what might had happened if John Gibb had not reacted so quickly.

"That's not all, though," Cora went on. "It was obvious he knew who had killed Sarah. You must do something about it."

Inspector Ramm moved uneasily in his chair. This latest incident would have to come first, but eventually he would need to tackle what else had gone on during this tragic fortnight.

Chapter Twenty Three

By the time Ramm returned to his office he found the Chief Constable had left, satisfied that the King was unscathed. The Inspector decided he would tell his superiors that the incident was an attempted assassination when he had a clearer idea of what had happened and, hopefully, had run the culprits to ground.

Ramm knew there was no time to lose. He told Sergeant Reynolds to find out where the Kilner Theatre had moved to, and then contact the nearest police station to ask that Orlando Kilner be detained. He wanted to interview the man himself. He also ordered messages be sent to all the rural constables to report sightings of the German gypsies.

"On no account reveal why we're after them. Say it's general lawlessness or something like that. No one must breathe a word about this outside the station or they will be for the high jump. We all will."

The next person he needed to speak to was Francis Cavendish. When he arrived at the Cottage Hospital he found John Gibb sitting beside the injured man's bed. The Scotsman looked rather uncomfortable when he saw Ramm approach and offered to leave, but Francis waved for him to stay.

Ramm could see that Cavendish, though still swathed in bandages, was more alert than the previous day. More importantly he appeared able to speak, though his voice was barely audible.

"I will waste no time, Mr Cavendish." Ramm was business like, struggling to hide his previous suspicions of the man. "I gather you knew about this damnable plot against His Majesty, but you chose not to inform the police."

Cavendish's breath rattled in his throat as he summoned the energy to speak.

"I am an agent for the War Office, not the police," he said haltingly. "My work is secret, Inspector."

"But you told Mr Gibb."

"I would trust John with my life. Thank God he was prepared to help." Cavendish looked across at his old comrade and began to choke with emotion. John reached forward and grasped his arm.

"Who was behind it all? The Kilners?" Ramm asked.

With John's help Cavendish took a mouthful of water, wincing as he swallowed. His reply was punctuated with gasps for breath. "We believe Orlando Kilner has been an agitator for German interests for years. The man's a fanatic. I was put on his tail when we discovered he would be in Leek at the same time as the King. His anarchist friends must have seen the Royal plans in official documents."

"But I thought Kilner was English," Ramm said.

"He's an actor and he can put on a good accent. His real name is Kleine, Roland Kleine. He was born in Germany and so was Mulder," Cavendish explained. "Kilner's son died in South Africa fighting for the Boers. According to our sources, he has been seeking revenge ever since. The younger son did as his father said."

"Was it one of the Kilners who attacked you?" said Ramm.

"It's highly likely to have been a member of the group."

"I shall arrest Kilner if it's the last thing I do!" Ramm declared.

There was a pause before Cavendish spoke again. "It might not be quite that simple, Inspector. We believe someone else was assisting him here in Leek."

"Another anarchist? Who?" The Inspector shook his head in disbelief.

"I am afraid I do not know," Cavendish replied.

Ramm began to realise that FJ Finch may have been right in thinking that James Broadhurst was murdered to prevent him revealing German sympathisers in the town. "Do you think Broadhurst was caught up in all this?" he asked Cavendish.

"Yes, but he never realised the risks he was taking," the agent replied.

When the Inspector left, Cavendish asked Gibb to send a telegram to the War Office. Once again he used pencil and paper to write out a message which John saw was in some sort of code.

Ramm was still coming to terms with the revelations about German fanatics as he walked back to the police station. He thought about the horrific train of events of the last two weeks. Two suspicious deaths, an attempted murder and now a plot to kill the King.

He sighed deeply as he realised the mistakes he had made. He had dismissed Finch's theories about James Broadhurst. He had ignored Miss Blake's pleas about Sarah Hulme. He had thought Cavendish was probably a criminal. Now he needed to try to put things right and he would start by finding Orlando Kilner.

When Nathaniel and Cora arrived at Portland Street, Edith pulled her daughter into a tight hug. The Blakes had nearly lost her two years ago and today she had been in peril again.

Edith told Cora she must lie down and then went to make tea. There was so much Nathaniel wanted to ask his daughter about, but knew now was not the time. Besides, he had work to do. Inspector Ramm had asked him to photograph the scene of the blast and he still needed to finish his pictures of the Royal visit for the next day's *Lion*.

Half an hour later he set out to cycle to Lowe Hill, calling at the newspaper office first. As he hurried into the news room with an envelope of photographs, he saw from Finch's tense reaction that the editor knew something dire had happened earlier.

Oliver Finch looked up from his typewriter and was the first to speak. "Is Cora safe?" he asked. There was no hiding his anxiety.

Blake hesitated, unsure where to begin or whether he was allowed to say anything at all. He himself was still recovering from discovering Cora's ordeal.

"So you have heard," he said.

"We know there was an unholy set-to at Lowe Hill. Was Cora involved? Tell us man, is she all right?" Finch senior urged.

"She has been most wilfully abused, but you know how strong she is. Time will tell how she copes with it all. But how did you know she was there?"

"Well, Cora had told me about the banner on the bridge," Oliver began cautiously. "When we heard about the explosion I went up to see what had happened. We were worried about her. Mr and Mrs Hurst at the farm told me there had been some sort of fight and two young women had been taken to the police station."

Blake frowned. "I still can't understand why they went all the way to Lowe Hill to hang a banner to greet the King."

"So you haven't seen it yet, Nathaniel?" FJ asked.

"No, I'm on my way there now. Ramm wants me to take photographs."

Father and son exchanged a look, imagining Blake's reaction when he saw the banner.

"So, do you know what this fight was about? Who set off the explosion? Nothing to do with the King, I take it?" Finch asked.

Nathaniel paused. "It's a shocking affair, FJ, truly shocking. Ramm is on to it, but I think he will want it keeping quiet at the moment."

Finch sensed there was a bigger story to be told and continued to press his friend. "The Hursts said there was a Scotsman involved. It sounded like John Gibb. What was he doing there? It wouldn't be because of his old friend Cavendish, would it?"

"FJ, I simply cannot go into details. I haven't had a proper conversation with Cora myself."

Blake told them that he had to leave and, after collecting his bicycle from outside the office, rode up the main road to Lowe Hill, his portable camera in a leather case attached to his handlebars. As he rounded the bend just before the bridge he saw why FJ had asked if he had seen the banner.

He braked hard and gazed open mouthed. 'Votes for Women' in letters two feet high was stretched across at the stone arch. "How did Cora get involved in this?" he asked himself. "Whatever did the King think about it?"

After all the worry over what she had gone through today, it was a fresh blow to find Cora had been keeping this secret from Edith and himself. "She knew we would be against it," Blake thought bitterly. He knew she was concerned about fair treatment for women, he just wished she had not made such a blatant protest.

Whether he agreed with it or not, he decided to take a photograph of the banner. Then he walked under the bridge, around the sharp bend and looked across the field where a constable was standing. Blake climbed the wall into the field. Where the ground sloped away sharply, he saw a crater of blackened earth.

"Inspector Ramm asked me to take photographs of the scene," he told the constable.

"You can proceed, Mr Blake, but please do not touch anything. Those are the Inspector's orders," the officer replied.

Blake drew nearer to where the blast had occurred. The

explosion had disturbed tons of earth and stones and there was still a lingering smell of smoke, explosive and something else Blake could not quite identify.

He shook his head in dismay as he imagined the death and destruction that would have occurred if the dynamite had landed in the King's motor car instead. He photographed the scene from several angles, including one showing the proximity of the road, then he stepped closer.

That was the moment when he perceived the gruesome sight around the crater and he realised that the unknown smell had been burnt flesh. To his horror Blake could now identify different parts of Thomas Kilner's body, some charred, some surprisingly intact. It was chiefly limbs – Blake was relieved he could see no sign of the head.

He thought back to when he had photographed the Kilner Theatre Company, a smiling Sarah and Thomas standing beside each other. Both were now dead. Blake pictured again the scene at the rag-and-stick that fateful evening when Thomas had helped him with the flash-lamp. There had been something haunted about the young man that night.

"Why did it have to end like this?" Blake said under his breath. All the melancholy and pain of the last few weeks seemed to collect in a single event. Once more he took out his camera, once more he photographed the mortal remains of someone he had seen alive. As he turned back to the road he hoped these weeks of trauma were coming to an end. There were culprits still to be caught, but for now at least, let the horror be over.

Inspector Ramm tensed as he saw the rag-and-stick tent on the green in the middle of Hartington. The scene looked peaceful enough, but he knew that somewhere in this village was the man who had plotted to assassinate the King.

Ramm was told the theatre's whereabouts when he had returned from the Cottage Hospital and had immediately ordered a carriage to take him to the village. Hartington, just over the Derbyshire border, was officially outside his authority and so he had informed Buxton Police of his intentions.

The dozen miles had taken longer than Ramm would have preferred and he had felt uncomfortably hot as the sun burned down on his peaked cap and tunic. On reaching the village he saw a tall uniformed figure stride towards him. Ramm had brought Constable Phillips with him from Leek, but was relieved to see the village policeman had been forewarned. After the violence at Lowe Hill he did not know what he faced at the Kilner Theatre.

The officer, who introduced himself as Constable Sheldon, said a group from the rag-and-stick had been seen going into The Charles Cotton Hotel earlier. From Sheldon's description, Ramm was satisfied that one of them was Orlando Kilner.

"Well, let us find the man," said Ramm, nodding towards the substantial three storey hotel, built from the grey limestone that was quarried locally. "Be on your guard. This fellow is a menace."

Ramm was amazed at Kilner's audacity. The man had masterminded a plot to kill the King, and yet here he was, setting up his theatre and then retiring to a hostelry as if nothing untoward had happened.

The Inspector clenched his teeth as he strode through the hotel entrance, glancing into the front parlour where a group of ladies were taking tea and scones, and then continuing into the wood panelled bar. Watched with some amusement by pipe smoking locals, Orlando Kilner was seated in a corner, sounding forth about the entertainment to be had in his theatre that night.

Kilner was about to bring a glass of spirits to his lips, but stopped suddenly when Ramm marched in flanked by the two constables, both with their gleaming black truncheons raised. The room fell silent as all eyes turned towards the officers.

That was the moment when Kilner's worst fears were realised. Over the last couple of hours he had been hoping to see Thomas arrive from Leek with news of the plot on the King's life, and he had become increasingly worried when his son, or any of the gypsies, had failed to turn up. He had thought of fleeing the theatre and taking Conrad with him. But he was loathe to leave the district until he knew exactly what had happened on Lowe Hill Bridge and, more precisely, what had become of Thomas.

"Orlando Kilner, I am arresting you on suspicion of attempted murder," Ramm announced. Without waiting for a response, he shouted. "Put the handcuffs on him, men!"

The constables charged forward, each grabbing one of Kilner's arms and hauled him out of his chair. The glass of whisky went flying as did pints of ale on a nearby table. Kilner's compatriots cried out in surprise. The theatre owner himself reared back in shock before gasping in pain as his arms were wrenched behind his back and the handcuffs clamped around his wrists.

"Inspector! What on earth is going on?" Kilner managed to utter as he was bundled out of the room.

Ramm ignored him, ordering Constable Sheldon to find a piece of rope so that they could secure Kilner in the carriage. When that was done, he stood guard over the prisoner while the constables ran over to the rag-and-stick to find Conrad Mulder. Ramm told them to use whatever force was necessary. Shortly after the officers disappeared into the tent he saw the huge figure of Mulder come through the canvas flap and lope off in the opposite direction.

"Damn it," Ramm muttered. Behind him he thought he heard Kilner stifle a laugh.

The two officers emerged with their helmets missing. Sheldon blew his whistle to sound the alarm and the two ran about, desperately looking which way Mulder had gone. An old fellow by a duck pond used his walking stick to point the way he had seen the man go, but by this time there was no sign of him.

Ramm realised that in his haste to get to Hartington he had come ill prepared to capture such dangerous characters. The constables hurried back, both out of breath.

"As soon as he saw us he made a run for it, Sir," said Constable Phillips. "I hit him with the truncheon, but he just knocked us out of the way. A proper brute."

"The railway station is up that way," said Sheldon, nodding towards the opposite end of the village. "He might be going to try to catch a train."

Ramm ordered the carriage driver to make for the railway station as quickly as possible and the constables clambered in.

The driver flourished his whip to urge his horse up the lane to the station about a mile from the village centre. Ramm and his men clung on as the carriage swept around several sharp bends. Kilner, who was tied to the seat, rocked wildly from side to side.

When they reached the station, the constables jumped down and searched the platforms and buildings, but there was no sign of Mulder.

Ramm sighed. One of the suspects had got away. He thought Mulder was probably lying low and waiting for darkness before making his move. He told Constable Sheldon to ask Buxton Police to issue an urgent search warrant for the man. "He should be easy enough to spot," Ramm added and then nodded at Kilner. "In the meantime we must get this one back to Leek as soon as possible."

"Isn't it time you told me what this is all about?" Kilner asked indignantly.

Ramm took exception to the prisoner's tone and replied angrily: "High treason, that is what it is about, Kilner! Or should I say Herr Kleine?"

At the mention of treason the constables exchanged a look of surprise, but said nothing. On hearing his German name Kilner appeared taken aback.

"Surely this is a misunderstanding. I think you are making a great mistake, Inspector," he said regaining his composure.

"No, Kilner, it is you who has made a great mistake. You and your son who is now dead," Ramm shot back.

"My son? You know nothing about Edward!"

"I am talking about Thomas, the son you left behind in Leek to carry out your plot."

"Thomas? Dead?" Kilner gasped. Actor that he was, he could not conceal his anguish. Although he had always known the jeopardy which his son was being placed in, he had been confident Thomas would escape. Surely, the plan was foolproof, he thought. Now he saw that his confidence had been misplaced. The plot had gone fatally wrong.

The journey back from Hartington was largely in silence. Orlando Kilner was sickened to hear of his son's death and sank in the seat groaning, his long black hair over his face, tears in his eyes. Now he had lost both Thomas and Edward, and he felt his own life had come to an end.

The Inspector sat stony-faced and quietly satisfied at the prospect of interrogating the traitor Kilner that evening. Now he had captured the fanatic, he would also inform his superiors of the plot. Admittedly, there were many matters to be cleared up, not least finding Mulder, the gypsies and another German agent in Leek, but the chief suspect was on his way to the cells.

After her father had left, Cora had spent the rest of the afternoon on her bed. Her arms and legs hurt and she found it difficult to get comfortable, so she lay on her back staring at the ceiling. Mother had come upstairs to offer her something to eat or drink, but she hadn't been able to face anything. When young William came home from school he had poked his head around the door and talked excitedly about seeing the King. She had managed not to burst into tears at the mention of the Royal visit.

Left alone again, Cora relived what she and Ellen had gone through on Lowe Hill Bridge. She felt guilty about landing her friend in such trouble, although there was no way she could have known what the Kilners were planning. The banner had seemed such a good idea, but now she realised it could have cost them both their lives.

After everything else that had happened, the banner appeared unimportant now. She still found it hard to believe that Thomas Kilner had tried to blow up the King. And if it hadn't been for John Gibb, he might have succeeded.

"I was a fool not to see through him," she thought. She recalled how Thomas had behaved towards her in the last two weeks. At first she had been fascinated by the idea that there had been something between him and Sarah. She found herself trying to see the handsome young actor through Sarah's eyes.

But she had always wondered whether he was telling the truth, especially when he said Sarah was struggling in the theatre. If Thomas could conceal a deadly plot, he would have found it easy to lie about Sarah, she thought.

Then she recalled what he had said on the bridge about his family and about Sarah. Perhaps he was being honest at last.

Once again, Cora started to go over all the things she had seen and heard and suspected. Then her eyes opened wider as the pieces began to fall into place. She realised what Sarah must have discovered when she spied on Professor Kilner, the reason she had died and the person who must be responsible.

Thomas was dead, but if Sarah's killer was still free then Cora knew her nightmare was not over yet.

As soon as they reached Leek, Inspector Ramm had Kilner put in the cells under guard and still in handcuffs. He made arrangements to circulate Conrad Mulder's description far and wide, but was disappointed to hear the German gypsies had yet to be located.

He gathered his wits before his call to Headquarters. He hoped to avoid blame for what had happened while taking credit for his quick reaction.

The Chief Superintendent on the other end of the line gave a cry of astonishment when Ramm told of the threat to the King. It was followed by a sigh of relief as Ramm explained that the would-be assassin was dead and the man who had planned it was in custody.

"I am confident we will track down the others," Ramm assured his superior. The Superintendent told him to hold the line and he then found himself going over the whole story again to the Chief Constable.

By the time the call was finally over, Ramm could imagine the storm he had whipped up at Constabulary Headquarters. Dropping the heavy handpiece into its cradle he glanced up at the wall clock and realised he had been on duty for more than twelve hours and had eaten nothing since breakfast. He called to Constable Knowles to make a mug of tea and then fetch him something to eat. He needed to revive himself before facing Orlando Kilner.

Half an hour later Ramm felt ready to question the prisoner and had him brought up from the cells. If Cavendish was correct, this was a criminal of a higher order than any he had ever dealt with and he felt under some pressure. He called in Sergeant Reynolds to witness what was said and to take notes.

The Orlando Kilner sitting opposite him was far different from the ebullient impresario the Inspector had first met two weeks' earlier. The previously immaculate hair was tangled, his clothes were stained with sweat, his neckerchief was raggedly undone and his demeanor was sullen. But it turned out he had lost none of his confidence.

"How did my son die?" he barked, leaning forward and glaring at Ramm.

"I shall be asking the questions, Kilner. We will come to

Thomas's death shortly, but first..." said Ramm in measured tones.

"Do you have any idea what it is like to lose both sons?" Kilner continued undeterred, raising his voice as if on stage. "They were heroes fighting for the things they believed in. Edward protecting our people in South Africa. Thomas here in this pathetic town, avenging his brother. Both of them were killed by the English!"

Kilner slumped back into the chair, drained by the outburst.

Ramm offered no sympathy. "Have you finished?" he asked calmly. "Perhaps now you can give me some answers."

"Do you honestly believe I will answer your questions?" Kilner shouted. "This whole affair is ludicrous!"

"You and your conspirators are responsible for the most heinous of crimes. A plot against the life of the King, to say nothing of the deaths of at least two others. But no matter how many lies you tell, you will be punished."

The handcuffs prevented Kilner's gesture of contempt and instead he scorned the Inspector's comment with a vigorous shake of his head. "You will prove nothing," he said haughtily.

The heated exchange was interrupted when Ramm was summoned to answer a call from his Chief Superintendent.

"The War Office has been in touch and they are sending one of their men for that fellow Kilner. And tomorrow two detectives from Headquarters will take charge of the search for the other miscreants. I'm sure you will give them your fullest support," the senior officer told him.

"Damnation!" Ramm muttered in frustration after slamming down the handset. Just when he had an important criminal in his grasp, the case was being snatched away.

At that moment a young messenger pushed through the station door and thrust a telegram into his hand. Ramm read it:

KILNER WANTED FOR CRIMES AGAINST CROWN. MAINTAIN CUSTODY UNTIL TRANSFER. DO NOT INTERROGATE. BY ORDER OF WAR OFFICE, LONDON.

Ramm guessed that Cavendish must have informed his colleagues in London and they were losing no time in getting involved. He sighed, realising he should have known this affair was far too important to be left to him and his men. An attempt on the King's life by foreign infiltrators could have an impact across the nation, perhaps across Europe.

Nathaniel Blake felt exhausted when he finally sank into his armchair that evening. He was drained after a day of emotional turmoil and frantic work. Having taken the pictures for Inspector Ramm at Lowe Hill, later he had decided to return on foot to collect Cora's bicycle. He also took down the Votes for Women banner, it brought back too many grim memories to stay there any longer.

"Oh my word! Whatever was she thinking?" Edith had cried when Blake arrived home with the banner and she saw just how dramatic Cora's protest had been.

Nathaniel and Ethel now sat opposite each other, the strain of the last few hours had almost robbed them of the energy to speak.

"I know this banner is not what we would have wanted, Nathaniel, but we mustn't press her about it," Edith said at last. "This whole affair will take a long time for Cora to get over."

"I am so angry about what happened to her," Nathaniel replied. He shook his head as if to rid himself of images of the last two weeks, the bodies and the injuries he had seen.

"Thank goodness John Gibb was there to save her. We owe that man so much," said Edith.

Nathaniel sat bolt upright. "I haven't even thanked him! At the police station I was too shocked. I must go to see him," he said. He stood up and started to pace around the room.

"You can do nothing about it tonight, my dear. Speak to him in the morning when you're rested," Edith advised.

Blake realised his wife was talking sense and sat down again.

Tired as he was, he could not stop thinking about the sickening events of the past fortnight. It had all started when the Kilner Theatre came to town and Sarah Hulme had become the first victim, he thought. He realised that Cora's instincts had been right and someone was responsible for Sarah's death. He was convinced Broadhurst had been murdered, too.

He sat with his eyes closed and thought about all the clues he had collected. Others beside the Kilners had been involved in this affair, he decided. James Broadhurst had suspected someone who was already in Leek. Perhaps that was the same person Sarah Hulme had been so worried about. Now, like Cora, Nathaniel believed he knew who else was to blame.

CHAPTER TWENTY FOUR

The Leek Lion

SATURDAY, JULY 23ʳᵈ 1904

PRIDE, HONOUR AND JUSTICE.

What pride and what honour came to our town when His Majesty King Edward passed along our humble streets yesterday.

Thousands gathered to line the pavements, not only townspeople but well-wishers from across the moorlands, and they were not disappointed as the smiling Monarch waved and acknowledged their greetings. Old and young joined in the throng for this memorable occasion. Streets, shops, houses and public buildings – all were bedecked with bunting, flags and banners of every kind.

Let us recognize the meticulous organization that made the day such a success. Police, Fire Brigade, Volunteers and Local Authorities worked together with admirable precision.

Sadly, one day of joy is not sufficient to lift the dark shadow that hangs over the town. Two weeks ago a young woman lost her life in a most public fashion. Ten days ago a businessman who has campaigned on German issues died in bizarre fashion. This week a gentleman was nearly throttled to death in the street and yesterday a mysterious explosion shook the town and, we understand, cost yet another life. Not since the murders connected with Dieulacres Abbey two years ago have we seen such distress in our peaceful community.

Two deaths have been explained away at inquests (see reports on page 4) and some would have us believe this spate of violence is nothing more than a coincidence. But the *Leek Lion* believes otherwise and this should not be the end of the matter.

Most thorough investigation is needed so that justice can be seen to be done. Without justice for the victims of these crimes, all the pride and honour of the King's visit will count for nothing.

A full report of the Royal visit appears on page 3.

CURIOUS EXPLOSION.

Mystery surrounds a curious explosion which occurred on the outskirts of Leek yesterday (Friday). The incident happened at Lowe Hill minutes at the time His Royal Highness was passing that point. One person is rumoured to have died, but this has yet to be confirmed by the authorities.

The blast is thought to have no connection with a nearby protest to draw attention to the campaign for women's suffrage. A banner bearing the words 'Votes for Women' was strung across Lowe Hill Bridge in full view of the King as he passed along Ashbourne Road.

Mr. Walter Hurst of Lowe Hill Farm told the *Leek Lion* that a disturbance had occurred on the bridge, but he did not know the cause. He and Mrs. Hurst attended to injured parties before police arrived. "We heard a great bang and found out that something had blown a great hole in one of our fields near the main road," he said.

The Manager of Leek Gas Works, Mr. Frederick Kirkham, discounted gas as the cause of the explosion.

Mr. Charles Bill, Member of Parliament for Leek, said he was appalled that women's campaigners had sought to stage a political protest during the King's visit.

"These women protestors are getting completely out of hand and I am sad to hear that dissent of this kind occurred on such an auspicious day for our town. We would not want His Majesty to believe that Leek people are mixed up in this sort of thing," Col. Bill said. "The question of women's suffrage has been fully debated in Parliament and has been wholeheartedly rejected," he added.

SERIOUS ASSAULT IN KING STREET.

Inquiries are continuing into a grievous attack which occurred in King Street, Leek during the night of Tuesday last.

The *Leek Lion* understands the victim was Mr. Francis Cavendish, a visitor to the town. He was found unconscious outside Loreto Convent on Wednesday morning by one of the Sisters resident there.

Mr. Cavendish had suffered strangulation and was admitted to the Alsop Memorial Hospital with injuries to his neck and head. It is believed he has now regained consciousness and is able to speak.

Leek Police said the reason for the attack and its perpetrator were unknown. They have issued an appeal for information from anyone who saw anything unusual in King Street on Tuesday evening or the early hours of Wednesday morning.

Saturday morning was filled with a bustle of activity in churches, chapels, schoolrooms and halls as final preparations were made for Club Day. In a few hours, many hundreds would be taking part and an equal number lining the streets to watch.

The church contingents would turn out in their finest clothes and there was rivalry as to who would look the best. Sewing had been going on for weeks to make sure dresses, blouses, bonnets and waistcoats were perfect.

From early that morning churches and chapels were filled with the smell of greenery as men carried in fresh flowers to be turned into the posies for the procession. In adjoining rooms, women were preparing mountains of meat or fish paste sandwiches for the tea parties when the parade was over. Others were busy cutting cakes, mixing jugs of lemonade and orange juice, or arranging tea cups. The men who would carry the colourful church banners, some of which were embroidered with religious scenes, were checking everything was firmly attached.

Nathaniel Blake had not had chance to talk to Cora that morning as she was still in bed when he left the house. There were many things he would have liked to ask her about what had gone on at Lowe Hill, but he and Edith had agreed that it was better to let her rest and recover.

Before going to the studio he had cycled to Abbey Green to give John Gibb his heartfelt thanks for saving Cora and Ellen. Gibb had been in subdued mood and still sore after the fight on the bridge.

"I only did what was necessary, Mr Blake. I feel sick to think what might have happened if I hadnae got there in time," Gibb had said. "Let's hope they catch up with the other devils."

"You mean Kilner and the gypsies?" Nathaniel had asked.

"Not just them. Francis said someone else was helping them," came the reply.

John's words were on Blake's mind as he came away from the farm. He was anxious to tell Inspector Ramm who else he believed was involved in the murderous affairs. But he expected the officer would be fully occupied that morning and he himself had many things to do. There were postcards of the Royal visit to print and then he would go out to photograph the Club Day activities. However he intended to stay at his most alert until he had spoken to Ramm.

At Leek Police Station, the Inspector was doing his best to co-operate with the new arrivals who had been sent to take over his investigations.

The first to arrive had been the agent from the War Office who had travelled from London to Stoke by night train. He was accompanied by a menacing fellow who looked like he had been a boxer. The agent divulged little, his companion said nothing at all.

Orlando Kilner was brought from the cells and handcuffed to the big man. As he was being led to a waiting carriage Kilner cast a final indignant look at Ramm.

The two detectives from Headquarters arrived next and Ramm gave them an exhaustive account of the previous day's events at Lowe Hill and Hartington.

It was agreed that their first priority should be the arrest of the gypsies involved in the incident on the bridge, as well as Conrad Mulder who was almost certainly Orlando Kilner's confederate. Ramm said he was also anxious to identify the mystery German sympathiser to whom Cavendish had referred. He thought there was also a chance that this person would lead to the truth about the death of James Broadhurst and Miss Hulme. He intended to start with the names on Broadhurst's list.

Minutes later a telegram arrived from Constable Mellor at Longnor stating that a group who looked like the German gypsies were camped near the River Dove at Hollinsclough. A carriage was hired and one of the detectives and two constables left immediately.

On the way they planned to locate John Gibb and take him with them to identify the culprits.

Next came a call from Buxton Police informing them that a man answering Mulder's description had been seen at a farm near Hartington. Ramm, accompanied by the other detective and a constable, set off in a trap for Hartington to meet up with Sheldon, the village constable.

By half past twelve, colourful contingents from sixteen churches and chapels were converging on the Market Place. Several were led by brass bands, the sun glinting on their instruments. When they reached the square, they were directed into position by the chief marshal.

Most of the women were in matching white dresses or white blouses and full black skirts. All wore straw hats, many of which were decorated with fresh flowers. The children were equally well turned out, girls in colourful summer dresses and boys in white shirts and dark breeches. Because of the sun, a good number of parasols and umbrellas were open.

The sounds of animated conversation, excited children and brass band music filled the square. On all four sides were crowds of spectators, many of the men in Sunday suits and straw boaters. At the lower end of the Market Place, handcarts were doing brisk trade in fruit and lemonade.

From the podium set up in front of The Red Lion, Giuseppe Manfredi looked out across a sea of hats, flowers, banners and flags. In a matter of minutes it would be his task to conduct this great choir in the singing of hymns in time with accompaniment from the Volunteers' Band.

Beside him stood Father Sperling, priest of St Mary's Roman Catholic Church who would officiate in the prayers. St Mary's were at the head of the parade this year and it was tradition that the leaders' clergy would also lead the service.

Manfredi gave an involuntary shiver as he caught sight of nuns from the Loreto Convent amongst the St Mary's contingent, their black habits a stark contrast to the summer dresses around them. They reminded him of his childhood and of something much more recent. Suddenly he felt the urge to flee. He snatched up his sheets of music and looked through them nervously.

The priest sensed his unease. "Is everything all right with you, Signor Manfredi?" he asked.

"Certainly, Father Sperling," Manfredi replied, regaining some of his composure. "I am a little hot, I think," he added, pulling out a handkerchief soaked in cologne and wiping his forehead.

Nathaniel Blake was watching Manfredi from his vantage point on the opposite side of the Market Place. People were leaning from the upper windows all around the square and Blake had taken his camera up to the top floor above a boot and shoe shop. The window gave him an excellent view of the gathering, but Nathaniel found his eyes drawn to the Italian. He was trying to spot if there was anything suspicious in the man's behaviour.

Last evening, as he sat mulling over his detective work, Blake had realised the dance teacher was central to the whole sad affair. His name had been top of the list that Broadhurst, it now seemed obvious, had suspected of spying. He was seen in Mill Street on the night of Broadhurst's death, and at the Horse Fair talking not only to theatre people, but to the gypsies. And when poor Sarah had written about 'M' in her diary, it was more likely she had been worried about Manfredi, not Mulder.

As Nathaniel looked out, he didn't know his daughter was amongst the spectators below him and she too was watching Manfredi.

The truth about Sarah's secret had dawned on her as she lay in bed last evening. She realised that Sarah must have overheard Kilner talking about the plot with Manfredi, the very man who had tried to persuade her not to join the Kilner Theatre. Lottie had said she thought Sarah had recognised the person she had seen with Kilner.

Manfredi must have been the one Thomas said they should never have got involved with. He had murdered Sarah to keep her quiet.

Cora had gone over the times she had seen the dance teacher since Sarah's death, how oddly he had behaved. "That wasn't grief, it was guilt!" she told herself bitterly.

And she had a sudden thought about the photographs of Manfredi at the Horse Fair. Cora was sure the gypsy he was talking to – the conversation he said had never happened – was one of those who had attacked Ellen and herself.

When she had woken that Saturday morning she ached all over from being manhandled and gagged at Lowe Hill. She had barely felt like getting out of bed, but she knew she had to do something. Although she could not bring Sarah back nor rid herself of memories of yesterday, she could try to prove her suspicions were correct.

Once she was downstairs, her mother had fussed over her while making sure young William was clean enough to take part in Club Day. Finally Cora had told her mother she felt well enough to go out and watch the procession herself.

When she reached the Market Place she had squeezed to the front of the crowd to get a good view of her dance teacher as he prepared to conduct the singing. Just like her father, she wanted to watch in case he did something to give himself away.

Printed hymn sheets were circulated and the service began. Manfredi swung his baton to keep time but in truth few people were taking much notice of him. At one point the singers and the band got completely out of step and the crowd sang on after the brass players had finished.

When the last hymn had been sung and the prayers mumbled,

the great procession began to thread its way from the Market Place and into Stockwell Street at the start of its circuit of the town centre. Blake left his viewpoint and went downstairs. He planned to set up his camera outside the Congregational Church in Derby Street ready for when the procession went past. He also knew that would give him a closer look at Manfredi.

Cora started to follow the procession. She dodged through groups of spectators on the pavement to catch up with the head of the great parade. She could see Manfredi, accompanied by Father Sperling and the Chairman of the Council, striding behind the Volunteers' Band. The dance teacher was wearing a straw boater and was staring straight ahead. In his hand, his leather music case seemed to be bulging more than usual.

Cora kept walking, keeping pace with Manfredi. She was determined to continue watching him. Afterwards she might even try to speak to him, she thought.

Oliver Finch was reporting on the event for the *Lion* and caught sight of Cora in the crowd as the procession reached Derby Street, the final part of its route. He hurried over to speak to her.

"Cora, how are you? I didn't think you would be here today," he said, his eyes searching her face. Cora's hand went instinctively to her cheek where face powder covered the marks left by the gag.

"I just needed get out of the house," she said. She tugged her sleeves over her wrists hoping he would not see her bruises.

"I don't really know what happened at Lowe Hill, but it must have been awful for you and Ellen."

"Oliver, I've so much to tell you," Cora began. Before she could say any more she realised that while she was distracted by Oliver she had lost sight of Manfredi. She darted forward and saw he was no longer walking behind the band. Looking around wildly, she stepped into the street and was nearly knocked over by a banner carrier.

Then she caught sight of someone in a straw boater barging

through the procession, hurrying against the stream of Sunday School contingents. She quickly turned to follow him, leaving a surprised Oliver behind.

Nathaniel was on the opposite side of Derby Street and had just taken a photograph of the Volunteers' Band when he saw Manfredi suddenly stop and swing round. He watched in amazement as the dance teacher started to retreat down the street, pushing past women and children. He became tangled in ribbons being held by some of the young people and snatched the silk away irritably.

Blake quickly took his camera off its tripod, took up his equipment in both hands and he too began to follow Manfredi as best he could along a pavement packed with spectators.

As he approached the bottom of Derby Street, Blake could see the steam omnibus was parked in front of The Talbot Hotel, a wisp of smoke rising from its chimney. The coke-fuelled bus looked to be waiting until the road was clear of the Club Day procession before setting off.

Blake was trying to keep his focus on the tall figure of Manfredi in the straw boater. He groaned as he saw the man break free of the parade and hurry across Sparrow Park towards the omnibus, clamber up the steps at the rear of the vehicle and disappear inside.

Blake was weighed down with his equipment and was finding it difficult to thread through the crowds. He realised he would never catch up with Manfredi. Seconds later he saw a young woman dash towards the omnibus, reach up to the handrail and haul herself aboard. Immediately afterwards the omnibus lurched forward and started to head out of town towards the Ashbourne Road.

Blake looked on in horror. Giuseppe Manfredi was on board the steam bus and so was Cora. "Oh no! She's chasing him," he said to himself.

Blake was faced with a dilemma. Should he go to the police station and raise the alarm, or should he give chase himself? He made an instant decision and hurried towards home. Cora was his responsibility and he knew it was up to him to protect her.

Edith was out watching the procession so the house was empty when he got home. He put down his equipment in the hallway and ran straight to the back yard for his bicycle. There was not a second to spare.

CHAPTER TWENTY FIVE

The omnibus, built like a small railway carriage with a steam engine in the front, had been operating between Leek and Waterhouses since the light railway along the Manifold Valley had opened a few weeks earlier. It had broken down on the railway's first day and had quickly become notorious for its unreliability and the disturbance it caused. The two-ton contraption earned the nickname '*The Earthquake*' in the *Leek Lion* after its iron rimmed wheels cracked cobblestones, its vibrations toppled shop window displays and its fearful noise scared horses.

After boarding at the rear, Giuseppe Manfredi had gone to occupy a spare seat at the very front. Although the omnibus was shaking and shuddering he felt more relaxed as he left the town behind. He planned never to return.

As they passed under Lowe Hill Bridge, he brooded over the plot that Kilner had drawn him into. He had worked with German sympathisers for years. Sometimes it meant breaking the law, but nothing like this, assassinating the King! Orlando was a fanatic bent on revenge, he thought.

Of course, he had been forced to silence three people. It was a shame about Miss Hulme, such a good pupil, he thought, but she was simply too inquisitive. He was not sorry about Broadhurst though, the man was a troublemaker, determined to denounce him. And there was no way they could risk having that British agent so close.

Manfredi smiled to himself as he recalled that using the bridge had been his own idea, a rather good one. But somehow things had gone wrong. He knew there had been an explosion but the King was alive and according to the *Leek Lion*, so was the British agent, the man he had left for dead in King Street. To make matters worse, there was talk of a new investigation into the deaths.

He had planned to leave Leek as soon as Club Day was over and he had panicked and seized the opportunity when he saw the steam bus.

Now he sat clutching the leather case he had stuffed with private papers that morning. He focused on the road ahead, oblivious of the other passengers, planning how to meet up with people he could trust.

Four rows behind him sat Cora, her eyes never wavering from the dance teacher. She was trying to hide from him, her bonnet pulled down tight on her head.

When she had seen Manfredi leaving the procession she knew she had no choice but to follow. Now though, she was beginning to worry. What would she do if he saw her? What if they left the bus and were alone on some country road? What if he attacked her as he must have done with Sarah?

Her thoughts were interrupted by the conductor asking for the eight pence fare. Luckily she had enough money in her purse, but when he asked where she was going she had simply shrugged. She had only a vague idea where the steam bus went and she did not know when Manfredi would get off.

She held her ticket tightly in one hand and clung on to the seat with the other as the vehicle bumped along the road. This was going to be a difficult journey and she did not know how it would end.

When Nathaniel Blake emerged on his bicycle into London Road there was no longer any sign of the steam bus. He began to pedal furiously, determined to catch up with Manfredi and Cora, whatever the cost.

By the time he reached Lowe Hill Bridge he was already out of breath. As he cycled under the tall stone arch he thought about what had happened a day earlier, the danger that Cora had faced there. Now she was in peril again.

He rounded the sharp bend after the bridge and looked across fields scarred by the blackened crater where Thomas Kilner had died. In the distance he could hear the sound of the steam bus as it climbed the Ashbourne Road towards the hamlet of Bradnop. Smoke from its chimney was floating above the roadside trees and he estimated it must be more than a quarter of a mile ahead. Catching up with it was a daunting prospect.

Blake was familiar with riding the rough roads of the moorlands. His bicycle was sturdy and, like most people's machines, it had a single gear. A long journey by bicycle usually involved pushing up the steepest hills and stopping when he needed to catch his breath. Today there would be no rest if he wanted to keep up with the steam bus.

He remembered seeing in the *Lion* that the omnibus took precisely an hour to travel the eight miles to Waterhouses. He expected to be much slower than the bus going uphill and so he would fall even further behind. However he might be able to close the gap by riding as fast as he could on downhill sections of the undulating road.

Although he had left his jacket at home, Blake was already

feeling the effects of the effort and the sun as he laboured up the steep incline past an old tollhouse. He was out of the saddle by now, standing on his pedals. His white shirt was soaked in sweat and he was parched from exertion and the dust of the stony road. He continued up the hill, hoping the steam bus had stopped at Bradnop, the first of three halts which were advertised. To his bitter disappointment he realised the omnibus had carried on.

When the road levelled out he was able to pedal a little more easily. He could now see the bus in the distance, but he realised he was getting no closer. He took the opportunity to rest his legs as he coasted into Cook's Hollow because he knew he would then face the most arduous part of the ride. The road climbed for about half a mile towards Bottomhouse crossroads and Blake was out of the saddle again, straining on the pedals to keep moving.

But the hill was too steep and he stopped almost immediately. He leaned over the handlebars panting and cursed under his ragged breath. He would have to push until he reached level ground again.

Although the steam bus was now out of sight, he could smell its smoke drifting back along the road and hear the steam engine as it chugged up the slope. Just like himself, the heavy vehicle was having to work much harder on this stretch of road.

Blake dismounted and with gritted teeth started to push the bicycle with what little energy he had left. He began to wonder if it had been folly to pursue the steam bus on two wheels. Now he would fall so far behind that Manfredi could be off the bus and gone before he caught up.

Peering ahead, he was surprised when he caught sight of the maroon painted vehicle. Instead of disappearing into the distance, it seemed that it was barely moving at all. Blake could scarcely believe his luck.

On board the omnibus, many of the twenty passengers began to grumble when the vehicle slowed down.

"Not again! Exactly the same thing happened last week. It

would be quicker to walk," said an overweight gentleman perspiring in a thick tweed jacket.

"Oh, I hope we do not miss the train. I've been so looking forward to it," said a well-dressed elderly woman who sounded like a visitor to the district. "Do not worry, Aunt. I'm sure it will be all right," replied a younger woman sitting beside her.

Cora glanced at her fellow travellers nervously, then saw that Giuseppe Manfredi was craning his long neck to look at the countryside on either side. She sank into her seat and tried to hide behind the man sitting in front in case the dance teacher decided to turn around. It was useful that she was shorter than most of those around her.

With a great discharge of steam, the vehicle came to a complete halt. The conductor climbed down the steps at the back and walked to the front where he engaged in a heated discussion with the driver. There were more complaints and groans of frustration from the passengers.

From what she had heard them saying, Cora realised that most of those on board intended to catch the Manifold Valley train at Waterhouses. She wondered if that was what Manfredi planned. The thought of getting on the train filled her with fresh anxieties. She doubted she had enough money for the ticket. She could finish up becoming totally lost. Manfredi could get away...

Cora squeezed her eyes shut and shook her head at her own foolishness in chasing the man like this. Then she remembered what had happened to Sarah and what Ellen and herself had gone through at Lowe Hill. The anger revived her determination to carry on.

Seeing that the bus had stopped gave Nathaniel new impetus to push on up the hill. As he was finally drawing near he saw a sooty cloud shoot from its chimney and heard the steam engine fire back into life. He had been tantalisingly close, but now the vehicle began to move away from him again.

Blake got back in the saddle and resumed pedalling as he approached Bottomhouse crossroads. The steam bus was still in his sights and he felt more confident of keeping up because the remaining two or three miles were mostly flat or downhill.

He passed Berkhamsytch Chapel on his right and saw trestle tables had been arranged outside. He guessed that tea was to be served when their Sunday School returned from Club Day. He remembered guiltily that he had completely missed William walking around the town because he had been too busy taking photographs and watching Manfredi.

Blake swooped down the road towards Winkhill and then pulled on the brakes when he saw the steam bus was coming to a halt. He stopped some yards behind and watched who was getting off. It turned out to be a heavily built fellow in a tweed jacket.

The vehicle started again and so did Blake, his mind now working on what to do when they reached their destination. He was desperate to know that Cora was safe, but was also determined to find out where Manfredi was headed. He didn't want this hard ride to have been a waste of time and effort.

Ten minutes later the steam bus ground its way through the middle of Waterhouses, putting a flock of chickens to flight. It stopped beyond some cottages past The Crown Inn, its fearful noise subsiding and the road dust settling around it.

A little further on, the Manifold Valley line crossed the main road and nearby was a wooden shed being used as a temporary station. The village's proper station would not be open until the railway line from Leek was finished.

Blake leaned his bicycle beside a cottage wall and watched what went on. The conductor was the first to get down from the bus and then he saw Cora appear on the rear steps. She jumped off the last step, looked around urgently and darted behind a fence at the side of the road. It was obvious she did not want the dance teacher to see her. In spite of his concern, Nathaniel found himself smiling at Cora's ingenuity as he tried to imagine how she had managed to stay hidden from Manfredi all the way from Leek.

The rest of the passengers began to descend and the conductor climbed a ladder to reach bags from the luggage compartment on the omnibus roof. Manfredi was the last to get out. He looked about with an uncertain expression and then followed other travellers who were walking along the road towards the level crossing gates. There was no sign of the train yet.

As soon as Manfredi was at a safe distance, Nathaniel stepped forward quickly and went to where Cora was crouching behind the fence.

"What in heaven's name are you doing?" he asked, keeping his voice low.

Cora looked up, shocked to see her father. She was guilty to be found out, yet relieved she was no longer alone. She stood up and hugged him and Nathaniel found it difficult to be as angry as he had intended.

"This was so very foolish, my dear," he said.

"But, Signor Manfredi..." Cora began, trying to keep her emotions in check. "I am sure he is to blame for what happened to Sarah. I had to stop him getting away."

Nathaniel realised his daughter had come to the same conclusion as himself, however he did not want her to think he approved of her rash behaviour.

"That is as it may be, but it was far too dangerous to follow that man on your own."

"But we can't let him escape after everything that has happened, Father!" Cora shot back. "And if you are going to follow him, so am I."

Nathaniel knew the train might be there at any minute. There was no time to argue with Cora nor to find a place she could stay until he returned. In fact he thought she would be safer where he could keep an eye on her.

He heaved a sigh of resignation and grasped Cora's hand. "I think we both need something to drink," he said, leading her quickly to a stall beside the road. Someone had set up a table selling homemade lemonade and punnets of strawberries to passers-by. Blake dropped tuppence in a cash box and undid the glass stopper on a bottle of cloudy lemonade. Cora drank half of it eagerly. He downed the remainder, although after such a ride he could have easily drunk the lot.

A shrill whistle announced the train's arrival at the station. They needed to follow Manfredi onto the train and Blake had to be prepared for anything.

CHAPTER TWENTY SIX

Nathaniel and Cora made their way cautiously towards the temporary wooden station where they could see Giuseppe Manfredi was amongst the passengers waiting to board the Leek & Manifold Valley Light Railway. Four passenger carriages were attached to the locomotive. On weekdays the train would pull waggons carrying milk churns to and from Ecton creamery half a dozen miles up the line.

As Blake got closer, he realised why folk had nicknamed it *'The Toy Railway'*. The chocolate brown locomotive and primrose yellow carriages were smaller than any he had seen at Leek Station and the track was much narrower.

However he knew he was not here to admire the train nor the scenery along the valley. He needed to keep his focus on Manfredi, who had boarded a carriage and was sitting in one of the high-backed upholstered seats in the first class compartment. Nathaniel guided Cora to the opposite end of the same carriage. They mounted two steps, went through a door bearing a large figure '3' and found a bench seat in third class. From there he could see Manfredi who was seated with his back to them.

Once all the passengers had boarded, the driver sounded the whistle and the fireman jumped down from the cab to close the level crossing gates across the Ashbourne Road. The train edged forward across the road and paused briefly while the gates were opened again.

So began a journey of bend upon bend, bridge after bridge as the train wound its way along the spectacular valley, crossing and re-crossing first the River Hamps and then the Manifold. The riverbed was bone dry and strewn with rocks because, as in every summer, most of the Manifold had disappeared into an underground channel. Soon there was a buzz of conversation as passengers pointed out limestone bluffs and dense woodland.

The guard came down the carriage asking where passengers wished to get off as it was his job to halt the train accordingly, as well as selling and checking tickets. Blake handed him a half crown coin for two return tickets to Hulme End, the terminus of the eight-mile line.

When the guard spoke to Manfredi, the Italian felt in his pockets for coins and then stood up looking flustered as he searched his leather case. At that moment he glanced down the carriage and froze when he saw Nathaniel and Cora watching him. He didn't acknowledge them and sat down again abruptly.

Up to that point, Manfredi had been feeling more secure on the train, especially as he had come up with a plan. He intended to get off the train at Hulme End and make for Hartington which was only two or three miles away. There he expected to find the rag-and-stick where he hoped to meet Orlando. If not, he would catch another train out of the area as soon as possible.

Now he had seen Blake and his daughter, his mood changed and he was on edge again. He dared not turn round in case they were staring at him and so he sat rigid in his seat.

He tried to think why Blake should be on the train. Perhaps the fellow was taking photographs of the railway. But Orlando had told him that Blake worked with the police. He had taken pictures of Miss Hulme's body and had probably been at the dye works, too. So was he working for the police today?

And what about Blake's daughter? Thomas Kilner had said she had been asking awkward questions about Miss Hulme. He himself remembered her asking about the Horse Fair and who he had been speaking to.

He decided to pretend he had not seen the Blakes and then try to get away from them as soon as he could.

Further along the carriage, Cora's stomach was in knots at the thought of what Manfredi might do.

"He knows we are here, doesn't he?" she whispered.

"I'm sure he does. But he doesn't know why, nor that we saw him dash away from the parade," Nathaniel replied, keeping his voice low. "I'm sure he will pretend that everything is normal. He certainly won't want any trouble on the train."

"So what are we going to do?"

"I will speak to him when he gets off. You must stay well out of the way." Although Nathaniel hoped to reassure his daughter, in truth he was less than confident himself. If Manfredi really was a murderer there was no way to predict how he would react if he thought he was cornered.

The train had been going for about 30 minutes when Blake caught sight of the yawning mouth of a huge cave in the limestone cliff high above the valley. They came to a halt next to a small wooden building with an impressive sign indicating this was the station for Thor's Cave and Wetton. In an adjoining field, a brightly painted shed was being used as a tea room.

The rest of the passengers in the carriage, apart from Manfredi, stood up to leave. Blake heard one say that they hoped to have time to visit the cave before the train returned.

Manfredi shifted in his seat and looked up towards the craggy hillside and the cave. It reminded him of the rocks he climbed in his youth, happy days in the Tyrol with his adopted family. Would he ever see the old country again, he wondered?

Blake tensed as he feared the dance teacher was thinking of getting off and disappearing into the woodland. However Manfredi remained seated when the train moved off.

Smoke from the engine drifted through the open window as the train picked up speed again. They passed another tiny station signposted Wetton Mill and soon afterwards the electric lamps in the carriage roof flickered dimly into life. Blake realised they must be approaching Swainsley Tunnel. He remembered Finch telling him the tunnel had been dug at great expense to satisfy Sir Thomas Wardle, the Leek industrialist and a director of the railway, who did not want to see the line from his country estate.

Although the train was still moving, Manfredi suddenly got up and opened the sliding door which led onto a small viewing platform at the end of the carriage. Bracing himself against the ornate iron railings, he leaned out to look in the direction the train was heading.

Immediately, Blake was on his guard. Manfredi had taken his case with him and he suspected the man planned to make a swift escape the next time the train stopped.

"Stay there, please," he told Cora before he went down the carriage and stepped outside behind the Italian.

Manfredi swivelled round in surprise and Blake was close enough to get a waft of his lavender cologne. He was instantly taken back to the tragic night at the rag-and-stick when he had detected the same aroma on Sarah Hulme's body.

Before either man could speak, they were plunged into darkness as the train rattled into the narrow tunnel. Suddenly the air was filled with the great noise of the engine and its choking smoke. Blake put a hand to his mouth and began to cough uncontrollably, at the same time trying to rub his stinging eyes. The next moment he was knocked backwards onto the wooden floor.

When Blake scrambled desperately to his feet he saw that Manfredi was gone. The man must have jumped from the carriage into the blackness of the tunnel.

He leaned out as far as he dared, but could see nothing except the dark tunnel wall rushing past. The smooth masonry was far too close for him to risk jumping after Manfredi.

As soon as the train was out in the open again, he lowered himself warily down the external steps and leapt off.

When Blake's feet touched the ground he fell forwards, tearing his trousers on the track bed and cutting the palms of his hands. Ignoring the pain in his knees, he stood up and started to make his way back to the black mouth of the tunnel. He was determined not to let Manfredi escape.

As the train had neared the tunnel, Cora had watched her father go to stand next to Signor Manfredi, but she had not be able to see what had gone on between them. Once in the daylight again, she could see neither of them.

She was on her own in the carriage. There was no communication cord to pull in an emergency nor any way to reach the adjoining carriages where the other passengers were.

Disregarding what Nathaniel had told her about staying in her seat, she dashed down the carriage and flung open the door to the viewing platform. There was no one there.

"Father! Father!" she shouted in panic.

She leaned over the railing and screamed for help, but the wind snatched her voice away and the train rumbled on. She dared not let herself think what might have happened to her father at the hands of Manfredi and, trapped in the carriage, she knew she could do nothing to help him.

Once again she looked out, desperate to see if there was any chance of the train stopping. Her heart skipped a beat when she saw one of the wooden station shelters up ahead, but the train carried on. Cora groaned in frustration as she saw a sign saying 'Ecton for Warslow' flash past.

After what seemed an eternity, but was only a couple of minutes, she finally sensed the train was slowing down. "At last! Now I can find someone who will help," she thought.

Manfredi heard footsteps approaching and sank into a recess in the tunnel wall, just big enough for a person to stand in. He hardly dared breathe in case he gave himself away.

His leap from the train had been another moment of panic. Blake had come up behind him and somehow he had known the photographer was on to him. He had taken his chance on a jump into the dark rather than be arrested.

When he hit the ground, Manfredi went sprawling. He had lain there, clinging to his case, as the train rushed past just inches away. There was a sharp pain in one of his ankles. As soon as the train had left the tunnel and the smoke cleared, he hauled himself upright and began to stumble away.

Looking towards where the train had gone, he was dismayed to see a someone else beside the line. It was Blake getting to his feet.

Manfredi realised his injured ankle gave him little chance of running away from the photographer. Instead, he would hide and get rid of Blake if he had to.

Once he entered the tunnel, Blake made slow progress in the darkness. There was a patch of light at the other end, more than a hundred and fifty yards away, but apart from that he could make out very little of what was ahead. He could see no sign of Manfredi, although he was sure the fellow had not had time to escape.

He frowned as his feet crunched on the limestone beside the track, the enclosed space seeming to amplify every sound. Soon the dim light behind him faded away and Blake found himself groping forward in almost complete darkness.

He began to feel afraid. When he started this pursuit in Leek he had no clear idea of what he intended to do. Once they were on the train he had hoped to confront Manfredi in some public place where there was a better chance of safety. Now he was alone in the pitch black with a man who may have killed two people and had done his damnedest to strangle a third.

Further along the tunnel, Manfredi reached into his music case as silently as he could and felt around for what he needed. It was a length of woven cord, the same one he had used on Sarah Hulme before Conrad had lifted her body into the stage rigging. He pulled it out and gently put the case back by his feet. He stretched the cord tight between his fists and waited for Blake.

Nathaniel heard a noise and stood stock still. Something or someone had moved. He staggered back startled by a rat scuttling across the ground by his feet. He waited, calming his nerves before he moved slowly forward again. He hoped to catch a glimpse of Manfredi, perhaps silhouetted against the smudge of daylight at the far end of the tunnel.

His eyes were becoming accustomed to the dim light and he perceived the shape of an arched recess in the tunnel wall. As he drew level with it he was aware of a sudden movement and before he had time to react he felt something tight around his throat. He began to choke.

Blake knew Manfredi was on him and he might have only seconds to live. Images of Sarah strangled, Broadhurst drowned and Cavendish unconscious, flashed through his mind.

He reached up to seize the cord and desperately twisted his body from side to side in an attempt to loosen Manfredi's grasp. Although the pressure on his neck was still firm he managed to tip his attacker off balance and then suddenly he could breathe again. Manfredi had let go of the garotte as his sprained ankle gave way and he toppled over with a cry of pain and frustration.

The Italian made a grab for Blake's legs and pulled him to the ground, too. Blake fell across the tracks and lay on his back, his breath knocked from him. Manfredi immediately seized him around the throat, intent on achieving with his hands what the garotte had failed to do.

Fighting for his life, Blake thrashed around wildly, trying to dislodge Manfredi's grip. The two men were locked together in a life or death struggle.

284

Blake used one hand to push against the steel rail of the track, levering himself against his attacker and finishing up on top of the lighter man, who was now beginning to tire. He twisted round, grasped Manfredi's head and with all his might slammed it against the rail. The blow knocked the man senseless and his grip went limp.

Blake rolled off him and lay on his back, gasping for breath. His heart was pounding. He had lost his spectacles in the fight and so could see even less in the gloom of the tunnel. He was aware of Manfredi lying next to him. He could hear the man's shallow breathing and was relieved he had not killed him. The Italian would live to face justice, but first Blake had to make sure he did not get away again.

He felt around on the ground for his spectacles, but instead his fingers closed around the cord that Manfredi had used to try strangle him. He decided to bind his attacker's hands, but before he could do so he felt himself losing consciousness and sank back to the ground.

The next thing he knew, someone was calling his name. He sat up slowly, peered around and saw a blur of light down the tunnel.

"Here! Over here!" Blake shouted as loud as he could manage.

The light moved closer.

"What in heavens has been going on?" asked the man in astonishment when he reached them. He shone his powerful railway lantern first into Blake's face and then over the prone body of Manfredi, who had begun to stir at the sound.

"Quickly, seize him!" said Blake. By the light of the lamp he reached for Manfredi's wrists and started to wind the cord tightly around them.

The railwayman hesitated a moment, wondering what to believe, then leant forward and grabbed Manfredi's shoulders to pin him to the ground.

"I work at Hulme End," he told Blake, breathlessly. "A young woman said her father had fell off in the tunnel. I come along the lane on the bicycle as quick as I could. They're turning the loco round, it should be here soon."

The next minutes passed in an awkward silence, the railwayman holding Manfredi firm. Then they heard the engine whistle as it slowed to a halt at the mouth of the tunnel. Blake was vaguely aware of more people running down the track, more lights, more shouts of surprise and finally he was being lifted to his feet.

In the waiting room at Hulme End Station, Cora sat with her eyes closed and her fists clenched. She was struggling to contain herself. She had no way of knowing if the railway workers had got back to the tunnel in time or what they had found.

At the sound of the locomotive returning she dashed outside and past the empty carriages which had been left behind. She looked up anxiously as the engine came to a stop. The cab was crowded and she could see her father was amongst the men.

The stationmaster was the first to climb down from the engine and he turned to offer a hand to Blake who stepped stiffly onto the platform. Cora threw her arms around him.

"Father, you're safe!" she cried, burying her head in his chest.

It was obvious Blake had been in a fight. A lens in his spectacles was cracked, there were cuts on his face and hands, his neck was red raw from the noose, his shirt and trousers were torn and covered in dirt.

"A little dusty, but I'll survive," Nathaniel reassured her.

They both turned to watch as Manfredi was manhandled from the cab by the train guard and the fireman. He was equally dishevelled, one eye swollen and his hands still tied. He avoided looking at the Blakes.

"I shall send a lad to get Constable Sheldon from Hartington," said the stationmaster.

An elderly couple who had been expecting to catch the train back to Waterhouses, looked on bemused as Manfredi, limping badly, was bundled into the waiting room. The Blakes sat on a bench outside, Nathaniel rubbing his neck where the cord had come close to doing its job.

Cora turned to her father. "He tried to kill you, didn't he? Just like he did to Sarah," she said.

Nathaniel took her hand. "I'm safe, Cora, that's all that matters. And the police will be here soon to take him away," he replied.

Cora stood up abruptly saying that she needed to find a lavatory. She took a few steps along the platform then darted into the waiting room where she flew at Manfredi in a rage.

"Sarah didn't deserve what you did to her!" she shouted.

Manfredi flinched back from Cora and the railwaymen guarding him looked startled. Nathaniel rushed in and tried to pull her away. She shook herself free.

"Sarah loved dancing, she dreamed of going on the stage and you took it all away!" Cora cried.

"I did what I had to, Miss Blake, there no choice for me," the Italian replied coldly. "Our plan, it more important than your friend."

Cora stared at him then, satisfied she had had the chance to confront him, turned away. She was not interested in his excuses.

When Constable Sheldon arrived, Manfredi was handcuffed to the officer and the two climbed into a wagonette to make the journey back to Leek.

Cora and her father sat opposite, holding hands and saying nothing. They were both exhausted. After what they had been through in the last few days, all they wanted was the comfort of home.

Epilogue

Two weeks later

Leek was alive with gossip after the *Lion* reported that Giuseppe Manfredi had been charged with the murders of Sarah Hulme and James Broadhurst and the attempted murder of Francis Cavendish. Families who had entrusted their children to him for music and dance lessons could barely believe how close they had come to a murderer.

But the newspaper would never be able to print the full story behind the crimes.

"The Home Office has banned us from mentioning the plot against the King," said FJ Finch as he walked with Inspector Ramm, Nathaniel, Cora and John Gibb.

The group had met at Abbey Green Wakes, an annual summer event held close to the farm where Gibb worked. Seeking some privacy, Ramm had suggested they stroll a little way beside the River Churnet.

"The Government won't risk news of the attempt on the King's life getting out. It could make matters worse on the Continent, some people would be sure to blame the Kaiser rather than a bunch of fanatics," said Ramm. "But I think I owe it to the four of you to tell you what we know so far."

"Kilner will face the death penalty, although I'm sure the case will be hushed up," he went on. "Mulder was arrested last week trying to board a ship at Hull docks, but tracking down the gypsies might take a long time. However we do have Manfredi, thanks to Mr Blake."

"It still seems strange that he was involved in all this," said

Blake, shaking his head. The photographer still bore the marks, both physical and mental, of his confrontation with the murderer in Swainsley Tunnel.

"Cavendish's people have discovered that Manfredi was an Italian orphan brought up by a German family. He's been a political fanatic for years, like his friend Kilner," Ramm replied. "And he has almost certainly been involved in murky business before."

"I presume he found out that James Broadhurst was on to him," said Finch.

"Yes, and because of this plot, he had to act quickly. He probably conspired with Kilner to write the false letter to lure Broadhurst, then he went to the dye house and attacked him."

"What about the others who were on Broadhurst's list?" asked the editor. He had not come to terms with the fact that his newspaper had encouraged Broadhurst in his fatal obsession with Germany.

"Mr Broadhurst suspected all sorts of people, but I have checked and the rest of them are perfectly law abiding," Ramm replied.

"Don't forget that Sarah was a victim, too," Cora interjected.

"My apologies Miss Blake. I should have taken more notice of what you said at the time. There's no doubt Miss Hulme overheard Kilner and Manfredi talking about the plot, and when they found out..."

"Manfredi murdered her," Cora cut in.

They paused and gazed at the waters of the Churnet as they thought back to the tragic night at the rag-and-stick, the start of an horrific train of events in the town. Cora had a distant look in her eyes, her mind on the eccentric dance teacher who turned out to be a killer. At least she had helped to catch him and gain some justice for Sarah.

Nathaniel was the next to speak: "Does the King know that John saved his life?"

Ramm turned to the Scotsman. "His Majesty has been informed

of your bravery, Mr Gibb, and I gather he intends to present you with a medal in person. There's also talk of a financial reward. You certainly deserve it."

"When I saw what was going on I knew I had to stop them," said Gibb, looking a little embarrassed.

"And you saved us, too, Mr Gibb!" said Cora. "Ellen and I will never forget what you did that day. Those people would have never let us live." Ramm and Finch murmured their agreement and Nathaniel gripped his daughter's hand.

"Let's hope we see nothing like it again," Ramm continued. He looked across the fields to where folk were enjoying an evening of wakes entertainment. Children were laughing as they joined in the games and a brass band had begun to play. "Perhaps life is already getting back to normal," he said.

The group dispersed shortly afterwards. Nathaniel and Cora were subdued as they walked back into town. Unlike Ramm, Blake thought it would be some time before he felt his own life was back to normal. However he was relieved the tragic episode was finally over and his daughter was safe again.

Cora was once more going over the fateful day at Lowe Hill when John Gibb had saved her and Thomas Kilner had lost his life. Had the King glanced up and seen the banner on the bridge? She hoped he might remember the Votes for Women protest, as well as this awful plot.

Their banner had been put away – the memories of what had happened were still too raw for her or Ellen to face looking at it yet. But the campaign would go on and they intended to be part of it. They had survived and they would not give up now.

HISTORICAL NOTE

The plot and characters of this novel are fictitious, however the background to the action reflects what life was like in Leek and the moorlands in mid-Edwardian times. Readers will recognise many of the buildings which are mentioned, although some have been demolished or changed in use:

Railway Station: site of Morrison's supermarket

Police Station, Leonard Street: converted to apartments

Cattle Market: site of the Smithfield shopping centre

Coffee Tavern: demolished when Smithfield centre built

Cottage Hospital, Stockwell Street: converted to apartments

Union Workhouse, Ashbourne Road: now the Moorlands Hospital

Fever Hospital, Ashbourne Road: site of senior citizens' housing

Lowe Hill Bridge: widened and rebuilt in concrete in early 1960's

Town Baths, Derby Street: site of The Co-operative Bank

Post and Telegraph Office, Derby Street: now Halifax Bank

Brunswick Methodist Schoolrooms, Regent Street: site of a car park

Cruso's Yard, off Stockwell Street: now the road entrance to Moorlands House

Fountain Street Methodist Chapel: site of an office building

Loreto Convent, King Street: now the Peak Weavers Hotel

Temperance Hall, Union Street: became the Majestic Cinema which burnt down in 1961, site now part of Buxton and Leek College

Talbot Hotel: rebuilt as a Premier Inn

The Spread Eagle, Mill Street: now The Dog and Rot

The Great Mill is based on the former Brough, Nicholson & Hall complex between Ashbourne Road, Cross Street and Fountain Street